Ace Books by Kasey Mackenzie

RED HOT FURY
GREEN-EYED ENVY
BLACKHEARTED BETRAYAL

BLACKHEARTED BETRAYAL

A SHADES OF FURY NOVEL

KASEY MACKENZIE

ACE BOOKS, NEW YORK

THE BERKLEY PUBLISHING GROUP
Published by the Penguin Group
Penguin Group (USA) Inc.
375 Hudson Street, New York, New York 10014, USA

Penguin Group (Canada), 90 Eglinton Avenue East, Suite 700, Toronto, Ontario M4P 2Y3, Canada (a division of Pearson Penguin Canada Inc.) • Penguin Books Ltd., 80 Strand, London WC2R 0RL, England • Penguin Group Ireland, 25 St. Stephen's Green, Dublin 2, Ireland (a division of Penguin Books Ltd.) • Penguin Group (Australia), 250 Camberwell Road, Camberwell, Victoria 3124, Australia (a division of Pearson Australia Group Pty. Ltd.) • Penguin Books India Pvt. Ltd., 11 Community Centre, Panchsheel Park, New Delhi—110 017, India • Penguin Group (NZ), 67 Apollo Drive, Rosedale, Auckland 0632, New Zealand (a division of Pearson New Zealand Ltd.) • Penguin Books (South Africa) (Pty.) Ltd., 24 Sturdee Avenue, Rosebank, Johannesburg 2196, South Africa

Penguin Books Ltd., Registered Offices: 80 Strand, London WC2R 0RL, England

BLACKHEARTED BETRAYAL

An Ace Book / published by arrangement with the author

PUBLISHING HISTORY
Ace mass-market edition / July 2012

Copyright © 2012 by Heather Faucher.
Cover art by Judy York.
Cover design by Judith Lagerman.
Interior text design by Kristin del Rosario.

ISBN: 978-1-937007-65-2

ACE
Ace Books are published by The Berkley Publishing Group, a division of Penguin Group (USA) Inc., 375 Hudson Street, New York, New York 10014. ACE and the "A" design are trademarks of Penguin Group (USA) Inc.

PRINTED IN THE UNITED STATES OF AMERICA

10 9 8 7 6 5 4 3 2 1

ALWAYS LEARNING   **PEARSON**

Dedicated to the memory of my mother, Debbie. You left us way too soon, but I know you're finally at peace, and *you* know I'll help our family carry on through the grief. We'll love and miss you always.

> *Death leaves a heartache no one can heal,*
> *Love leaves a memory no one can steal.*
>
> —FROM AN IRISH HEADSTONE

ACKNOWLEDGMENTS

This section is going to be long again because this book has been, without a doubt, the absolutely hardest to write of my life. Many personal challenges kicked me around this year, culminating with the heartbreaking death of my mother, Debbie, on Thanksgiving night. I want to take this opportunity to thank each and every person who, in whatever way, helped my family deal with this tragedy, from those who gave their support and love to those who made sure my baby boy had a wonderful Christmas. Both old and new friends helped ease my heart during the toughest crisis of my life. Sorry there's not room to list you all by name, but just know that you are all appreciated so much more than I can express. Thank you!

Thanks again to my ever-patient editor, Jessica Wade, and everyone at Ace who was so understanding as I dealt with all the trauma this year; to my awesome rock star of an agent, Ginger Clark, who never doubted I could get this book done; to my amazing cover artist, Judy York, and Ace's fantastic art department, who all amaze me more with each book; and to the enthusiastic readers, librarians, and booksellers who have connected with this series and make what I do possible.

Last but not least, thanks to my beloved family: my loving husband, Shawn, who has more faith in me than I could ever have in myself; my adorable son, Zack, who is the sweetest and best baby boy a mother could ever have; my stepfather, Larry, who loved my mother so much and whom we love for that and many other reasons; my baby sister, Kelsey, who has become such an amazing mother and dealt with so much the past few months with grace and love; my brothers, Dustin and Chris, whom I may not always see eye to eye with but love tremendously; my future brother-in-law, Scott, who is an amazing man; my new nephews and niece, who gave us all reasons to smile even in the darkest of days; my grandparents, uncles, aunts, cousins, and in-laws, who pulled together to help us deal with Mom's passing; and my best friend, Julie, who is just as much of a sister to me as my biological sister. Much thanks and love also to my fabulous friends in the writing community, including (but not limited to) Jill Myles, Gretchen McNeil, Cindy Pon, Chris Marie Green, Wen Spencer, Jackie Kessler, Heather Brewer, Cole Gibsen, Shawntelle Madison, Chloe Neill, Team Purgatory at Absolute Write, my chat buddies at Forward Motion for Writers, and the St. Louis Writers Guild.

Remember to hold your loved ones tight and tell them how you feel about them: You never know when it will be for the last time.

CHAPTER ONE

NOTHING KILLED A POSTPARTY BUZZ LIKE waiting all night to jump your lover's bones only to have a Harpy bust into your home while you're getting frisky on the sofa. Even worse, a *pregnant* Harpy, whose enormous belly, swollen ankles, and raging mood swings served as a walking billboard for conscientious birth-control use. I let out a choked scream and covered my nakedness with an afghan when the Harpy Queen waltzed through my front door *entirely* too early in the morning. Scott Murphy, the love of my life, became alert—er, the *other* kind of alert—and lunged to his feet, fortunately still wearing his tuxedo pants.

I grabbed his arm before he could strike. "Down, boy; it's Serise." The only Harpy neither of us would attack on sight. Normally, when a Fury—like me—became so overcome by Rage, she couldn't control it and

Turned Harpy, which was bad news. But Serise had earned my trust enough that I'd programmed my magical wards to allow her inside without raising a dozen alarms. Something I was very much starting to regret.

"Somebody had damned well better be dead, *Your Majesty*, or you may well soon be, baby bump or no."

She blinked yellow-green eyes and laid a protective hand upon her stomach. "Have I interrupted something important?"

Trust a Harpy to completely miss any and all social cues, like the half-naked couple *getting busy* on the sofa. She might be slightly saner than her sisters thanks to her status as Queen, but that didn't make her any less socially awkward. "Seriously, Serise, you have like five seconds to get to the point before I kick you *out* of my house."

"Nobody is dead, but I believed the two of you would wish to know about the man I caught shadowing me after I dropped off your nieces at their home."

My hackles rose in a more figurative sense than those of my Warhound lover beside me. "You let some strange man *follow you* to my brother's home?"

Serise finally seemed to clue in to the absurdity of conducting a serious conversation while Scott and I were half-naked in the living room. "Perhaps you would prefer to clothe yourself before—"

"Gods damn it, Harpy Queen, are my nieces in danger?"

"Of course not." She actually sounded offended. "Firstly, I never claimed the man was unknown to me. Secondly, you should know I would never be so clumsy as to allow anyone to trail me while on guard duty, especially not my children's sisters." Serise's children—the one already born, Rinda, along with the unnamed bun in her oven—shared the same unknown father's DNA as my adopted niece, Olivia, who was a biological cousin to my niece, Cori. In Serise's eyes, both girls shared kinship to her own children, which meant they were to be protected. Came in damned handy, considering all the recent abduction and assassination attempts aimed at my family.

"Furthermore, this man was already at your family's home in Salem. He followed *me* back to Boston, where I led him on a fruitless chase until I knew the wedding reception would be over and you would be home." We had just come from the wedding of Scott's old flame. Of course, a serial killer had almost gotten in the way, but that was another story.

I leaned forward with narrowed eyes and yanked the afghan up when it started to slip. "Who the *hell* do we know that would follow you from my family's home into Boston without trying to talk to you?" *Or, as was more likely since most arcanes hated Harpies, to kill her?*

Serise's disconcerting gaze moved from my face to Scott's. "The man you've been looking for since the night your sister Fury died, the missing Warhound, Sean Murphy."

THE UNEXPECTED REVELATION HIT ME LIKE A combat boot to the stomach; and yes, I knew how *that* felt from personal experience. My duties as both member of the Sisterhood of Furies and Chief Magical Investigator for the city of Boston came with hazard pay for good reason. With everything I had experienced over the years, few things took me completely by surprise anymore, but hearing that Scott's baby brother had transformed from missing person to Harpy stalker managed to wallop me right upside the figurative head.

Sean had vanished in the chaos when I led a group of allies against the mortal scientists who'd been experimenting upon arcanes like Vanessa, my childhood friend and sister Fury who died giving birth to Olivia. We'd believed Sean to be captured by the brainwashed Sidhe serving the scientists, but shadowing Serise from Salem to Boston indicated he possessed at least a modicum of freedom. Considering we'd been turning over every stone we could to find him for months and he hadn't had the courtesy to let us know he was still alive, that didn't sit too well in my stomach.

Scott's sudden growl hinted he didn't like the sound of it, either. "You saw my brother tonight, and you're *just now* telling us?"

Serise gave a careless Harpy shrug. "I did not recognize him until I circled back to shadow *him* for a time."

Scott clenched his fists, and I could just picture him counting to ten beneath his breath so he wouldn't lose his cool. Hound tempers may not have anything on the supernatural Rage that fueled both Fury and Harpy magic, but they came in a *close* third. "Did you talk to him? Are you *sure* it's him?"

"I did not approach lest I scare him away before *you* could speak with him. I did, however, memorize the address of the building he went into."

She scrawled the details onto a piece of paper, and Scott frowned like it personally offended him. I touched his arm. "Problem, sugar?"

He shook his head and looked up at Serise. "Thanks for the info. Can you do me a favor and keep this between us?"

"Of course, if you feel that's the wisest course of action." Her gaze grew suddenly fierce as she curved her hand against her belly again. "Provided you inform your brother that continuing to shadow *me* will be extremely hazardous for *his* health. Only the fact I recognized him as your kin kept me from eliminating the potential threat to my children."

Scott nodded. "You have my thanks for sparing him, Your Majesty." He nodded to the door in a not-so-subtle hint, not that his lack of tact would particularly bother the Harpy. "Do you need an escort home?"

Serise shook her head. "No. Two of my sisters accompanied me tonight and await me outside." Then, without further ado, she made good her escape. Not too big on niceties like *hello* or *good-bye*, that one.

I let the afghan drop once the front door clicked shut and snatched the scrap of paper from his hand. Reading the numbers and letters didn't shed any light, however. Years of working Boston's streets helped me identify the address as being inside the city's magical Underbelly, but that wasn't terribly revelatory. "Spill it, Murphy. I know that something about that address has you spooked."

He dropped back onto the sofa and shook his shaggy auburn hair. "Not spooked so much as surprised. We've got a job scheduled at this address starting tomorrow night."

By *we*, he meant the Shadowhounds, a group of mercenaries founded by his father, Morgan, which Scott now led. At least until his big sister, Amaya, recovered enough from her run-in with those aforementioned mad scientists to resume her position as Shadowhound *Numero Uno*. At which point I planned to recruit him to the MCU.

"Okay, no way is *that* mere coincidence. Who's the job for?"

His expression grew slightly sheepish. "An Anubian priest."

I forced myself not to scowl from the reflexive disgust that swept over me anytime someone mentioned my least favorite immortal, Jackal-Faced Anubis. Just my typical bad luck that the one god who detested me also happened to be my lover's patron deity.

Back when my best friend, Vanessa, had first disappeared, I'd crashed Anubis's slice of the Underworld and gotten the *tiniest* bit snippy with him. Okay, maybe a whole lot of snippy, but who could blame me? My closest friend in the world had been missing for months; I couldn't find any sign of her *or* a body and had been convinced her narcissistic ex-lover had murdered her. In order to bring him to justice, I needed confirmation that she was indeed among the deceased, and Anubis could have given me that very thing. Instead, he'd become a whole lot of divinely wrathful with my ass and kicked me out of the Underworld. Scott didn't know just how bad the blood between his deity and me ran, but he *did* know Anubis was nowhere near being on my Christmas-card list.

Not that I was ever organized enough to send *those* out on time.

"Do you think Sean is trying to ambush you via the priest?"

Scott's generous lips tugged downward. "Now why would my brother want to *ambush* me, Riss?"

Because he was getting kinda crazy stalkerish with me before he disappeared? Because he started acting like he kinda hated you and wouldn't be too sad to see you out of the picture? Not exactly suggestions I could pose to Scott at the moment seeing as how I'd never found the right time or words to come clean about the things his brother had done and said in the time leading up to his disappearance.

"Er, by ambush, I mean ask you for help without letting anyone else know he needs it."

His expression changed from annoyed to thoughtful. "That would make sense. I mean, if he's in trouble and can't risk bringing it back home, the Anubian temple is a damned good choice to arrange a rendezvous."

His sudden distracted air had me letting out an inner sigh. If Serise's abrupt appearance hadn't already killed our amorous mood, his brotherly concern would have hammered the last few nails into its coffin. Not that I could blame him. One of the things we had most in common was our deep love of family.

"You may as well go back to your place tonight, then, so you can get an early start on figuring out what the heck is going on with your brother."

Sheepishness gave way to a look of gratitude mixed with guilt. "You sure?"

I brushed a kiss on his lips. "Of course I am. I'll be busy all day tomorrow getting Trinity up to speed for my leave of absence, anyway."

"That's right; Cori all ready to swear her oaths to the Sisterhood?"

My fifteen-year-old niece had finally Fledged as a Fury after several anxious years where we waited to see if she would follow in both her aunts' arcane footsteps or instead remain a magical skip like her parents. "More ready than you can even imagine. Mom's meeting us the day after tomorrow to make sure no little *accidents* happen during the trip to the Palladium."

The Palladium existed in the slice of the Otherrealms controlled by the Sisterhood of Furies and was where we conducted most official business. It also happened to be one of the few places in the Otherrealms not currently debilitated by a strange supernatural plague. The fact that the Otherrealms were slowly but surely dying off was the primary reason arcanes had traveled en masse to the mortal realm several decades ago, which nowadays kept me gainfully employed as Chief Magical Investigator in charge of all crimes committed by or against arcanes.

Scott wrapped his arms around me and squeezed. "You afraid of another attack?"

Discord had broken out among the Furies in the past months, pitting sister against sister in deadly strife, something I once would have thought impossible. "It would be foolish not to anticipate that as a possibility. I'd rather be prepared and not need to be than the alternative."

"That's what I like most about you, baby. Always thinking ahead."

I shifted against him, pressing my bare chest against his own suggestively. "Really? *That's* what you like most about me?"

His earlier distraction faded, and golden Hound eyes glowed with rekindled desire. "*One* of the things I like most."

"Oh, yeah? What *else* do you like?"

"I can think of at least a few things." His voice grew husky, and his warm, callused hands caressed my lips teasingly. "Like your beautiful smile." Those amazing hands moved several inches lower. "And your delectable neck." He leaned forward and nipped the sensitive flesh in question, before trailing his fingers down to the serpent heads tattooed onto each of my shoulders. "Not to mention your sensitive shoulders." I moaned when he dragged his fingernails across them, then down to my quivering chest. "And most especially your perfect, gorgeous breasts." His mouth soon followed caressing fingers, and I was most gratified to discover that the Harpy Queen hadn't been a *complete* buzzkill after all . . .

THE OBNOXIOUS SOUND OF "WHO LET THE Dogs Out?" had me clawing for my cell phone and cursing Cori's prankster ways at an hour that felt *way* too early the next morning. One of these days I was going to learn how to prevent her from changing my ringtone when I wasn't paying attention. "This had *better* be important," I barked into the phone after my bleary eyes registered it wasn't even 7:00 A.M. I'd gotten used to sleeping in until the decadent hour of 8:00 ever since I'd hired Kale and Mahina, the husband-and-wife Night Owls who oversaw the Magical Crimes Unit's night shift, meaning I rarely had to pull eighteen-to-twenty-four-hour shifts anymore.

"Now, is *that* any way to greet the loving mother who was only restored to you a few short months ago?"

My lips twitched upward, and I relaxed back into the plush pillows behind me. "It is when she wakes me up more than an hour before my alarm goes off."

"Oh, is it *that* early in the mortal realm?"

The feigned innocence in her tone made my lip twitching turn into eye rolling. "You know damned good and well what time it is here."

Her voice lost its teasing edge. "I *do* know how little

sleep you usually get and wouldn't disturb your rest unless it *was* important. New rumors are flying among the Elders that the Alecto Prime has cut off ties with the Tisiphone Prime." Alecto, Tisiphone, and Megaera were the classes of Fury, and I was a Tisiphone.

I frowned. "Officially or unofficially?"

"Either way spells trouble, especially considering the Megaera Prime's attacks upon our family and a new, even more disturbing development."

"So when exactly are you ever going to call me with new, even *less* disturbing developments?"

"So when exactly are you going to give me another grandbaby?"

Oh, touché, Mom. She knew just how much the thought of bringing children into the world at that time freaked me the hell out—and wasn't adverse to throwing that in my face to shut me up. Something I might have done were the roles reversed: I was *so* my mother's daughter.

"Okay, so tell me about this new, *more* disturbing development."

"Maylin refused to appear before the Conclave when summoned yesterday."

I sat up straight in bed, nearly dropping the phone in my rush. "Whoa, wait, what? Can she *do* that?"

Maylin Chang had the distinction of serving as Tisiphone Prime, meaning she ruled over the class of Furies both Mom and I belonged to with pretty much an iron fist. That being said, *all* sisters were subject to the authority of the Conclave of Fury Elders, our governing body, up to and including the Primes. The closest analogy among the mortals might be the difference between the state and federal governments in the U.S. Traditionally, each class of Furies kept the identity of its Prime secret from the other classes—and most especially from non-Furies—but when the Conclave summoned, Primes were supposed to appear before a closed Conclave session under a cloak of anonymity, at which point they revealed their identity to the fifteen sisters who served on the Conclave's Lesser Consensus. Those sisters were sealed under oath *not* to reveal the identity of any Prime.

"What did Maylin say when you asked her what the *hell* she was thinking?"

"She's refusing to see me now, too."

My heart sank because Mom was right; this really *was* a disturbing development. Mom and Maylin had become close friends during the Great War several decades earlier—what the mortals euphemistically referred to as the "Time of Troubles." Our Prime had been one of the first to welcome Mom back from her MIA status with open arms and had pushed hard for the other Tisiphones to elect Mom to our vacant seat on the Conclave's Lesser Consensus. She'd not yet been officially voted onto the Lesser Consensus, but things were looking pretty promising.

"Are you telling me that *Maylin* is the one pulling Nan's puppet strings?"

My grandmother, Maeve (whom my family had called Nan for as long as I could remember), had miraculously awakened from a prolonged magical coma not too long ago, which *should* have been as amazingly good news as Mom's being rescued from those mad scientists. Unfortunately, Nan wouldn't talk to either of us and had inexplicably challenged Ekaterina, the sister serving as the head of the Lesser Consensus, to a duel for her seat on the Conclave's ruling council. The levelheaded Nan Mom and I knew would *never* return from the brink of death only to challenge another sister to a potentially deadly duel over what amounted to mere *politics*. Mom and I suspected that someone else had used dark magic to wake Nan from her coma and manipulate her into those bizarre actions, or else had killed Nan and was impersonating her magically. Not completely far-fetched, since Furies had impressive shape-shifting abilities.

"I'm not sure, but I don't believe this is all coincidence any more than you do. I think it's more important than ever that you bring Cori to the Palladium as soon as possible. I'll feel better if you're both here where I and my allies can watch over you until we figure out what is going on in our class—not to mention the strife with the other two classes."

I glanced at my bedside clock. "I have to finish filling Trinity in on some administrative details before I start my official leave, but I can grab Cori first thing in the morning and meet you at the rendezvous point."

"Will you be able to drag yourself out of bed early enough to meet us at 9:00 A.M.?"

I ignored her gentle dig. *"Us?"*

Her tone turned grim. "Given the number of near *accidents* we've had lately, I recruited Laurell and Patricia for escort duty."

"Oh, good, I've fought beside those two before. Wicked fierce in battle."

"Exactly why they were my first choice. That, plus their staunch support of my bid for the Conclave seat the past few months."

"I better get going so I can finish everything I need today and make sure Cori will be ready in time. See you at nine tomorrow morning, then?"

"Sounds good. You take care, darling, and bring Cori to me safely."

"Will do, Mom. Love you."

"Love you, too."

I couldn't help the goofy grin that spread across my face whenever she said that. Having her back in my life after more than twenty years of believing her dead was hands down the best thing to happen to me in ages. Granted, getting back together with Scott had made me ecstatic, but nothing and no one could compare to your mother—or love you quite the same. Which made Nan's incomprehensible behavior to her own daughter all the more unbelievable.

We'll figure out who *has screwed with her head, and we'll make things right again.*

I had to believe that—any other result was simply unthinkable.

TRINITY LARUE LOOKED UP FROM A BOWL OF gruel when I leaned against the doorjamb of her office next door to mine in the PD. "*How* on earth can you eat that squirrel food?" She finished chewing with what had to be pretended bliss. I refused to believe anyone could actually *enjoy* eating sugarless granola cereal with fat- and taste-free milk.

"It's good for you. Much better than all that sugar and caffeine *you* ingest."

"Yeah, well, I've got to keep my Fury metabolism fueled, thank you very much."

"You're such a lucky bitch that you *never* gain an ounce despite all that junk you shovel into your face."

"Yes, well, that souped-up metabolism comes along

with assassination attempts every other day and the danger of Turning Harpy whenever I channel Rage."

She wrinkled her nose sympathetically. "True, I'll take the health food and my newfound gym-addict status over the constant death threats and uncontrollable anger."

"Don't forget: *You're* the one with the Spyder." Her eyes went a little dreamy at the mention of the electric blue sports car her older brothers had rebuilt for her thirtieth birthday not that long before. It sure as hell beat the MCU's land whale of a stakeout van that I commandeered whenever flying on my own two wings or taking the subway just wouldn't do. "You ready for me to get you up to speed on where everything stands?"

Trinity and I had worked together on the Boston police force for several years before we officially formed the MCU, with me as chief and her as deputy chief. She'd been assuming more and more responsibility as I managed to loosen up my controlling ways and conquer my fear for her safety as the lone 100 percent mortal on our team. Once she called me out on that tendency to coddle her, I'd done my best to curb the habit. She'd proven herself on every occasion, and she sure as hell deserved my respect.

She spooned up the last bite of squirrel food and popped up to come around her desk. Her office was *nearly* as compact of mine—minus the conference table and chairs squeezed against the wall—so I immediately noticed the oversized vase of calla lilies when she brushed past the credenza upon which she had placed it. The extremely *expensive* vase of calla lilies, which I knew were her favorite flower.

"Well, *somebody* must have gotten lucky last night."

A smile spread across her face as she gave a saucy wink. "Oh, like you *didn't* after you and that Hound of yours got half-drunk last night."

"Me *less* than half-drunk and him *more* than half-drunk, thank you very much." Thanks to that whole Fury metabolism I had going on, which gave me the opportunity to play designated driver with Scott's zippy red Ferrari. "But wait, I didn't see you leave the reception with Penn's brother."

"That's because I didn't."

"You little vixen, you! So if things didn't pan out with Tariq, who are the flowers from?"

Her smile took on a mysterious edge. "That's for me to know, and you to *maybe* find out, if things keep going as well as they have been the past little while."

"Damn tease. At least tell me if I know the guy."

"You have previously made his acquaintance, I believe." She pushed me gently away from her doorway. "Now, that's all the info you're allowed until you get back from your leave, or we'll *never* get any work done because you'll be busy hounding me or, even worse, the poor guy who may very well at *some* point get lucky."

Trinity dated a lot—with her good looks, sharp brains, and sly sense of humor, no surprise there—but she guarded her heart carefully and took her time before deciding whether a guy was worth getting more intimate with. She was like me in that regard, probably one of the reasons we had connected so well as partners. For all our differences, we had a lot of the same core values. Like our dedication to the MCU and protecting the people of Boston from various and sundry magical crimes. I couldn't think of a better person, mortal *or* arcane, to entrust my city with during my absence. Good thing, too, because there really wasn't anyone else I *could* entrust it to.

We spent the next few hours going over various mundane—but necessary—administrative minutiae, with me trying like crazy to ferret out more details from her regarding the guy who had sent her such lovely flowers. She didn't crack the slightest bit, taking extreme pleasure in watching me try without success to guess who the new man in her life was. I finally gave up when we knocked off for the night, she presumably to head off for a dinner date with Mr. Mysterious, and me heading to Scott's apartment so we could hopefully enjoy a repeat of the night before—minus the overbearing Harpy Queen—before I left for gods knew how long to clean house in the Palladium. A Fury's job was just *never* done.

CHAPTER TWO

WITH AS MANY PEOPLE AS HAD TRIED TO KILL me over the years, you'd think I would get used to it. Then again, the fact I hadn't *completely* gotten used to it was the reason nobody had yet managed to do me in, not permanently anyway. Temporary death—there'd been a few of those. Nothing I'd like to repeat anytime soon—especially considering how much I'd pissed off Scott's Jackal-Faced god that last time. Being two times a cop—Fury and Chief Magical Investigator—meant two times the psychos out for my blood. Of course, getting that very real threat through my fifteen-year-old niece's head at precisely nine the next morning was easier said than done.

"Aunt Riss, I just don't understand wh—"

I turned from the subway entrance and narrowed my eyes at my soon-to-be apprentice. "What part of *be quiet* did you *not* understand, apprentice?"

She flushed when I used her title rather than name and had the sense to actually shut her trap. Stubborn she might be (hmm, wonder where she got *that* from?), but she learned quickly, a quality that would serve her well during her training. Assuming I could keep her alive long enough to swear her oaths to the Sisterhood. A flash of red teased my peripheral vision, and I whirled, in-stinctively placing my body in front of Cori's. Normally, the red leather uniform of a Fury meant safety and sup-port, but not so much these days, with civil war brewing among the three classes of Furies.

The hint of red *did* prove to be a Fury's uniform, but no threat to Cori or me. My mother swept out of the sub-way station's door, flanked by the two Furies she had mentioned the day before. Mom zeroed in on us straight-away. She nodded to each of her informal bodyguards, who took up posts at the sides of the doorway while Mom jogged the last few feet separating us. We exchanged smiles, but she focused most of her attention on Cori, drawing her into a bear hug and murmuring into her ear. Cori alternately grinned and flushed, torn between ado-lescent pride and embarrassment over the big deal Mom was making over her. No surprise she made such a fuss; it was the first time she'd seen Cori since the teen Fledged into her Fury powers a few days before.

"While your aunt and I *are* proud of you, Concordia Joy," Mom said, "you'll also find we expect a great deal from you. To start with, you must remember to treat us always as elder Furies first, your aunt and grandmother second."

Cori let out a huff of air. "Now you sound like *her.*"

Another arch of the brow. "Where do you think *she* got it from?"

I laughed outright. "Oh so true, I'm afraid. Stacia may have been my official mentor, but Mom taught me a lot about being a Fury before she disappeared."

Mom and I exchanged a grim glance. That was another of those shared griefs that would never fully go away.

The hair on the back of my neck stirred, and my body tensed in response to a sudden surge of adrenaline. Someone was channeling magic nearby. It might have been a mere coincidence, but . . .

Trusting survival instincts honed over the past two decades, I nodded toward the door. "We should get a move on."

Mom placed an arm along Cori's shoulder and nudged her forward. "Of course. Laurell will serve as our rear guard while Patricia clears our forward path." The second-named Tisiphone nodded before vanishing in the direction from which they had appeared. Laurell waited until we followed and fell in behind us.

Passersby who caught sight of Mom's red leather (Cori and I were wearing more anonymous street clothes) gave us a wide berth on the staircase to the subway platform. Halfway down the steps, we channeled Fury magic to camouflage our little entourage. While not technically invisible, we became nearly impossible for mortals—and most arcanes—to detect, as much for the mortals' peace of mind as our safety. They tended to freak out when winged demigoddesses leaped atop speeding train cars to reach the magical portals sprinkled throughout Boston's underground railway system.

Despite my sudden sense of unease, we made it to the platform unaccosted, other than my bum knee's pitching a fit as I jogged down the stairs. Magical and medical remedies, including physical therapy, promised a brighter prognosis than when I had originally injured it, but both would take time to pay off. For the moment, I just had to grin and bear the pain.

Patricia waited for us at the empty end of the platform, eyeballing the area for any signs of danger. Laurell no doubt did the same from behind. While I only knew the two vaguely, what I *did* know reassured me. One of those rare mated pairs of Furies, they were unfailingly loyal to the Sisterhood and, most especially, other Tisiphones. Knowing they had watched Mom's back when I couldn't had given me enough peace of mind to finish up my police duties on the serial-killer case and now made me feel better about getting Cori safely to the Palladium. Of course, that thought no sooner crossed my mind than trouble struck.

Goose bumps pricked my skin as the hair on my neck rose once more. Someone had once again channeled the barest hint of magic nearby. I didn't waste time thinking, just shifted to full Fury form. Mortal honey blond hair surrendered to charcoal locks that snapped in the magical breeze caused by transformation. Boring blue eyes changed to glowing green orbs meant to inspire terror. My jeans and T-shirt became identical to Mom's red leather pants, sleeveless vest, and flat-heeled, knee-high boots. Most impressive of all were the twin tattoos along each upper arm that morphed into living, breathing serpents: the magical familiars called Amphisbaena, who amped up my own arcane abilities.

Nemesis and Nike hissed in response to my mental warning of potential ambush and wound their way from upper arms to lower, ready to aid me if needed. Mom and the other two Tisiphones picked up on whatever bad vibes I'd caught, and we drew a protective circle around our most vulnerable member.

Cori gulped and shot me an uneasy glance. "Aunt Ri—I mean, Marissa?"

"Shh," I murmured, and tried to figure out what had set my inner alarms blazing. Barely a dozen mortals stood at the opposite end of the platform, also waiting for the next northbound train. A couple of arcanes—shifters of some sort—stood across the tracks waiting for the next southbound train. No magical currents vibrated in the air other than the eddies left behind by my sudden transformation. Why, then, was I so sure something bad was about to go down?

I turned to confer with Mom, only to notice Laurell stepping close to Cori. My skin crawled even more when I saw her serpent tattoos flash briefly, seeming to shimmer from Tisiphone red to Megaera green, then back again. *Shit, an imposter.* Managing to mask the sudden flicker of realization from my face, I sent a magical feeler toward Patricia. The arcane feedback bouncing from her to me screamed purely Tisiphone, so that was one less worry; though when she figured out someone had taken out her mate long enough to impersonate her, there would be hell to pay.

All this transpired in a few breaths' worth of time, but it was just long enough for the imposter to yank Cori away from my mother's side and aim a magical weapon at the Fury she considered the biggest threat. No big surprise that turned out to be me. I had a reputation for shooting first, asking questions *never* when it came to loved ones.

Mom whirled, confusion on her face, but froze when she saw Cori held in front of Fake Laurell and the

weapon pointed at me. Patricia's breath hitched, and she
let out a choked, "Laur?" before registering the inescapable conclusion. *This wasn't Laurell.*

"Drop it!" I growled.

Knowing what I meant, the imposter allowed her dis-
guise to fall away, revealing someone I *should have* but
hadn't expected: Durra, the bitch who'd been infatuated
with Vanessa and irrationally blamed me for her death.
Durra had also tried to abduct Cori just days before.
Some people apparently never learned.

"This is becoming a habit of yours, Megaera." She
took my insult of using title rather than name without
batting an eyelash. "But really. Ambushing me twice in
subway stations? How pathetically predictable." Fake it
till you can make it, I always say. She didn't need to
know just how fast fear for Cori had my pulse racing.

Patricia hissed when she recognized the dark-skinned
Megaera facing us. "If you've harmed Laurell, *sister*, I'll
carve you into pieces with my bare claws!" No idle
threat, considering that her Fury talons had broken
through her skin the moment she spoke.

"Peace, Tisiphone. Laurell has merely been—
detained—upstairs. She is unharmed."

"She better be," came the growled response.

Mom bit out a growl of her own. "Do you *have* a death
wish, Durra of the Megaera? Interfering with an Elder
Fury escorting a candidate to the Palladium—days after
attempting to abduct the same candidate—who is also
that Elder's granddaughter by blood. I could flay the flesh
from your bones, and none would gainsay me."

Durra winced, skin paling several shades. Still, her
weapon never wavered. "I appear in the name of the
Megaera to summon you two sisters of the Tisiphone into

her presence. This candidate will stand hostage for your goodwill until you leave the Megaera's presence. Safe passage to and from the Megaera's hall is granted. Failure to answer the summons means that this candidate shall remain hostage until such time as you do appear."

Mom and I glanced at each other with deer-trapped-in-headlights expressions. Prime Furies typically only had the power to compel sisters from their own classes to appear before them. It was an absolute power but finite in that it applied only to the class over which they ruled. The only exceptions to that were when two Primes issued a summons jointly—virtually unheard of—or during times of war. As far as I knew, no such war had been declared.

Surely we would have heard *if a formal declaration had been . . .*

That thought faded when reality intruded. In all the millennia the Sisterhood had policed the arcane races, one thing had always held true: The Sisterhood stood united against the other species. Never once had we devolved into warring among ourselves, not to the extent that civil war had ever been declared. Even now, when sister fought against sister, would that unspoken rule be broken? No; to the outside world, appearances must be maintained. Formal war would never be declared if that war was waged within. The Sisterhood *would* stand together as far as others were concerned.

Among ourselves, however, battle lines were clearly being drawn.

"M—Marissa?"

That choked comment came from a shaken Cori. She looked like she wanted to open a can of kickass on Durra the way she had before, but at the same time she trusted me to handle things so that she wouldn't have to. I would *die* before I let her down.

"What assurances do *we* have that the Megaera will keep *her* word?"

Durra shook in Rage, taking the insult toward her superior much worse than the one to herself. Holding on to her temper took visible effort. Finally, she managed to grit her teeth and let out a sharp whistle. Moments later, a half dozen Megaeras strode down the staircase and stopped just behind Durra. Make that five Megaeras and one pissed-off Tisiphone.

Patricia let out a relieved breath when she recognized Laurell. All I could notice was the fact that we were outnumbered, barely, but outnumbered all the same. Especially considering that, in a fight, Cori would be way more hindrance than help.

One of the newcomers held out a ceremonial olive branch, the arcane version of a white flag and far more respected by our kind than its mortal equivalent. That they carried it meant they truly wished us no harm. Betraying its promise of safety would make them oath-breakers in the eyes of the gods and mark them for death—nasty, not-at-all-quick death. The Megaera with the olive branch nudged Laurell, who stalked past Durra without a word and took her place beside Patricia. That Megaera then stepped in front of Mom and went down on one knee. "I stand hostage for the Megaera's good-will while you appear before her."

Mom opened her mouth to make some no-doubt-diplomatic response, but I beat her to the punch. "And who are you to her that we should give a shit?"

The other Megaeras bristled at this outright insult, but Durra hushed them so the branch-bearer could answer. "I am the Megaera's great-aunt and mentor. She will not break her word, and any Megaera who violates her edict shall be executed."

I blinked, then blinked again. Prime Furies *did* have the right to execute traitors to their classes without trial, but it was a right even more rarely exercised than summoning sisters outside their own classes. The Megaera was playing hardball. This *had* to have something to do with Nan, recently awakened from her twenty-year coma only to jump into a political hotbed, not to mention the Prime Tisiphone refusing to appear before the Conclave. Why else would the Megaera first try to kill me, abduct Cori, and blockade my mother only to seek a conference with those she opposed?

My pulse picked up speed when I realized the Prime Megaera's offering a reciprocal hostage gave us another bargaining chip to hold over her head should the necessity arise. Each class jealously guarded the identity of its Prime sister to prevent others from tampering with her sovereignty. With the Megaera's great-aunt as hostage, however, it would be easy to discern the identity of our hostage and work backward to discover the Prime's identity as well. The Megaera knew this and was making a clear statement. Her desire to speak with us was great and, should treachery arise, it would *not* come about on her end. Of course, by claiming Cori as hostage, she guaranteed it would not come about on *our* end, either.

I touched Mom's arm and nodded slightly. She let out a deep breath before speaking. "We two sisters of the Tisiphone accept your standing as goodwill hostage for the Prime Megaera and further accept her summons and offer of safe conduct."

Cori let out a breath of her own and shot an uneasy

glance from Mom to me. Further demonstrating that she *could* be taught, however, she kept her lips zipped. The branch-bearer nodded and moved to stand between Patricia and a still-simmering Laurell. I stepped closer to Cori to offer her reassurances. Durra bared her teeth but made no move to stop me.

I kept my voice low and calm. "I'm afraid you'll have to spend some time with these—sisters—of ours while Allegra and I meet with the Prime Megaera. My previous instruction still stands." I.e., *be quiet.* "We'll be as quick as we can."

She gave a brave nod and even managed the ghost of a smile, falling back without protest when Durra nudged her toward the Megaeras behind her. "If you two will come with me?"

Like we had a choice.

While I reassured Cori, Mom wasted no time giving instructions to Patricia and Laurell. They would head on to the Palladium as planned while we went along with the Megaeras like good little girls. Yeah, just *thinking* that had me rolling my eyes. I was about as far from being a good little girl as, say, the Jackal-Faced god was from being a cute and cuddly puppy dog.

CHAPTER THREE

I EXPECTED DURRA TO LEAD US AWAY FROM our former destination, and she didn't disappoint. She and three of her sisters escorted us up and out of the subway station. The remaining sisters of both classes stayed behind to accompany their hostages to the Palladium. What *did* surprise me was the fact our escorts didn't lead us to another Otherrealm portal. Instead, we wound a circuitous route through Southie, around the South End, then into Chinatown. At that point, our ultimate destination became clear: Not the Otherrealms at all but Arcane Central here in Boston, the predominantly arcane neighborhood known as the Underbelly. I opened my mouth once or twice but shut it when Mom shot me an expression much like the ones I'd given Cori. She really *had* taught me most of what I knew about being a Fury—attitude wise, anyway.

Nearly an hour after we left the subway behind, Durra approached a building deep in the Belly that seemed a likely spot for a meet-and-greet with her superior, a pantheon, or temple dedicated to all the gods and goddesses. Fitting, considering that's who Furies were officially sworn to serve. Some of us had our personal favorites, of course, but we owed allegiance to no one god in particular.

It wasn't a big shocker to discover that the pantheon crawled with Megaeras. Hell, with an undeclared civil war brewing, their Prime would be an idiot to venture away from the Palladium without a substantial guard force to watch her back—and front—and both sides. So far, no matter how much she'd pissed me off, the Prime Megaera hadn't struck me as the slightest bit stupid. Bitchy and treacherous, yes; stupid, not so much.

Durra exchanged inaudible murmurs with one of her sisters before turning back to Mom and me. "The Megaera awaits us just beyond this antechamber. I assume neither of you carries spell-worked silver?"

Even though that was a big no-no on sacred ground unless one was a temple guardian, I couldn't blame her for checking. Her ass would be in just as much trouble as ours should she bring us before her Prime carrying the metal lethal to our kind. She didn't take us at our word, of course—the slight tingle of a magical scan washed over us before she was satisfied we spoke truly. Durra nodded to the sister closest to the door, who then swung it open. Mom and I followed the assassin-turned-kidnapper-turned-escort without a word.

Modern-day pantheons were more like Christian churches than their predecessors. We passed from the cold marble antechamber into a warmly decorated chapel consisting of a dozen rows of pews leading to a carpeted dais—the chancel—on the far side of the room. Gorgeous tapestries lined the chapel walls in between elegant stained-glass windows throughout the room. Several tense-looking Megaeras sat in the front pew, staring up at the chancel's sole occupant: a tall, dark-skinned woman in full Fury form who bore a vague resemblance to the olive branch-bearer-turned-hostage. *The* Megaera.

As if she could hear my mental identification, she turned emerald eyes toward Mom and me. My steps faltered slightly as I followed in Durra's wake, but I tightened my lips and turned the stumble into an outright strut. I was a *Tisiphone*, dammit, and no way would I let another Fury intimidate me as if I'd just Fledged yesterday. Not even *the* Prime Megaera.

I forced my gaze back to her Furied-out eyes and finished looking her over. Her dark brown skin set off the red leather uniform way better than my pasty white skin did. Her hair, while the typical Fury's charcoal in color, had been plaited into several dozen braids wound into tight buns jutting out from her scalp, no doubt in homage to her homeland. Based upon her great-aunt's slight accent and Durra's fanatic devotion, I was willing to bet her birthplace was somewhere in central Africa.

Durra reached the foot of the dais and distracted me from my unabashed appraisal. She went down on one knee, placed a hand upon her heart, and muttered something in an unfamiliar language too rapidly for me to channel magic to comprehend. Definitely sounded like Swahili or something similar. I tried to remember exactly where Durra was from, but we hadn't been close even *before* she tried to kill me.

The Megaera's sudden sharp voice belied the pleased nod she gave her sister. It also matched her great-aunt's in accent. "Keep to English, Durra, so that all present may understand." *And to lower the chance we might pick up enough clues to figure out who she was in case we needed to track her down again later.*

Durra nodded. "Of course, Prime. I bring with me Allegra and Marissa Holloway of the Tisiphone to answer your summons, as requested."

Ten to one that hadn't been the phrase originally spoken.

The Megaera accepted Durra's announcement with a graceful flick of her wrist. Durra rose smoothly, bowed first to her Prime, then—to my surprise—Mom and me, before joining her sisters on the front pew, leaving mother and daughter Tisiphone to face the imposing Megaera alone.

Fortunately for my still-developing diplomatic skills, tradition dictated that the seniormost sister—in this case, Mom—spoke first. "As your sister Megaera indicated, we two of the Tisiphone stand before you in answer to your summons. By what right do you summon sisters not of your own class?"

The Prime touched her palms together and inclined her head respectfully. "By my right to serve as Voice of the Triad."

Shocked whispers behind us demonstrated that the other Megaeras felt as much surprise as Mom and me. She and I shared a look before focusing on the Megaera again.

Mom's voice sounded much less accusatory and more awed this time. "The Triad has spoken to you directly?"

The Prime nodded, expression more serene than I

could have managed under the same set of circum-stances. Serving as leader of the individual classes was only one function performed by the Prime Furies. Their more sacred duty was to act as messengers for the gods and goddesses on those rare occasions they chose to communicate with the Sisterhood directly. The last time I personally knew of its happening came only from sec-ondhand stories told to me: Upon the night of Hazuki's assassination, the Moerae who finally succeeded in bro-kering that blood-soaked Peace Accord ending the Great War only to be murdered by a splinter faction of arcanes who did *not* want peace on any terms. After her assas-sination, the Sisterhood's first instinct had been to hunt down and slaughter her assassins, something that would have plunged us straight from one war into another. The Deities had forbidden that act by speaking through all three Prime Furies, leaving the Sisterhood no choice but to obey. Of course, the Deities might speak with the Primes more often than word got out, but still. That was a pretty startling statement.

The Megaera's abrupt reversal from trying to kill us to suing for peace made all-too-much sense. The Deities themselves had intervened. Rather than be merely grate-ful, however, I was a whole lot of scared shitless. For them to exercise a rite so rarely used, things had to be even worse than any of us expected, like the difference between the *Titanic* heading toward an iceberg and a moon-sized meteor hurtling toward earth. Mom's fin-gers clutching at my hand showed that she, too, was terrified.

The Prime turned her attention from Mom and me to the sisters behind. "Leave us," she commanded.

Several of the Megaeras shot us uneasy glances but

scurried to do her bidding. Durra, not surprisingly, pro-
tested. "But that would leave you defenseless, Pri—"
The Prime's eyes flashed a brighter shade of green that
had Durra scrambling toward the door. *Nobody*—
however well-intentioned—accused a Prime of being
defenseless and got away with it, not to mention gainsaid
a direct order. "As you wish," Durra choked out before
vanishing after her sisters.

The Prime gave a deep sigh when the chapel door
thudded shut. "If only children would *think* before they
speak."

Mom gave me a sardonic glance before smiling
slightly. "If *only*."

An answering smile flashed across the Megaera's
face before she became businesslike once more. "Now
that we are alone, I can prepare you."

That didn't sound particularly good.

"The Triad desires to speak with you both."

My knees buckled but not due to the injury I'd suffered when saving Scott from insurmountable odds.
Drumbeats sounded inside my ears in sharp staccato for
several seconds before I realized it was my pulse pounding in fear. Funny, in a not-ha sort of way, since a minute
earlier I thought myself incapable of being any more
scared.

Just as the Sisterhood had its hierarchies—apprentices
like Cori, sisters like me, and Elder Furies like Mom, so,
too, did the Immortals. Demigoddesses such as Furies
who *barely* counted and were usually classified with the
other arcanes, lesser gods and goddesses who were *truly*
immortal (meaning they could not be killed in any way,
shape, or form) but had either little magical or political

power, and the greater gods and goddesses who were referred to as Deities-with-a-capital-*D*. The divine beings falling into this category were those who possessed a shitload of power both magically *and* politically (as reckoned by fellow immortals). The Triad referred to whichever three Deities currently had enough magical and political power among Their fellows to be elected as nominal leaders. While They didn't rule over their peers in the strictest sense of the term, They *were* responsible for serving as Tribunals against any immortal thought to have committed crimes against other immortals.

Mom's hands squeezed my fingers tightly, and her ragged breathing indicated she was no less fearful than I. Nan hadn't raised a fool any more than my mother had.

This time, I was the first to find my voice. "But that— that's—*impossible*. The Triad doesn't speak to—we're not *Primes*!"

The Megaera inclined her head in agreement. "You are not." She tilted her head, then murmured with a thoughtful tone, "Not yet."

My poor, skittering mind could take no more, and my body shifted from partial to full Fury form out of pure instinct: glowing green eyes, huge feathered wings, hissing Amphisbaena writhing along my arms, and razor-sharp talons bursting from my fingernail beds.

Amused emerald eyes met my own, and the Megaera let out a soft laugh. "You've half prepared yourself already."

Her matter-of-fact response to my uncontrolled shift lessened the embarrassment—a little. Only Furies in full-on demigoddess form could withstand a meeting with *true* Immortal beings. We would be unable to see them at all in mortal form, and in partial Fury form, we would see them but be unable to withstand their sheer magical glory. Mom shifted to help lessen my faux pas even further, something that made me love her all the more. She also expanded on the Megaera's response to my incoherent babbling. "It's not impossible for them to speak with non-Primes, Marissa, they just rarely choose to do so, especially outside of a wartime Conclave." The Conclave consisted of all Elder Furies, who were eligible to vote in the Greater Consensus, and the fifteen Furies—five from each class—elected to serve on the Lesser Consensus.

I blinked at Mom's revelation. Apparently Elders kept all kinds of secrets from junior Furies. Although, really, considering how much more we worked in the outside world, that only made sense. Just like the mortal PD I worked with, the Sisterhood kept its secrets from outsiders as much as possible. Mom was only 'fessing up now because she *had* to. My mind finally finished its panic attack and logical thought kicked back in. If the Deities rarely chose to speak with non-Primes outside a wartime Conclave and were about to break that usual pattern, that could mean only one thing. The Sisterhood's brewing internal war had the potential to spill out across the arcane world as a whole. And the Triad thought *we* could do something to stop that.

I licked my lips and stared at the Megaera intently. "Why?" Meaning: *Why us?*

She didn't dissemble, but neither did she answer my question. "Let us finish preparing for their arrival, and I will let the Triad explain."

Goose bumps broke out all over my body, and I couldn't help the shudders that followed. True, I had confronted lesser gods before—case in point, my lover

Scott's patron deity, Anubis—but they were just a step above Furies on the magical food chain. A big step, to be sure, but the step dividing *them* from the Deities-with-a-capital-D was ten times greater than that between Furies and the lesser gods, maybe even a hundred. The thought of facing not just one Deity but *three* was almost too much for me to handle.

Still, I guess I should have been grateful they were giving our puny little brains time to prepare for their arrival and limiting their number to three. A magical number; a sacred number—and the reason Furies had been divided into *three* classes—and even more interesting when I really thought about it. The Triad would carry the authority of the immortals as a whole, which meant that somebody had been a *very* bad boy or girl since the only reason the Triad could have to confer with the Sisterhood directly was to serve as Tribunal against someone of true immortal blood.

Mom broke into my reverie by shaking me slightly and nodding toward the Megaera, who had opened a concealed door behind the chancel. She held her arms out in a formal gesture, sweeping them from us to the doorway. "Come, sisters, let us prepare to receive the counsel of the Deities who would aid us."

And who would have us aid them, the cynical side of me couldn't help but add silently. I shoved that irreverent piece of my personality way, way down inside. If ever there was an absolutely worst time to give in to one's Inner Snark, meeting with the Triad would be it. Only once I was sure I had ironclad control of my emotions did I follow in my mother's footsteps through that doorway, feeling very much like Alice stepping through the looking glass.

CHAPTER FOUR

THAT FEELING ONLY INTENSIFIED OVER THE next hour as the Megaera—at some point I *really* needed to find out her actual name—helped us fumble through rituals we'd never heard of, much less needed to learn. We also had to bathe in magically cleansed water that seemed to sear away all signs of inner exhaustion along with outer grime. I couldn't remember the last time I'd felt so refreshed, especially considering I'd been pulling bone-draining shifts for a month on that serial-killer case. My skin continued tingling even after I stepped out of the water and slipped into the snow-white toga the Megaera handed me.

She smiled at the dubious look I gave it, gesturing to the matching garment she wore. "That old saying *when in Rome* had its origins even earlier than most etymologists would believe. Many of the Deities adopted the

Roman gods' style of dress for formal ceremony. So do
we when meeting with them."

Mom gave me another *mom* look as she finished
draping her toga with expert tucks and folds. My brow
furrowed. Where the heck had she learned to wear a
toga? Granted, she was around a century and a half old,
but *still* . . . She opened her mouth to speak—more like
nag—but I rolled my eyes and allowed the Megaera to
start wrapping the white fabric around me in an even
more expert manner than my mother's. Once *that* was
done with, we slipped on flimsy gold sandals with straps
that wound halfway up our legs. Good thing there were
no mirrors nearby because I didn't want to see how
ridiculous I must have looked decked out *à la Caesar.* I'd
made it through college without ever once getting roped
into a toga party for more than one good reason. *Not* a
good look for me.

I had to admit, though, that both Mom and the
Megaera looked regal in their Roman getup. They'd also
refreshed their hairstyles. The Megaera's braided buns
had been jazzed up with colorful beads, and Mom had
shifted her hair from its typical simple style into an updo
that would have done any Greek goddess proud. My fingers touched my own charcoal locks hanging loose in
humidity-inspired waves, but I straightened my spine in
sheer stubbornness. The Deities could damned well take
me the way *they* created me, or not at all. I'd jumped
through more than enough hoops for one day.

Not that I would ever be stupid enough to say that out
loud.

My au naturel hairdo—or lack thereof—must have
passed muster because the Megaera guided us from the
bathing chamber, down an empty hallway, and into a

room that could have been copied directly from the Palladium's Conclave, the imposing chamber that hosted the meetings for the Sisterhood's voting council of the same name. Of course, this was a *much* smaller version, but all the elements were there: ornate marble floor and walls as white as our togas, a solid mahogany table in the center of the room, and the same overwhelming sense of grandeur that grabbed you by the throat and made you feel about six inches tall.

One unexpected element caught my attention: a golden chalice resting atop the table on the end nearest to us. It was to that spot the Megaera led us. She took the chalice into her hands and held it toward us.

"The ancients spoke of ambrosia, the nectar of the gods that granted them their immortality. This is the ambrosia they spoke of, though our forebears were only partially correct. Ambrosia is the drink of the gods only in that it contains the essence of true immortality—or rather, a portion of it—and comes from the Deities themselves. For three days you will become as true demigoddesses with the senses the immortals possess. You will feel, hear, and most importantly, *see* the world as they do, allowing you to commune with them as you would not otherwise be able to do."

My breath hitched at the enormity of her words. Furies were called demigoddesses by many—even ourselves—but it was more a figurative title than literal, seeing as how we could be killed like any other arcane. If what the Megaera was saying meant what I thought it did . . .

"And yes, for a time you will truly *be* as the Deities are—immune to death's touch. But be warned: The Deities exact a high price from those to whom they grant this gift—and it is finite. The effects will wear off three days after you partake of the ambrosia, and you will become as weak as a babe for some time afterward. A final caution: While you two will be divine for that period of time, those you care for *will not be*. Never forget this. Your enemies will not."

I clenched my fists at her warning. As high an honor as the Deities were granting, she was right. Whatever job they had in mind for us to do, it would undoubtedly suck big-time, and since I was sure it involved the turmoil in the Sisterhood and my grandmother, our enemies could easily get to us through our loved ones. Then again, that was just about par for my course.

"Do you understand?"

Mom and I nodded. "We do."

"So be it. Let us drink, and so doing, become as our Makers for a time."

She took an unladylike swig from the chalice, turned it slightly, and held it to Mom's lips. Mom took a matching gulp but didn't react with quite so much savoir faire. Her eyes watered, and she staggered back a step, a dark red liquid dribbling from her chin and splashing onto the pristine white of her toga. Funny, I'd always pictured ambrosia as looking more like honey than blood. I watched as the crimson drop burrowed into the fabric, but to my shock, it didn't stain it as I expected. Instead, the ambrosia was absorbed into the garment, which briefly glowed with a silvery sheen before fading to duller white once more. I blinked but didn't have time to wonder exactly what that meant because the Megaera rotated the chalice again and pressed the surprisingly warm metal to my mouth. I stared into the dark red liquid that swirled much like the butterflies stirring inside my stomach, bracing myself; not that it helped a whole heck of a lot. I reacted even more violently than Mom when molten fire burned its way across my tongue, down my throat, and into my belly, drowning every one of those butterflies in incandescent heat. My eyes flooded with tears that ran down my cheeks in torrents as coughs racked my body hard enough that I saw stars. I didn't merely stumble, either. I fell flat on my ass on cold white marble and convulsed.

Mom barked a terrified question I barely heard, although I did catch the Megaera's response more clearly. "She is not an Elder so of *course* it affects her more!"

Several moments passed while I oozed every ounce of spare moisture from my body and coughed up both my lungs. The ambrosia tasted like nothing I'd ever experienced and didn't think I'd ever want to experience again. It didn't hurt—exactly—just saturated every fiber of my being in a pulse-pounding rush that took my breath away. Almost literally, since I went several minutes unable to take in a bit of oxygen and yet didn't notice its lack until the coughing subsided and I could finally *think* again.

Mom reached down to help me stand, and my mouth dropped open when I noticed a familiar silvery light dancing across her skin. For that matter, the glow shimmered along her toga again, too. My gaze flew to the Megaera, who glowed even more brightly than Mom. *Because she's ingested ambrosia more than once?* Then I noticed something even more disconcerting: Eerie silver light edged itself around both of their glowing emerald eyes.

I managed to stumble to my feet with Mom's help,

noticing that silvery light now played across my skin as
well—and, I assumed, also rimmed my eyes. The fire
inside began cooling somewhat but not entirely. As much
as the bath moments ago had energized me, it paled in
comparison to the vitality buzzing inside my blood and
bones. I felt jazzed, pumped up, buzzed—like being
drunk without any of the downsides. It felt like I could
take on the world with both hands tied behind my back
and one eye closed, injured knee and all. My eyes widened as realization kicked in. For the first time in
months, my knee felt—completely normal, without the
slightest hint of pain or even discomfort. *Who needs
Jack Daniel's when they have ambrosia? Enough of this
stuff, and I really* could *take on the world!*

Then I remembered what was to come and managed
to sober my thoughts, if not my emotions. Because,
amped up on ambrosia, I might well be able to take on
all comers, but one truth was inescapable. This sense of
indestructibility was extremely temporary. Eventually,
reality would set in once more, including the incessant
knee pain.

As if she could hear my irreverent thoughts, the
Megaera judged me sufficiently recovered to continue.
She guided us to the far side of the table. A pentagram
had been engraved into the marble floor just past the
table, in front of a dais much like the one in the chancel
where we'd first encountered the Megaera. The notice-
able difference was the enormous mirror framed in
silver gilt that was suspended from the wall, towering
over both dais and pentagram. My flesh prickled with
goose bumps as I recognized it as a summoning circle.

Circle was a magical rather than literal term and referred to the sphere of arcane energy that would surround

both pentagram and mirror once the summoning began. I'd seen summoning circles before—hell, I'd summoned spirits from the hereafter myself—but never one involving a mirror, much less one so large and overflowing with magical energy. The reason for that was simple— it required a phenomenal amount of power for a living being to travel from one mirror, through the arcane maelstrom separating the various realms, and out of another mirror without frying to a flaming-hot crisp.

The Megaera positioned Mom at the southwestern point of the five-sided star and me at the southeastern. She moved to the northern point, keeping her back to us so she could face the mirror. Her hands shot into the air, and magical energy roared up all around us. Sapphire blue Fury's magic swirled from her hands to mingle with a thousand sparks of silver I was learning to identify as divine in nature. The Megaera then chanted in some language even more ancient—and powerful— than the Latin most spellcasters used. My focus narrowed to the mirror on the wall as it rippled with myriad colors and shuddered as if something was trying to break through it— and then something *did*. Or, rather, some*one*. Three of them, to be precise, each as overwhelming and awe-inspiring as the next.

Flash.

A woman with night-dark skin and crescent-shaped eyes rimmed in silver strode onto the dais, toga snapping in the magical breeze whipping inside the circle. Somehow it seemed appropriate that her raven black hair had been braided into a multitude of knots much like the Megaera's. Unlike the Fury's hairstyle, however, hers was adorned with glittering emeralds, rubies, and sapphires rather than beads. A belt of woven crescent moons—each bearing a precious gem at its center—encircled her shapely hips. My eyes widened when I saw a shimmering, multihued python tattoo wrapping from each of her shoulders to fingertips. The colors and size were different, but I couldn't help but be reminded of my own Amphisbaena in ink form. She clutched a shimmery silver sword in one hand, an emblem that leaped out at me immediately. While I didn't recognize the goddess by name, I knew what she represented in her current guise: The Rebuker.

Flash.

A man who was more light-skinned than the woman but just as obviously an African Deity sauntered to the opposite side of the dais. His eyes were scarlet bolts of lightning, rimmed in immortal silver, and his black hair sprang from his head in tight curls that seemed to crackle with barely restrained energy. Like the goddess, he bore twin tattoos on his arms running from shoulder to wrists, stylized white rams with eyes the same scarlet lightning bolts as his own. His belt was formed of silver storm clouds winding around his waist. A golden shield hung from one of his arms, giving a clue to his current role despite the fact I didn't know his name: The Defender.

Flash.

Another woman emerged, this time a pale-skinned redhead of obvious Celtic heritage, with silver-rimmed, ice blue eyes that resembled Scott's Hound eyes in all but color. Her titian hair rioted around her head even more wildly than my own au naturel style, resembling nothing so much as a horse's mane. A particularly apt image, since I recognized her the moment she stepped between the other two Deities: Epona, Celtic horse-goddess, who had also been worshipped by many Romans.

My identification was verified by the twin horses that seemed to gallop across her arms, not to mention the golden hounds chasing each other across the belt at her waist. She ruled over not just horses, but also Hounds, the European branch, at any rate. In her current guise, however, she represented an even more important role made evident by the balanced set of scales dangling from one hand: The Mediator.

Brilliant silver light flashed once more, and the mirror went quiescent, leaving the three Deities staring at us with impassive expressions carved into immortal faces. I felt guilty just standing there, much like a child confronted by disappointed parents. Even reminding myself that *I* wasn't the one in trouble didn't really help. Not only was I standing in the presence of three real-life Deities, but they were in all-out Triad mode. Rebuker, Defender, and Mediator; the immortal version of the Supreme Court. No, more than that, because bearing the symbols of office as they did, they were authorized to act as judge, jury, *and* executioner.

The Megaera chanted another unfamiliar spell, and the summoning circle faded much like the mirror's portal had. She immediately sank to one knee, placing hands over heart; Mom and I followed suit. The Deities accepted this as Their due, and we waited until Epona motioned before rising to our feet. "Greetings, Megaera, and Tisiphone's Daughters." Our classes were named for the first three Furies of the same names, the only three of our Sisterhood to become *true* immortals as reward for their centuries of service. We became their figurative daughters during the ceremonies in which we pledged ourselves to the Sisterhood.

The Megaera—who represented a stand-in for her

namesake here on earth—bowed less deeply before responding. "Greetings to the immortal Tribunal. We of the Sisterhood stand ready to serve You."

The Rebuker narrowed her eyes and bared her teeth in a downright unfriendly manner. "Do you really, Daughter? All *three* of you?" She turned her glare onto first Mom, then me, and my suddenly weak knees barely managed to keep me upright.

The Deity currently serving as Defender stepped in. "Peace, Ala. You already know these two of the Tisiphone remain steadfast, or the ambrosia would have smote them instantly."

Oh. My. Gods. *That* would have been nice to know *before* we slugged it down like Jack D. Or—maybe not.

Ala—I recognized the name as that of an African fertility goddess associated with justice—sniffed as if not completely convinced but dialed back the divine wrath a few notches. "Perhaps *they* remain steadfast, but the same cannot be said for their entire class or even all those who share their maternal bloodline."

Mom and I shared a silent, miserable glance. Ala could only be referring to Nan, since Cori had not yet pledged herself to Their service. We had a few distant cousins still active in the Sisterhood, but none close enough for the Deities to classify as belonging to our *maternal* bloodline.

Epona leveled a no-nonsense look on the Rebuker. "These two have been *chosen* to serve as our Nemeses among the Tisiphone. So, as your husband said, peace."

If I remembered my African mythology correctly— definitely not my strong suit since there were so many different tribes on that continent—Ala's husband was a thunder god who enforced the law the same way she was said to actually give the law. Ironic, then, for her to draw the role of Rebuker to his Defender.

Ala sniffed again but relented. "Fine, then, Kamanu. *You* proposed these two as Nemeses. *You* give them their charge." The words were civil enough; but her tone most definitely was *not*. Seemed immortal spouses could annoy each other just as much as mortals.

Nemesis—also the name of one of my Amphisbaena—was a Greek goddess who never actually existed, at least not as her own separate entity. The title referred to whichever of the Furies the Triad selected to carry out their investigations—or punishments—against whatever immortal had sinned against the Deities as a whole. I didn't know much about them for one simple reason: Rare were the immortals stupid (or powerful) enough to piss off enough of Their brethren to the point that the Triad needed to move against them. I did know this much, though: Serving as a Nemesis meant a Mandate to end all Mandates, one that would drive a Fury to pursue her charge with quicksilver speed and Rage riding high until the sinner had been brought to justice. To fail didn't risk mere madness—it meant certain death.

Kamanu turned his lightning-bolt eyes in our direction. His role of Defender should have lent him a comforting air, but it didn't. Those crimson eyes edged in silver looked nothing so much as demonic. Plus, just knowing that *he* had been the one to suggest Mom and me for what would be a ridiculously dangerous job prevented me from feeling any warm fuzzies toward the man. God. Whatever.

"Allegra and Marissa Holloway, you have been Chosen by the *Gens Immortalis* to serve as Nemeses against one of its number. For millennia, he numbered among the lesser gods rather than greater, serving as one of the Death Lords governing a portion of the Underworld. Recently, however, he has been amassing large amounts of power, forging bonds with other lesser gods, and becoming something rare in the immortal world: their liege lord."

I blinked. The concept of pledging fealty to an overlord had originated among the Deities rather than mankind, though medieval mortals had taken to the concept like ducks to water in a time of upheaval. The immortal world had once been even more chaotic than the mortal realm; not so surprising considering the sheer number of gods and goddesses ruling over similar spheres. For quite some time, weaker gods had pledged to serve stronger gods, carrying out their orders in the divine, arcane, and earthly realms. Eventually, those stronger gods became the dozens now known as full-blown Deities, and the lesser gods began serving them as a whole rather than individually. Much like we Furies did, actually.

For a *lesser* god to pledge other immortals to him as their liege lord was more than just rare, come to think of it. I had *never* heard of lesser gods accepting another lesser immortal as overlord.

Apparently, Mom hadn't, either. "I don't understand. I thought only a greater god—a Deity—could forge the bonds required for liege lordship. I also thought liege lordship had been done away with at the same time that arcanes reached the Peace Accord with mortals. For an immortal to bond others to himself now must surely be an act of . . ."

Her gaze flew to mine and realization sank in. *Well*, duh. *An act of war, thus the whole Triad needing to recruit Nemeses bit.*

Kamanu nodded. "Indeed. Greater gods have been forbidden to pledge lesser gods to Themselves as liege lords. However, it was never expressly forbidden for lesser gods to do the same since none have ever possessed the power to do so. Many of us now believe that for this lesser god to convince other immortals to swear oaths of fealty must mean one essential truth: He is no longer a *lesser* god at all."

Mom let out a hissing breath. "So you believe he has made the transformation from lesser god to greater."

All three Deities nodded although Ala looked distinctly sour at having to do so.

Kamanu gestured with the Defender's shield. "By our laws, if he is still a lesser god, then he has not *technically* broken any precepts and cannot be punished for swearing others to himself. If, however, he has broken some other precept—such as gathering an immortal or arcane army with the intent of using it against other immortals—or if he *has* made that transformation from lesser god to greater, then he must be brought before the Triad to answer for his crimes."

Those were an awful lot of *ifs*. Especially if—ha—they planned to send us out into the world as Their Nemeses. Surely they had something more concrete to go on.

"If, for instance, the Prime Tisiphone now refuses to serve as Voice for the Triad and, in fact, has not answered any summons for the past several weeks, and it can be proven that she has pledged to serve this particular immortal individually, we would have all the proof of wrongdoing we need to make him answer for his crimes."

This inspired another shocked glance between Mom and me. *Whoa. Whoa. Whoa.* We knew that things had gotten tense among the Sisterhood; suspected some in our own class had manipulated Nan into challenging Ekaterina, the current Moerae; and knew that Maylin had blatantly refused to appear before the Conclave. But to hear that she had actually had the audacity to refuse a summons from the *Deities* Themselves boggled the mind beyond belief.

I found my voice but kept it calm and respectful. "The faction split in the Sisterhood. You believe it is this lesser god pledging Furies to himself much as he has other lesser gods?"

Kamanu nodded.

Whoa to infinity, then. Mr. Lesser God may have found a loophole allowing him to pledge other gods to himself lawfully, but *all* immortals, whether lesser or greater, were forbidden to pledge Furies to themselves individually. For him to do so meant he was either bat-shit insane—rare, among immortals and arcanes (except Furies who Turned Harpy)—or he was damned sure he stood a good chance of winning against all other comers. Starting, but not ending, with the Triad, which meant he had a whole hell of a lot of power, magically and politically speaking, and most likely *had* made the transformation from lesser god to greater.

But the Triad still has to prove *that or some other crime, thus why they need us.* Ancient tradition dictated that Furies were the ones to track down immortal criminals to bring them before the Triad for Reckoning, in large part because only *we* could both channel magical Rage and draw upon the powers of those immortals who bound us to them through a Mandate. These two facts gave us a tremendous advantage against our quarry, not to mention the fact we were the seasoned investigators and enforcers of the arcane world.

Ala shot her husband a pointed look. "Tell them about the portals. They must know exactly what they are up against before they agree to serve as Nemeses."

I suspected she was more concerned with not recruiting weaklings who would wuss out on Them later than with our delicate sensibilities, but still, I always appreciated full disclosure.

Kamanu complied. "Around the same time that the Prime Tisiphone fell out of communication with us, several Death Lords reported that another Lord's sections of the Underworld had become closed off from the areas under their dominion. They attempted to bring us proof that this Lord had turned traitor, but this proved impossible. Not long ago, a group of priests sent by one of the lesser Death Lords vanished after journeying into his territory to investigate the portal failures. Those closed-off areas have only increased over the ensuing time since until, just recently, portals between the Underworld and the Divine Realm began shutting down as well."

The *supposedly* lesser god they wanted us to investigate not only had enough power to pledge other lesser gods to himself, he had enough juice to cut off *other* Death Lords from his part of the Underworld? *And* had enough spare power to start closing off those areas from the greater gods? Jeez. Us. Forget the *Titanic* and moon-sized meteors; we were onto supernova scales of disaster already.

Mom clenched her hands and looked as displeased as I felt. "And may we hear the name of this—lesser god?" The pause in her voice came through loud and clear, but she kept her tone a lot more smooth than I could have managed.

Ala and Epona both focused their gazes upon my face as Kamanu opened his mouth to reply. I had no clue why until his unwelcome words reached my ears. "Anubis the Jackal-Headed, Egyptian Lord of the Underworld."

CHAPTER FIVE

SHOCK STABBED STRAIGHT TO MY BELLY, making me distinctly weak in the knees. *They think bloody freaking* Anubis, *the god who hates me because grief and Rage made me bitch him out in front of his priesthood, is plotting an immortal coup and believe Mom and I are Their best hope for thwarting it? The two of us barely-even-demigoddesses up against a lesser god who drummed up enough power to challenge every other Death Lord—and win? Who now has enough power to command other immortals who should be his equals? What the hell kind of drug are They smoking— and, more importantly, where can I get me some?*

My penchant for sarcasm in the face of danger helped me straighten my spine and stare at the Triad with every bit of incredulity pulsing through my body. Mom knew me all too well, despite our twenty-year separation, so she grabbed my hand in a viselike grip and mouthed the words *Calm down!* as if they had a prayer in hell of working. Hell. Exactly where these out-of-Their-minds Deities wanted to send us on a suicide mission.

Rage at Their seeming callousness toward two Furies who had already sacrificed plenty—like, say, twenty years of a mother-daughter relationship we could never get back—quickly caught up to and beat the snot out of former shock. Nemesis and Nike hissed in response to the white-hot flood of anger they could feel as strongly as I did. They probably saved me from certain doom because settling *them* down distracted me long enough that I missed my chance to immortally offend the Triad.

Mom spoke up while my attention was diverted. "Just to be sure we understand, Your Graces . . . Not only has Anubis sworn both other lesser gods and a faction of the Sisterhood to his personal service, but you believe he has closed off most of the Underworld to other Death Lords and now to the Divine Realm? And you want the two of *us* to find proof of his crimes where the other Death Lords have fa—been thwarted?"

Ha. That showed Mom's greater gift for diplomacy clearly enough. I would have just spat out the word *failed* to two of said Death Lords without bothering to pretty it up. Because, dammit, that's exactly what Epona and Ala had done—screwed the ever-living-heck out of the pun-so-intended pooch, in the form of Anubis. Also known as the god who told me if I ever set foot in his domain again, he'd rip my entrails out and eat them in front of me with a side of fava beans and Chianti. And he hadn't been kidding.

Any other Deity would have taken into consideration

the fact that I'd been consumed with Rage and grief over Vanessa when I'd, um, *requested* help in figuring out whether she really *had* been murdered, but not Mr. Jackal Face. He and Mercy were not only strangers to each other, but I was willing to bet he couldn't even spell her name, *with* a dictionary.

What sucked even more hard-core was the fact my lover, Scott Murphy, and the entire Murphy clan considered Anubis their personal protector in addition to his position as Warhound patron deity, even the distant cousins who had actually sprung from Epona's Celtic line. I'd thus far managed to conceal how far I was in the immortal doghouse (ha) from them because, hey, it hadn't come up. But it damned well *would* if I accepted this Mandate to drag Anubis before the Triad currently out for his figurative blood.

Assuming I survived.

And you talk like you have a choice here, Marissa, like you physically could *turn down a gods-given Mandate. Even one they're nice enough to discuss with you ahead of time.* Then I remembered that Nan was somehow a puppet in this whole mess, and I steeled my spine again. *As if you* would *refuse if you could.*

Because, when it came right down to it, I had enlisted to serve as the arcane version of a soldier, not been forced into it. One thing to be said for the immortals: They were completely honest and up front about what could be asked of you as a Fury *before* you pledged those unbreakable vows. Until that point, you could always choose to go back to being 100 percent mortal again. But I hadn't made that choice, and I wouldn't change my mind if I could. Because, as they were now proving by recruiting us to serve as Nemeses, they held each other to just as high standards as they did their arcane children.

Again, Kamanu nodded. "We are well aware how dangerous the Mandate we would place upon you shall be; thus, why we propose to make you Nemeses. You shall be true demigoddesses until you fulfill the Mandate, and have the special powers that coincide with that title."

Wait, we would continue as full demigoddesses while fulfilling this suicidal mission of a Mandate? And get special powers with the gig? Suddenly, it didn't sound *quite* so suicidal. True demigoddesses shared one particular attribute with full gods and goddesses: namely, they couldn't be killed.

Of course, that didn't mean Anubis couldn't capture and torture our asses, but hey, small favors and all that.

Mom took another deep breath. "If we do agree to this Mandate, agree to serve as your Nemeses, we'll be going up against sister Furies of our own class, not to mention possibly against my mother, Marissa's grandmother. Neither of us will kill her should that be asked of us."

Epona cut in. "It will not be asked, not of you, hopefully not of anyone. We believe she is being somehow manipulated by Anubis; thus, she has not committed any crime that cannot be laid directly at *his* feet."

Mom relaxed slightly. So did I although I hadn't realized until then that I'd become just as tense as she. Epona had basically pardoned Nan for any crimes she might have committed—or would commit—while acting as a pawn of Anubis. Now, we just had to prove she *was* one of his pawns and not a willing participant.

Ala's expression grew slightly more sympathetic at the mention of going up against sister Furies, including Nan. "Even those who pledged to serve Anubis willingly may find forgiveness if he coerced or threatened them into serving him. Mere arcanes cannot be expected to stand up to the full force of an immortal's commands."

"That is exceedingly merciful of Your Graces, and I don't mean to cast doubt on the wisdom of Your choice, but . . . how exactly can two demigoddesses prove Anubis's guilt against the combined might of his arcane and immortal subjects? While stealth and strategy can make up for superior numbers, in this particular situation . . ."

The Megaera spoke for the first time in several minutes. "It will not be you two alone, Allegra. Several of my sisters will pledge to serve you as you fulfill your Mandate, up to and including giving their lives so that you might succeed."

I had the sneaking suspicion that my least favorite of her sisters would count among that number, but it was a generous offer, one we couldn't afford to refuse.

Kamanu bestowed an approving smile upon the Megaera. "Indeed, the Megaeras will assist you in your endeavor, and I suspect you already know several Tisiphones who can be trusted as well."

Like Laurell and Patricia, to start with.

Mom ventured a question that hadn't even occurred to me. "And what of the Alecto? Do they stand as loyal to the Deities as the Megaera and we two of the Tisiphone?"

Kamanu hesitated, and his wife took advantage of the pause to speak. "We believe so, yes, although that shall be the first task of your Mandate. To ascertain for sure."

Mom furrowed a brow. "What do you mean?"

"We have been unable to contact the Prime Alecto for several days now. However, unlike the Tisiphone, she had been cooperating fully before that. It is our hope that Anubis has somehow prevented the Alecto from either receiving or responding to our communication attempts but that she remains loyal. It shall be your task to ascertain whether this is true, Allegra. If it is not, then you shall bring her before us for judgment. When we bind you to your Mandate, you alone shall have the knowledge of the Alecto Prime's identity—which you are not to reveal to anyone else unless completely unavoidable."

Kamanu picked up the thread of instructions. "Once finished with that, we desire that you bring the Tisiphone Prime before us. She *will* answer for her disobedience."

I swallowed at the thought of what awaited Maylin, such a good friend of my mother's but now persona non grata with our immortal Makers.

Ala turned her sour gaze upon me. "To you falls the duty of journeying to the Underworld to find proof of Anubis's crimes and bring him before us for judgment."

That time the swallowing was all for me. I'd barely made it to the Underworld and back with my life the last time and wasn't looking forward to doing it a second, souped-up Nemesis powers notwithstanding.

Ala dismissed me with a sniff, then glanced pointedly at her husband. "Well?"

Kamanu remained unruffled but stepped forward. "The time has come for you to choose. Will you serve as our Nemeses, obtain the proof we need that Anubis has committed crimes against the *Gens Immortalis*, and bring him before us?"

I took Mom's hand in mine and squeezed, nodding when she looked at me. A ghost of a smile flickered across her lips but was gone when she turned her attention back to the Triad.

"Yes, we shall accept this Mandate you lay before us, Your Graces."

Epona nodded as if she'd expected the answer, and Kamanu appeared pleased. Ala, on the other hand, seemed as disapproving as before. I wondered whether one of us had done something to personally piss her off or whether she was always this bitchy. Not that *that* seemed terribly likely, either: Most earth goddesses lived up to their whole nurturing, motherly-type reps. Then again, there was *always* an exception to every rule.

The three immortals stepped close together, clasped hands, and began chanting in that unfamiliar language the Megaera had used to summon them what felt like hours earlier. The hair on the nape of my neck stirred as pure magical energy crackled in the air. Brilliant silver beams danced around the Triad, arced toward the three of us, and snapped into our bodies. Pleasure so intense it bordered upon pain burst through me, inspiring an unintended moan that sounded extremely sexual. No big surprise, really, considering the thousand pinpricks of sensation that vibrated along my every nerve ending felt better than any orgasm I'd ever experienced.

Not that I'd ever admit that fact to Scott.

The better-than-an-orgasm eventually faded to a dull roar. Mom and the Megaera had again recovered before me—something that was beginning to grate on my nerves. Once they satisfied themselves that I'd survived what I assumed had been the Triad's granting us official status as Nemeses, they focused on the immortals, who dropped their arms and separated. Surprisingly, Ala's big, fat sour expression had mellowed into something resembling not satisfaction so much as acceptance. Of course, the deed was done, and I was willing to bet that only the combined forces of the Triad could now revoke our demigoddess status *or* the Mandate I could feel buzzing through my veins once the metaphysical wallop had dulled somewhat. Huh. Weird I hadn't felt it immediately—it was way stronger than any of the three I'd felt before. It didn't hurt—exactly—but the persistent itch at the back of my brain was by no means pleasant, either.

Epona motioned with the scales in her hand. "Go forth as our Nemeses and seek the information we need. Anubis will not dare strike you directly, but beware his followers, who may have no such compunction. We recommend you strike swiftly and silently when possible. You will also find that the next time you shift to Fury form, you will carry our Mark as Nemeses quite clearly. You will enjoy increased abilities in this form and, most importantly, be truly immortal—but take care. You *can* suffer tremendous amounts of pain, and those you care for shall remain as vulnerable as ever."

Kamanu nodded gravely. "We have faith in you, our Nemeses, but know this: Your status as demigoddesses will last for three days only. At that time, you shall revert to your natural form, and we shall have no choice but to choose new Nemeses."

Oh, *lovely.* What he left unspoken was the fact our Mandate would remain the same, if the pressure from leaving it unfulfilled didn't drive us to insanity—or death. And even if we survived, we probably wouldn't make it long trying to carry out that Mandate as normal— very killable—Furies. I resisted the urge to roll my eyes or snark my thoughts out loud, but barely. The Triad was bound by rules every bit as much as we—perhaps even more—and failure came with consequences. Their

dubious gift of making us their Nemeses had to come
with a finite limit unless they were willing to make us
permanent demigoddesses, something we did *not* want
at this point in our lives even had they been willing to do
so. Besides which, doing that meant we'd become ineli-
gible to serve as Nemeses since, technically, we would
no longer be Furies.

Ala met our eyes one by one. "Do not fail us, children. You will not like the results."

With that encouraging piece of advice, she turned to
the mirror, spoke several incomprehensible words, and
reactivated the summoning circle with as little effort as
I might have opened a physical door. Compared to the
tremendous amount of work the Megaera had gone
through to activate it originally . . . I couldn't hold back
a shiver at the reminder of how very powerful these
beings truly were and how much our continued health
and happiness depended upon pleasing them.

*Guess now I know how spiders feel when they see me
coming . . .*

Within moments, the Triad had disappeared as
quickly as they came, leaving behind a magical vacuum.
The Megaera sprang into action, banishing the silver
motes of energy with what appeared to be greater ease
than before. My eyes narrowed as I thought back over
the past several minutes. The Triad had spoken of choos-
ing only Mom and me as their Nemeses, but that atom
bomb of immortal magic had blasted all three of us. The
Megaera shone with just as much silver incandescence
as Mom and I now did. Which must mean . . .

"They made you a Nemesis, too." Mom's mouth pursed
in surprise, but the Megaera merely nodded. "You knew
they were going to?"

"Yes. They asked me if I would be willing to serve yesterday when they requested I bring you before them."

My eyes widened. "But if we fail—which is a possibility no matter how much we don't want to consider it—that means that . . ."

"I'll die along with you, yes. Or Turn Harpy, which is worse."

I couldn't understand her unruffled calm. "Yeah, you'll die and leave your class without a strong, clearly uncorrupted Prime. How can you risk—"

She turned an intense gaze my way that had me squirming nearly as much as the Deities had before her. *So* not good for my Fury ego. "If we can't stop Anubis from bringing outright civil war to the Sisterhood, who serves as Prime Megaera will be the least of our concerns. Once he seizes control of enough Furies to take war to the immortal realm, our struggles will seem petty in comparison."

I shuddered at the reminder. While the Sisterhood could boast never having gone through a civil war, the Deities could do no such thing. Unfortunately for us, however, the rare times war *did* break out among immortalkind, *our* world was the one to suffer. Immortals were truly that—exempt from death—and power plays in their realm *always* spilled over into the others. They became the undying chess masters moving us insignificant pawns across the game board of life. As bad as civil war among the Sisterhood would be, war among *them* would be a hundred times worse.

Rather than speaking those fears out loud, I merely nodded.

Mom let out a heavy breath. "I must admit this was *not* how I intended to spend the next few days."

A choked laugh burst past my lips before I could stop

it. "Oh, I don't know; we *have* accomplished one of our goals for the week: making sure the big, bad Megaera stops trying to kill or kidnap our family members."

The *big, bad Megaera* arched a brow, the hint of a smile glinting in her eyes.

I shrugged. "Hey, it's not like you ever gave us a *name* to use."

Her lips twitched ever so slightly and she relented. "Adesina." She pronounced it "Ah-day-see-nah," the syllables rolling off her tongue with deceptively easy grace. Pretty name, not that I planned to say that out loud. Partners we might now be, but she *had* tried to have me killed. Or so I had been assuming . . .

"What exactly *were* Durra's orders that day in the subway?"

She didn't play any pointless games. "She was to subdue you by whatever means possible—short of death—and bring you to me."

I noticed her deliberate use of *she* rather than *they*. "Then the explosion—"

Her expression darkened. "Was a traitor working for Anubis. She was supposed to cast a sleep spell when Durra pushed you down the stairs. The goal was never to murder you but to use you as leverage against your mother and grandmother."

"Nan I understand—she's obviously being used by Anubis somehow. But why my mother?"

Adesina—weird to have a name for her finally—looked at me like I should know better.

Which I really *should* have. "Mom's miraculous reappearance from presumed death months before Nan's equally miraculous awakening made you suspect they *both* were working for Anubis."

Mom pursed her lips thoughtfully. "A logical assumption, really. Had we both been pawns of Anubis and succeeded in winning Lesser Consensus seats, our influence would have been considerable."

Adesina nodded. "Indeed."

All right, so knowing that Durra had meant to injure rather than kill me softened my emotions toward her somewhat, but that didn't solve our immediate problems.

"So, exactly who else can we trust to get this mission impossible accomplished? Do we only involve sisters, or should we seek outside help?" Much as I loved him, Scott was, for once, not at the top of my list. He was too close to Anubis spiritually for my comfort—and safety.

"Good question," Adesina said. "I have trusted only those of my class I know beyond doubt remain steadfast with any details, but unfortunately that number is very small; smaller after our sister's betrayal the other day. I trust Durra and those who escorted her today, and perhaps three or four others, implicitly. The others here today I wish I could wholeheartedly vouch for . . . but I just can't."

Well, at least she was honest; and several trusted sisters was better than none.

"Sounds like we should keep the numbers of our posse small, and we're definitely going to have to split into two groups."

Mom agreed. "It would be most unwise to go against the division of labor proposed by the Triad, who no doubt had Their reasons to give us each our assignments. Still, we have to decide where you should begin your investigation in the Underworld."

They turned their silver-rimmed gazes upon me. I forced myself not to fidget this time. While it felt weird to have two Elders—one a *Prime* and the other very nearly a member of the Lesser Consensus—look to *me* for direction, it made sense. Neither of them had been involved in active investigations for years, while they had been my bread and butter since just after I Fledged.

"Well, the Triad said we have to find proof that either Anubis has made the power transfer from lesser god to greater, meaning he illegally bound other gods to himself, or that he has sworn Furies to his direct service—also illegal. I say we prove *both*. If we try to prove one--and fail—that means we still have a chance to prove the other."

They nodded in approval, something that had a flush of pride touching my cheeks. When neither interjected, I took that as encouragement to continue. "I would recommend that you two work together to convince the Alecto Prime to work with us if she *didn't* fall out of contact with the Triad willingly. Having the three of you working together to confront the Tisiphone Prime will give you a much greater chance of success. Once that's done, I suggest going after Anubis's weakest link."

Adesina tilted her head, curiosity brightening her eyes. "Which would be?"

Mom caught on to my intention. "My mother. Either it's an imposter posing as her or actually my mother being magically manipulated. In whichever case, she will be much easier to break and interrogate for information. If she's an imposter, we can threaten her with immediate execution for falsely impersonating a sister with the intention of stealing a Conclave seat. If she's actually my mother, we stand a good chance of breaking whatever magical spell holds her in thrall and gaining her active cooperation."

"What if we can't?"

·Mom faced Adesina squarely, fingers clenched but face composed. "Can't break the spell?"

Meaning, really, what if there *were* no spell to break?

"Then we have no choice but to . . . treat her as we would any traitor."

A slight tremble of the voice was the only indication of what that statement cost my mother. Both Adesina and I noticed it but didn't comment. Me because I felt the same grim determination as Mom, and Adesina out of respect. We three Nemeses had been charged by the gods to *stop* civil war, and we would damn well *do* that, no matter the cost.

Even if that meant losing Nan before we could truly get her back.

Adesina broke the tense silence. "And how precisely do you intend to accomplish your own task?"

"Oh," I said with false lightness in my voice and a twisted smile, "I happen to be sleeping with the son of an expert on Egyptian mythology. I suspect she'll be able to give me an idea or two on where to start before I recruit some muscle to accompany me into the Underworld."

I found myself exceedingly grateful that Mom had no clue about the bad blood between Anubis and me. Well, you know, the *preexisting* bad blood. Once he found out that the Triad had sent Nemeses after his ass, there'd be all kinds of *new* bad blood to contend with.

Mom being Mom, she pointed out the glaring flaw in my plan. "I'm afraid *that's* going to prove difficult, to say the least, Marissa. Or have you forgotten what Kamanu told us about the Underworld?"

"Not at all. He said that portals between the Divine

Realm and the Underworld had been shut down. He said nothing about those in the mortal realm."

Adesina made a clicking sound with her tongue. "A valid point, Allegra."

Mom narrowed her eyes and took a step forward, no doubt intending to intimidate me. Apparently she'd forgotten we were now damned near the same height. "Do not even *suggest* that you use the usual means of accessing those portals." Her tone suggested that, similar height or no, she could still turn me over her knee if the occasion warranted. I didn't really doubt her chance of success either—moms can be *scary*.

By *usual means* she meant the method I'd used previously and was glad she didn't know about: dying. Temporarily dying, to be specific, which was a huge pain in the ass to accomplish without it turning into permadeath. The only reason I'd managed it the last time was because I'd coerced two Oracles into helping me kill myself, then placing my body into magical stasis before healing me, something that took a crapload of magical power and tended to earn negative points on Ye Olde Karma Meter. So *why* had those Oracles helped me? Let's just say that even mostly neutral, supposedly altruistic healing types have secrets they want kept. Yeah, there's more than one reason most Oracles hate me.

While temporary death was a workable method, it wasn't the one I planned to use this time. One (which Mom obviously wasn't considering): As true demigoddesses, we *couldn't* be killed. Two: I intended to bring arcane backup this go-round, a couple of Furies and at least three or four others. No way would we be able to find enough Oracles to pull *that* off for that many people. Besides, Furies were easier to heal after temporary

death than any other species. There'd be no guarantees
anyone else would survive. Three: Traveling to the
Underworld in spirit form made you way weaker than if
you went there in body. Last time I'd merely gone there
after information, so I hadn't cared about strength. This
time I'd need to retain as much ass-kicking potential
as possible. And reason number four: As Nemeses, we
could commandeer temple portals for our own use; including, say, the portal to Anubis's Underworld territory
housed in his official Underbelly temple—not too far
from our current location.

I reminded Mom and Adesina of those facts, which
seemed to satisfy the Megaera but only partially pla-
cate Mom.

Mom grimaced as something occurred to her. "I
assume you won't be able to involve Scott."

My conscience stung at the thought of having to hide
something so big from him. "No, and I won't be able to
tell Liana why I'm suddenly so interested in Egyptian
mythology, either. For my Underworld expedition, I was
thinking about bringing Mac and Charlie, if I can convince them, and possibly one of my people in the MCU
who is distinctly qualified in matters pertaining to death
and the Underworld."

Adesina didn't bother questioning my choices—
either because she already knew all about my usual allies thanks to assassination recon or because she trusted
me to get the job done.

"Mac you can trust implicitly, and he's been raring to
get involved with . . ." Mom let her voice trail away and
gave a meaningful roll of her eyes toward Adesina. Only
Mom and I currently knew what we'd been keeping
secret from the Sisterhood for fear someone would try

to cover the truth up before we could ensure his safety: Patrick "Mac" MacAllister was more than just Mom's half-Sidhe son who had been genetically and magically forced upon her; he was half-something the world had never seen: a *male* Fury. Part of this week's original plans had been to pave the way for announcing that fact and inducting him into the no-longer-aptly-named Sisterhood. *That* had gone all to hell, pun intended.

Mom hid her near slip by nodding decisively. "Yes, and Charlie will have no particular qualms about taking on Anubis."

Charlie Andrulis belonged to the race of oversized and superstrong individuals known as Giants. He was also one of my best friends and had helped me with several tough cases in the past. He'd only recently completed a six-month gig pulling guard duty in Gunmetal Alley— the Belly's version of a black market—so I was hoping he'd be willing to take another freelance job helping me. As a Giant, he held no particular affection for Anubis. That plus his loyalty to me and the fact I paid well should mean he'd agree. The daredevil in him would thrill at the chance to journey to the Underworld at the side of a real-life Nemesis. Not too many mercs (if any) could put *that* on their résumés.

"Yeah, thank the gods (ha) that Giants are very much into earth worship and not particularly fond of Anubis." Mom seemed more resigned to my proposal, but something on her face indicated she still wasn't completely sold. I elaborated on my trump card in the hopes of changing that. "The other person I want to bring is a Bhairavi Raga. One of the world's strongest, actually."

Her eyes widened. "You mean you'll ask . . ."

"Sahana to step outside the morgue finally? I'd say

desperate times call for desperate measures in this case. She may not be able to stand up to Anubis himself, but anyone short of a full-on immortal . . . Let's just say I wouldn't want to be in *their* shoes." I glanced down at my old-school footwear and made a face. "Sandals. Whatever."

Adesina turned to Mom and arched a brow. "Are you merely concerned that one of us is going to the Underworld alone, or that the youngest of we three Nemeses should go alone, or that the one to go alone is your daughter?"

Nice to have someone *besides* me be the recipient of a chastising tone for once. The Prime made a valid point. While it was only natural for Mom to fear for my safety more than other Furies since I *was* her flesh and blood, it wasn't okay for her to allow that concern to color how she carried out her duties to the Sisterhood. When Mom clenched her firsts and scowled at Adesina, however, I found myself grateful that *I* hadn't been the one to point that out to her.

Remember that whole scary-mom thing? Furies most of all.

Mom opened her mouth to make a no-doubt-angry reply, then gave a resigned shrug. "Probably all three. Any one of which would be bad enough, but all together?"

Adesina smiled slightly. "Well, we can share our concerns over our daughters' being set loose in the Underworld while we make our own way in the Palladium."

That seemed to settle Mom's ruffled feathers even further. I felt clueless since I had no idea what the Megaera was talking about. She had a daughter? One who had to be a Fury if she planned to send her with me. But who? . . . *Oh, no freaking way!* And yet, it made all too much sense. The age was right, they bore more than a passing resemblance to each other, they shared the same faint accent, and who had Mommy Dearest sent after our family more than once? "Don't tell me *Durra* is your daughter!"

Mommy Dearest turned her little smile in my direction. "Whether or not I *tell* you, she *will* be accompanying you to the Underworld."

Mom nodded, an adamant gleam in her beady little Nemesis eyes. "As will Laurell and Patricia."

I scowled. "How can they do that while pulling guard duty in—"

She waved her hand dismissively. "Under the circumstances, I believe we can dispense with the goodwill hostages." Adesina nodded. "While you gather your other allies, I will arrange someone to keep an eye on Cori until we can see her pledged and send Durra, Laurell, and Patricia to you in the mortal realm. I assume you plan to assemble outside the Temple Anupu?"

Anupu—an old name for Anubis, one often used by Egyptian purists among his Warhound worshippers. I gave a grudging nod. "Fine, have the three of them meet me just outside the temple half an hour before midnight tonight. *Just* those three. The smaller our number, the better our chance to get in, find the proof we need, and get back out undetected." Fat likelihood of the *undetected* part, but a girl could dream. Otherwise, I would have given up on life long ago.

Though if we *didn't* make it into and out of Anubis Central undetected tonight, life might very well give up on *me*.

CHAPTER SIX

RECRUITING MAC TO THE CAUSE WENT AS smoothly as expected. I merely had to call him and say Mom and I needed his help for a dangerous mission, and he leaped at the opportunity. That boy had a Fury inferiority complex that wouldn't quit—not until (I refused to think *if*) we managed to get him inducted into the Sisterhood. Then again, considering that his fifteen-year-old niece would automatically make it into the Sisterhood by virtue of her double-X chromosomes, perhaps the inFuriority made perfect sense . . .

On the other hand, he didn't take the need to keep the mission secret from his wife, Elliana, quite so well. "Wait, you're saying I can't even *tell* Elle I'm going? She's going to notice when I don't come home tonight."

"Thought you said Ellie"—(oh, how she *hated* that

nickname, which was why I *loved* using it)—"was on some overnight job with Scott. He told me yesterday he had some bodyguard gig for the next few days." By now, he might even have managed to find out what the hell was *up* with his baby brother.

"Yeah, but normally we text each other when we leave unexpectedly."

Aw, what conscientious spouses. Of course, considering their risky employment for the Murphy-run mercenary company, the precaution made sense. Ellie served as Scott's second-in-command in the Shadowhounds.

"Just tell her you're helping me out with family business that might take a day or two and you'll call her tomorrow."

"I don't like lying to my wife, Marissa."

Two could play the annoying sibling game. "It's not *lying*, Patrick. What I need your help with has *everything* to do with Mom and Nan, so very much *is* family business. I need someone I trust at my back, and it can't be Scott or Elle." It took everything I had to use her preferred nickname, but I figured every little bit of persuasion helped.

"Can't? I figured you didn't want to involve them because they're otherwise occupied."

I checked my watch and impatience flared. Quarter past seven. Not a whole lot of time to rally the troops, show up unannounced on Liana's doorstep, and make it to Temple Anupu for our midnight rendezvous. On the plus side, being an official demigoddess meant I didn't have to stop for meals or other pesky mortal concerns. "Look, Mac, this is too complicated to get into on the phone. Can't you just trust me as your sister and let me explain in person?"

"Well, when you put it that way, it's not like I can say no without being a complete jerk-off. So yeah."

"Great. Why don't you meet me at my MCU office in, say, three hours? I'll leave word with the front desk to expect you."

"Fine. See you soon. But be ready to spill it, big sister."

I clicked *end* on my cell without responding. *Two troops down, one to go.* Mom and Adesina had left the Pantheon for the Palladium a while earlier thanks to their Super Secret Elder Travel Power, while I had commandeered the room where we'd—okay, Adesina had—summoned the Triad in order to make my phone calls. Sahana, unsurprisingly, was still buried liver deep in some unfortunate arcane's corpse and would meet us at my office. The next discussion, however, was one best done in person since Charlie was weird about answering his cell phone. Go figure. A seven-foot-tall, several-hundred-year-old warrior who didn't embrace cell phones with the same enthusiasm as my fifteen-year-old niece, who had hers practically grafted to her hand.

My pulse picked up speed as I made my way out of the by-then-quiet Pantheon. *Oh yeah, time to test drive the new superpowers.* Okay, so maybe I had a little teenager of my own lurking inside. It wasn't every day that one became (even temporarily) immortal. Evening breezes caressed my skin as I slipped out into the Pantheon's rear courtyard. I'd chosen a backyard retreat for the privacy, knowing my new form might take a little getting used to. In light of the way ingesting ambrosia had kicked my ass earlier, *might* was most likely an understatement. I braced myself and initiated the shift before I could scare myself out of it.

On the plus side, it didn't hurt like becoming immortal had. Shimmery silver light spread along my body in place of the normal Fury sapphire glow, and breathing became a little harder. *Funny how I no longer need to eat or sleep, but my body still thinks it needs to breathe.* My skin seemed to stretch uncomfortably—no, that wasn't really right. It felt as if muscles I'd never known existed suddenly roared into use, like magic I'd never touched beat against my outer flesh in an attempt to escape its inadequate confines. Silver light vanished, leaving me to stare down at my arms and body beneath the courtyard's dim safety lights. I'd expected something different, but what I saw had me gaping. Glittering black serpents with ruby red eyes twined along my arms, tongues flicking furiously and chaotic thoughts bombarding my brain. They *felt* like my Amphisbaena—my magical familiars—and yet, they were different. The simple mental pictures and emotions that made up our usual form of communication seemed more sophisticated. Practically verbal.

And why not? an amused voice whispered into my brain. *We are very verbal creatures; you are simply too unskilled to hear us usually.*

I stared down at my left arm in amazement, certain she had been the one to *speak*. "N—Nike?"

Her tongue flicked out in clear amusement. *Very good, Marissa. You may make a proper Nemesis yet.*

Not to be confused with me, a differently *flavored* mental voice inserted.

"N-nemesis, of course."

Dizziness had me move my gaze from my arms to the leather uniform clothing my body. It was way darker in color than my usual bloodred vest, pants, and knee-high boots, a black as deep as my made-over serpents although not as shimmery. Other than the color, though, it seemed the same as ever. I stomped my low-heeled boots experimentally and ran my hands along my upper thighs. *Check and check.* I wondered if anything else about my new form was outwardly different but couldn't be sure without a mirror.

Nike laughed inside my mind. *If you're done admiring yourself, Marissa, I believe you have an appointment to keep.*

Okay, *that* was definitely going to take some getting used to. I'd always suspected that Elders could communicate with their Amphisbaena on a level we younger sisters couldn't manage, but I'd never dreamt *this* was possible. Not only could they speak directly into my mind, they apparently could read it without my conscious intent as well.

Nemesis let out a little hiss. *We always could, silly Fury.* You *just didn't know it.*

"Okay, well then, guess we'd better track down Charlie."

Magic responded to my touch in a seething torrent, inspiring a miniature cyclone that hurled me a hundred feet into the air before I could even blink. "Shit!" I screamed, fighting down panic to beat my wings double time and catch my balance midair.

Gently, my Amphisbaena admonished in unison.

No shit! I thought it but kept the words unvocalized. Not that it *really* mattered . . .

Remember, you are much stronger now. Nike, who seemed the more—motherly—of the pair; if a magical serpent who was born of the blood of a dying predecessor could be considered motherly.

Stronger, but not correspondingly smarter. Nemesis, it seemed, played the annoying big sister to Nike's *mother.* Gee, just what I never wanted . . . Amusement flooded my mind, and, just like that, communicating with them on a verbal level felt natural—as if we'd always done it this way. I turned my attention to our flight, having to adjust for my greater magic, strength, and speed. The trip to Charlie's apartment building on the opposite end of the Belly took half the time it normally would have. I suspected I could have shaved the flight time even further had I been actually used to my new abilities. For all I knew, I could have *teleported* there in another eyeblink, but it was too late to find out. My feet touched down roughly on Charlie's tenth-story balcony, and I sent thankful prayers skyward. This Nemesis thing wasn't coming quite as easily as I'd hoped.

Wait, you mean there's a learning curve to becoming immortal, just like there was when you became a Fury? Shocker!

"Okay, the more you talk, the more you sound like me," I muttered to Nemesis. "And the world only needs *one* of me."

Amen, came Nike's calm response. The *yin* to Nemesis's *yang*? The two could have been opposing sides of an alternate version of myself, a serpentine alter ego. For all I knew, they actually were.

How do you know you're *not* our *alter ego?* Nemesis wanted to know.

"Enough," I said out loud. "We have work to do!"

Trying to hide my involuntary smile at the mental banter, I leaned forward to knock on Charlie's sliding glass door. Three loud raps, two soft, four loud, two more soft knocks. The TV, which had been blaring on the other side of the dark blue curtains obscuring my view, suddenly clicked off. Funny how he couldn't be bothered with his phone half the time, but he didn't have the same problem when it came to the boob tube. Not that I could really cast stones, considering I used to ignore my own cell and worshipped at the altar of situational comedy.

I stepped back and waited. Footsteps thumped along the hardwood floor, then the curtain peeled back a few inches. I stuck my tongue out ever so maturely. Several seconds passed, and I started worrying that my face *had* changed as radically as Nemesis and Nike, until the balcony door finally slid open.

Charlie's dark eyes peered down at me. "Riss?"

"Of course it's Riss. I used our secret knock, didn't I?"

He shifted his considerable weight from one foot to the other, clearing his throat several times, almost as if uncertain of himself. A very distinctly un-Charlie-like behavior, to be sure. His eyes widened as they took in my new style. "Holy shit. You went all Nemesis on me."

Ha. Not a huge surprise he caught on so fast. Giants were nothing close to the slow dimwits human folklore made them out to be, Charlie least of all. The reason he was the top-paid mercenary of his race. The guy had a bachelor's *and* a master's degree in engineering "just because," for gods' sake.

"You gonna just stare at me all night or invite me in already?" He rubbed a hand over bleary-looking eyes— tiredness could have explained his failure to invite me in sooner—and stepped back so I could slip in past him. "Jeez, Charlie. You look exhausted."

He led the way through a utilitarian kitchen and into the much cozier living room, decorated in stereotypical bachelor chic although I did catch sight of a few homey touches—like art on the walls and a couple of vases of flowers—that hadn't been present the last time I'd visited. Apparently he'd finally decided to do a little nesting. Way past time, since he'd owned this place for several years already. *Hmm, or he could have a new love interest hiding in the bedroom.* That *could explain why he stalled a little before letting me in.* I couldn't hold back a tiny grin at that thought. Charlie loved love, and his *dry spells* tended to be few and far between.

I settled onto a beat-up but extremely comfy recliner while he plopped down on the fortunately sturdy sofa. "I *am* exhausted. Pulling fourteen-hour shifts for several months will do that to a guy."

I cleared my throat with a guilty flush. "Ah, yeah, about that. I know you only *just* finished that other gig, but . . ."

His lips quirked upward. "But you find yourself unable to resist my delectable charms and want to hire me."

"Um, yeah. Something like that."

Some of his exhaustion seemed to magically evaporate, and he sat up straighter. "Done."

"But—wait. You don't even know what the job is."

"Doesn't matter. I've only had boring-as-hell grunt work since we blew the cover off that illegal cloning factory. Work with you is *never* dull."

You can say that again, Nemesis snarked silently. I couldn't really argue that sentiment. The *illegal cloning factory* referred to the fact my traitorous mentor, Stacia, had founded and manipulated that rogue group of mortal scientists intent on creating genetically-and-magically enhanced supersoldiers (like my brother). *They* had intended to use the resulting army to send all arcanes back to the dying Otherrealms; whereas *Stacia* had planned to turn on her mortal underlings and conquer earth in the name of arcanekind. In her defense, losing her entire Wing of Furies in the mortal vs. arcane war fifty years ago had driven her batshit insane.

Not that *that* had stopped me from taking her psycho ass out.

"This job *won't* be boring, but it *will* be way more dangerous than anything we've done before, which is saying something."

He rubbed his hands and gave a distinctly maniacal grin. "*Ex*-cellent."

"Dammit, Charlie, I'm serious."

"So am I. You should *know* that by now, darling."

I let out a long-suffering sigh. "You are hopeless, Andrulis."

"So my mother claims. But, just like her, you love me anyway.

"Yeah, yeah, yeah. Well, since you're obviously so completely bored out of your mind, you'll be happy to hear we need to get going like five minutes ago."

"Wait, the job is tonight?" He glanced to the over-sized flat-screen TV that currently had some reality show paused midscene. "But we'll– I mean, I'll—miss the rest of *Surviv . . .*" *Aha! So he does have someone stashed inside his bedroom.* Funny how much he sounded like Trinity, who never missed an episode of the nation's ultimate reality show. His voice trailed off at the mock glare I turned upon him. "Okay, okay, shit. You're such a slave driver. At least let me change."

Less than five minutes later, he had presumably said his good-byes to his clandestine lover and was garbed in black cargo pants, matching tee, and biker boots, and we were speeding in his very large Hummer toward the branch of the Boston PD that housed the Magical Crimes Unit. My *baby*, if anything could be called that, since I'd cajoled and pushed until Boston's Finest finally approved the budget and gave me the go-ahead to form the unit from the ground up.

The MCU now consisted of me as Chief Magical Investigator; Trinity, as deputy chief; Milo Cass, the supposed mortal who possessed a tiny amount of War-hound blood, giving him several minor supernatural perks, which he concealed from everyone except Trinity and me because of discriminatory disclosure laws; a husband-and-wife pair of literal Night Owls (the form they shape-shifted into thanks to the Hawaiian goddess Hina), Kale and Mahina Iwalani, who covered the night shift; and three other part-time arcanes I called in to cover shifts as needed.

Despite his greenness, I had high hopes for Cass. He was the only mortal (okay, mostly mortal) besides Trinity who we hadn't scared off in a matter of days.

We stopped by the Arcane Morgue in the basement to pick up Sahana, who would work herself into the grave (ha) if I didn't keep careful watch. Her Death magic would consume her life force if it could, but I was in the process of pulling as many strings as possible to hire her some arcane lab techs she couldn't accidentally kill if they had to interrupt her work. In the meantime, we arcanes in the MCU made it a point to check in with her regularly. A less than ideal stopgap, but it'd have to do.

Sahana had fortunately ditched the corpse she'd been working on when I called and moved to paperwork in her office; just because I didn't puke at the sight of dead bodies didn't mean I enjoyed watching autopsies.

"You forget about the meeting already, Sahi?"

She blinked up at me, unfocused eyes slowly clearing as they settled upon mine. "Ah, no. Course not. Though I *am* surprised you called one for tonight. Aren't you supposed to be over in La-La Land."

La-La Land. The pet name some arcanes gave to the Fury slice of the Otherrealms that outsiders so rarely saw. "This has to do with my business there."

Sahana's gaze sharpened even further. As caught up as she got with her powers, the woman was no fool. "Spill it then, Riss. What on earth can *I* help you with that touches on Fury business?"

My lips twisted wryly. "You mean what *under* earth can you help me with?" She just looked confused, as did Charlie, but no way was I repeating myself more than necessary. "Come on, our fourth is meeting us in my office. I'll tell all there. Scout's honor." Ignoring the fact I'd never been any kind of Scout.

The PD was relatively quiet at that time of night, though by no means deserted. Mortal officers nodded as we passed, giving a double take at my being dressed in black leather rather than red but being too intimidated to comment out loud. Sahana, however, had no such qualms. She shot me a sidelong glance after the third officer stared as we passed him on the steps leading toward the MCU several floors above the morgue. "I thought something seemed different, but seeing everyone look at you like you're wearing only underwear just made it click. Black leather and black tats can mean only one thing. You're in Nemesis mode. No *wonder* you called an emergency meeting."

Just then one of the last voices I wanted to hear at that moment drawled from the top of the stairs. "Gee, how *nice* of you to call an emergency meeting without me. And here I thought *we* were partners."

My heart sank, but I forced myself not to show it. "Hey, Trin, thought you'd be home by now."

She seemed slightly out of breath, as if she'd hurried there from somewhere else. Knowing her, that probably wasn't far off the truth. "I *was*, but Kale and Mahina called me back for an abduction case. Some idiot pedophile snatched a half-Sidhe girl who looked about fourteen years old."

I winced. "Mortal, of course."

"Of course. An arcane perv would have *known* better. The *fourteen-year-old* turned out to be closer to fifty; some vigilante who'd caught the creep snooping in her neighborhood and decided to make an example out of him. Dude's still alive—barely—but his family's making noises about charging the *girl* with attempted murder."

I snickered. "They're welcome to have his attorney explain to a jury exactly *why* he snatched and tried to molest an apparent fourteen-year-old."

"Yeah, exactly."

We'd reached the top of the stairs by then. Her glance slid past me to Sahana, paused briefly upon Charlie, before turning back to me. "Nice new threads."

I shifted uncomfortably, bracing for the knock-down, drag-out to come. "Hey, Sahi, Charlie, mind waiting for us in my office? Mac should be there."

Trinity nodded, expression excruciatingly blank. "He is."

They gave us measuring looks but didn't argue, clearing the stairwell landing and disappearing down the hall and leaving me to face someone who could be every bit as scary as my mother, mortal or not. She didn't mince words, either. "What the hell, Riss? I've got to find out you called an *emergency meeting* behind my back by catching your little brother sneaking into your office? I thought we were past your trying to *protect* me."

"I'm not—"

"Bullshit!" She smacked the fire door so hard that the sound echoed up and down the stairwell. "It *always* comes back to your thinking mortals can't pull their weight against arcanes. Here I thought you trusted me enough to hold down the fort while you did your Fury thing, and you're back here checking up on me *already*— and in secret—"

"Jeez, Trill, would you *shut up* for a minute and *listen*?" My exasperated tone and none-too-polite words had her doing just that. The way her lips trembled in rage signaled it wouldn't last for long. "I *do* trust you to look after things. I'm *not* here to check up on you. This has *nothing* to do with police business and everything to do with my *Fury thing*, as you so charmingly put it. We're just meeting here because the fewer arcanes who see me in my *new threads* right now, the better."

"Oh." Her voice grew really small, and her cheeks flushed. "Um, sorry for jumping to conclusions. It's just—"

I waved that off. "I've given you reason to doubt in the past; I know that."

"So then, what's up with all the black? Not that it isn't hot, but I thought—unlike your tats—Fury leather only came in one color."

"Usually. With one exception. I—right now I'm serving as a Nemesis."

She frowned. "What, like your snake?"

"Same name, whole 'nother ballgame. A Nemesis is like . . . kind of like a U.S. Marshal drafted by the gods to investigate and hunt down one of their number who has broken immortal law." Trinity twitched at that. How she could *still* claim to be an atheist after everything she'd seen and heard was beyond me. "Just focus on the Marshal bit. I'm tracking down a badass for my arcane superiors. The new threads are temporary, and I'm on a deadline."

She got a determined look on her face. "I could—"

I shook my head emphatically. "No, I'm sorry, but you can't. I need you here, Trin. Honestly. It's not busy-work. Someone's got to smooth over things with the pervert's family."

She sighed. "True, that."

"And you literally *can't* come where we're going: Mortals wouldn't survive the trip."

She still looked none too happy but didn't press the issue. "Fine, then, I'll just get back to Kale and Mahina. At least I know you'll be in good hands with Charlie."

Something in her voice seemed odd, but I passed it off to residual prissiness from the whole being mortal thing. "Yeah, you saw how much ass he kicked at the illegal cloning factory."

"Yeah, there *is* that. Seriously, though, watch your back."

"You, too."

She took off down the stairs—I assumed Kale and Mahina were waiting for her at Mass General's arcane emergency room—and I decided to switch to mortal form to keep a lower profile the rest of my time in the PD. Probably should have done it sooner, but that damned Fury vanity streak had done me in; being a Nemesis was just so freaking cool. Yeah, yeah, I can be as big an idiot as anyone else.

I turned to open the door and head down the hall to my office. Or at least, I *tried* to, only to bounce backward when the door wouldn't budge. "What the—" Instinct kicked in and I spun, expecting an ambush of some kind. Instead, I saw someone unexpected coming up the stairs behind me. My newly awakened and possibly traitorous grandmother, Nan.

CHAPTER SEVEN

SHOCK PUNCHED ITS WAY STRAIGHT TO MY stomach, and I staggered. Decades had passed since I'd seen her looking so hale and hearty, this lovely and *alive*. In the hospice she'd always been a frail pile of bones lying unresponsive upon her bed. The Oracles moved her regularly, of course, cared for her to the best of their abilities, but even among arcanes a coma patient was a coma patient. Now, however, Nan stood tall and proud, a good half foot above my own height. She wore the red leather Fury uniform I hadn't seen her in since my childhood—back on that fateful day she and Mom went hunting Nan's sister, Medea, who had lost her battle with magical Rage and Turned Harpy. They'd succeeded in their quest—putting the former Fury out of her misery—but at too high a cost. Losing Nan to her coma just before my mother vanished for years had been agony to endure. It also left me to Stacia's nefarious clutches, which I'd only later learned had been precisely her plan.

"My, my, my, lassie," Nan said now in her lilting Scottish accent, "but aren't *you* a sight for sore eyes?"

Hearing her speak helped me conquer my bewilderment. "N-Nan?"

She stopped a step below me—putting us on eye level to each other—and smiled. "Of course it's me, lassie. Surely you've been expecting me?"

"I—I . . ." Okay, maybe I'd only *partially* conquered my bewilderment. "Of *course* I've been expecting to see you, but Mom said—"

Nan shook her head sadly. "You shouldn't believe everything you hear, lassie, not even from your mother."

Okay, that *lassie* thing was starting to unnerve me. Nan *had* often called me *lass* growing up, but rarely *lassie* after I explained why her doing so made me want to bark like a collie. I had vague recollections of someone else's calling me that, but couldn't quite dredge up a face or name. I focused on Nan's flowing red hair—odd, she'd always worn it tightly braided along the crown of her head—and familiar blue eyes. The exact shade shared by Mom, Cori, and me; a thought which had me remembering our shared danger. "*What* is going on, Nan? What were you *thinking* to challenge the Moerae days after waking from a coma?"

She raised a hand and gave a soft chuckle that sounded huskier than usual. Déjà vu struck again. That wasn't Nan's laugh, but it *did* seem familiar. "Slow down, lassie. I *am* only newly awakened." When this didn't produce answering amusement, she sobered. "Gods' truth, Marissa, I hadn't planned for things to go this way, but since they have . . . I hate to be the one to break this to you, but your mother just can't be trusted. Something's *wrong* with her."

I managed to mask true emotion behind a poker face. If *that* wasn't the pot calling the kettle black . . . The more Nan spoke, the more convinced I became that Mom was right. This wasn't Nan—not the Nan we'd known and loved. "Why do you say that?"

She gave a heavy sigh. "Haven't you wondered *why* she suddenly changed her mind about hating politics after the debacle where she lost the election to Ekaterina, only to go after a Conclave seat again once freed from captivity?"

"Couldn't the same be asked about your changing *your* mind about politics?"

A calm expression came my way. "I have little interest in the Moerae's seat, Marissa, and more concern in bringing a traitor to justice."

I couldn't hide my frown this time. "Traitor? The Moerae?" I'd suspected her of that very thing myself, blinded by my loyalty to Stacia and innate dislike of Ekaterina, a mistake I would *not* easily repeat.

Nan nodded gravely. "Aye, the Mocrae. *She* gave your mother and me the information leading us to Me— Medea twenty years ago. *How* else could she have such intimate knowledge of Harpy identities and locations if she weren't in collusion with the nasty creatures herself? Your mother and I found Medea—along with several other Harpies waiting in ambush—exactly where *she* said we would."

I blinked at that revelation. Mom had never let that tidbit slip; but, then again, barely a year went by before she disappeared, and I'd been too young for her to share

many of the details with. "So you think that—what—
Ekaterina set you up?"

She nodded again. "Wholeheartedly. She and
Stacia—" Her words cut off when I gave a jerk at the
unexpected mention of my mentor. "You didn't know?"

"Know what?"

"That Ekaterina and Stacia were—lovers—before
Medea became involved with Stacia. Ekaterina never
got over her jealousy; she did everything in her power to
break the two apart."

Her words—though unexpected—had the ring of
truth in them. I didn't necessarily believe everything she
was saying, but I *did* buy Stacia and Ekaterina having a
romantic past. The Moerae was openly bisexual, and it
would clearly explain why she later grew to so resent
Stacia—and by extension, me. Before, I thought it had
just been the fact that she and Mom had once vied for
the same Conclave seat, but now . . .

"That still doesn't explain why you think something
is wrong with Mom." Or, as sudden paranoia had me
realize, *why* she'd tracked me down here at the PD to
discuss her concerns, alone. Or *was* she alone? I pulled
in the tiniest hint of magic and enhanced my physical
senses. Sure enough, I could now hear the softest of foot
scuffles and rustles on the flight of stairs below, enough
to make me think there were at least three or four people
concealing themselves. Concern for Trinity pricked, but
then I registered that I had heard the fire door on the
next landing open and close and knew they'd let her
leave before rushing in.

Nan didn't catch on to the sudden tensing of my
body—or my infinitesimal use of magic. "I believe
Ekaterina is manipulating her, has been since her return.

If you'll just return to the Palladium with me, I'll show you the proof."

Oh, for the love of gods. Now I had to worry about *family* abductions? She'd obviously brought the backup below in case she couldn't persuade me to go along quietly. I didn't have time to accommodate her, either. Time was a-ticking, as the insistent Mandate buzz in the back of my brain reinforced. My mind whirred, trying to come up with a feasible plan to get rid of Nan and her goon squad without bloodshed (mine) or breaking my cover. I could easily shift to Nemesis form and take on all of Nan's friends, but that would ruin the element of surprise. If they *were* all working for Anubis—as now seemed likely—and saw me in Nemesis form, they'd warn him, and he'd reach the logical conclusion: The Triad was gunning for him. He'd find out soon enough, of course, but I at least wanted to get through that portal before he did.

I decided to go with one of the things I did so well: BS. "I find it hard to believe . . . Okay, okay, I guess it's only fair to hear both sides of the story." I made a show of glancing at my watch. "But I have some loose ends to tie up here. I'm meeting several mercs in my office to go over some work for the PD. How about I meet you tomorrow morning?"

She fell for it—not that Nan had any reason not to. When she'd last dealt with me, I'd been a younger, more biddable version of myself. Not to mention a preadolescent not yet dealing with Fury Rage way worse than any PMS. "You can't cancel this meeting?"

I let a smile touch my lips. "Yeah, cause it'd be *such* a good idea to drag badass arcane mercs to the PD this late at night only to cancel on them."

She smiled in turn. "Fair enough. Then I will look forward to seeing you tomorrow, lassie." Gods, *who* used to call me that? "Just ask to be shown to my quarters when you arrive."

My turn to nod, then—because it would be weird for me not to—I reached forward and hugged her. It felt stranger than when I'd first embraced Mom after her unexpected return. Nan didn't hug me back initially, which didn't help the sense of awkwardness. After several seconds, she patted my back slightly, as if we were mere acquaintances. I was seriously picking up on the same *off* vibes Mom had. Something was wrong with Nan; and as soon as I got done laying down the smack with Anubis, I'd find out *what*.

ONCE I GOT RID OF NAN—PRETENDING ALL the while to be unaware she had been prepared to abduct me if I hadn't given in gracefully—I hurried to my office, half-fearing another ambush or catastrophe to waylay me although I made it unaccosted. Charlie and Sahana sat around the table shoved against one wall while Mac lounged in my office chair, doing gods knew what to my desktop. The shiny new computer he and David had set me up with had gone a long way toward making me *not* loathe computers with every fiber of my being as I once had. Not that they would ever replace Jack D in my heart.

I shot Mac a pointed look. "Comfortable?"

"Extremely so. And you're late."

The door slammed behind me when I kicked it, inspiring Sahana to jump and Charlie to raise an eyebrow. "Problems, darling?"

Besides apparently brainwashed grandmothers willing to kidnap me if I didn't do what they wanted me to? I activated the room's spell against eavesdropping with a quick touch of magic. "You have no idea. Okay, so, I'll make this short and not so sweet. Mac: You at all familiar with Nemesis?"

He pushed slightly away from the desk. "You mean, like your snake?"

Good thing they both were in tat form since people kept calling them *snakes* like they were ordinary creatures—and now they could verbalize dissatisfaction when that happened. "Same name, different story. I'm talking Nemesis as in the immortal version."

"Ahhh, you mean those Furies chosen by the Triad to hunt down immortal criminals. Yeah, Mom told me all about them when . . . you know."

When he was still under Stacia's brainwashing and Mom was held captive by the mortal scientists—back before Mac busted her out.

"Yes, exactly. Well, long story short, the Triad chose Mom and me to serve as Nemeses because one of the lesser gods has been a very, very bad boy."

Mac blinked several times, then stood, disbelief in his expression. "Wait—whoa—what? I thought you and Mom just had to do a little housecleaning in the Sisterhood. Are you saying that an actual *immortal* is behind all this?"

"Afraid so. Well, at least we think it's all connected. Nan's awakening, her refusing to speak with Mom, her challenging the Moerae, the split within the Sisterhood . . . The Triad believes one of the Death Lords is making a power play, swearing Furies to himself individually, not to mention other lesser gods."

Charlie let out a piercing whistle. "What's he trying to do, start a war?"

"Pretty much. There's no other logical explanation, really."

Mac frowned. "So, *which* Death Lord?"

I looked him straight in the eye. "Anubis."

He let out a sharp breath. "F-uuu-ck."

"My sentiments precisely."

Mac understood why this sucked so bad on a personal level in a way no one else could. "Gods, Riss, no wonder you didn't want me to say anything to Elle."

Charlie cleared his throat loudly. "Ah, correct me if I'm wrong, Riss, but didn't Anubis threaten to kill you if you stepped near him again?"

Damnation. Of *course* Charlie knew about that. I must have confided to him after the first time we'd saved each other's lives. Too much postadrenaline Jack Daniel's.

"Death is the last thing *I* have to worry about now; I'm a Nemesis, remember? Full-on demigoddess while working for the Triad." At least for the next three days.

He looked slightly reassured. Sahana and Mac, on the other hand . . . Not so much. She opened her mouth to speak, but I raised a hand. "It's a done deal; I have the Mandate, which is nonnegotiable. I get that you guys are concerned for my safety, but here's the reality: If we don't nail Anubis's ass to the wall quickly, war is pretty much guaranteed. Not just among the Furies, either. We're talking *Clash of the Titans Take Two* without any Hollywood ending."

Sahana heaved a sigh, then stood with a resolute expression. "How can we help?"

No hesitation. No prevarication. She just calmly assumed that her pitching in was a guarantee. Pretty humbling, really, especially considering we were mostly colleagues who had just became friends over the past few weeks.

Mac, not to be outdone, stepped around the desk and touched my shoulder. "Yeah, Riss, what can we do?"

My eyes felt a suspicious stinging sensation that I shoved aside for the moment. Plenty of time to get all sappy *after* we headed off yet another looming war.

"Okay, so . . . The down-and-dirty answer is that Mom's looking for evidence that Mr. Jackal-Faced *has* sworn Furies to himself, which will probably be all kinds of boring. I, on the other hand, have the much more exciting—and dangerous—task of looking for evidence against him on his home turf."

Charlie's eyes got as big and excited-looking as a Goblin in front of a malfunctioning ATM. "You mean . . ."

"I'm headed to the Underworld, and you all get to come along for the ride."

After I made a quick telephone call to my mother, letting her know about my little run-in with Nan. If we got lucky, Mom might be able to corner her when she returned to the Palladium. Hey, a Fury could *hope*, right?

MY CLAIM THAT I HAD TO GET SOMETHING from Hounds of Anubis before we hit the Underworld—which was the truth, but not the *whole* truth—didn't faze any of them. They waited out front while I—disguised once more in mortal form—popped into the oversized, block-long building that housed Liana Murphy's arcane antiquities store along with the Murphy mercenary headquarters. I cornered Scott's full-blooded

Egyptian Warhound mother in her office next to the store.

"Liana, just the woman I needed to see."

A sincerely pleased smile crossed her face as she rose from her desk and moved to hug me. She'd made me squirm—just a little—in the weeks after Scott and I reconnected, but she knew we truly loved each other, and that was all that mattered to her. No big surprise, considering she'd given up her rich and snobby Banoub relatives in order to marry Scott's mortal father, Morgan.

"To what do I owe this unexpected surprise, Marissa?"

"I'm on official Fury business, and I need to ask you a few questions, but I can't tell you why."

She didn't even bat an eyelash. "Ask away, then."

I let out a breath, grateful that she had granted me the same unwavering loyalty all Murphys showed each other. Of course, I felt a little guilty knowing I would use whatever expertise she shared with me against her personal deity, but I didn't exactly have a choice.

I'd had time to ponder what strategy might work best for not only proving Anubis's guilt but managing to capture him on his own home turf, where his powers would be the strongest. Only one possibility immediately sprang to mind. *Every* religion among mortals and arcanes had some sort of belief pertaining to the divine judgment souls would face upon their deaths. I planned to use that fact against old Jackal-Faced.

"I need to know whatever you can tell me about Egyptian Reckoning lore as it relates to Warhounds." Since they numbered among the few to still worship Anubis almost precisely the way Ancient Egyptians had way back when.

She blinked. "The long version or the short version?"

I glanced at my watch. Just after eleven. "Whatever you can tell me in—say—thirty minutes or less."

Never one to mince words, Liana proceeded to do just that and gave me precisely the strategy I'd been hoping for.

BOSTON JUST BEFORE MIDNIGHT—ESPECIALLY in the Underbelly—bore so little resemblance to its daytime self that one often felt as if the border between this world and the next had been unknowingly traversed. This was, strictly speaking, an impossibility given the fact that no one, whether mortal, arcane, or divine, could ever *accidentally* pass from one realm to the next. On the other hand, it wasn't a complete non sequitur, since the thresholds between worlds did become *easier* to cross at certain times of the day and year—thus the timing of our midnight rendezvous.

The most obvious difference consisted of the vast number of shadows lining each side of the cobblestoned sidewalk upon which we now strode. While full darkness benefited our desire to pass quickly and quietly from Hounds of Anubis to our destination, it also increased the odds for someone hoping to make a nighttime ambush before we reached the Temple Anupu. Of course, none of the three traveling with me would make that easy, increased hidey-holes or no.

My companions fanned out around me in an obviously protective manner; laughable for the mere fact they thought they were being subtle. Sahana walked at my side—but close enough I could have smacked her shapely derriere with little effort if she or I pinch-hit for the other team. Charlie scouted the sidewalk ahead, all seven-foot-plus of him casting such a long shadow that Anubis himself might have thought twice before tangling with the Giant. Mac, in contrast, ghosted so far behind, I was tempted to ask if he had to stop to use the little boys' room. In reality, he couldn't resist channeling Fury magic every few moments to check for any unwanted followers. I was torn between amusement he thought he could hide his efforts from a full Fury and gratitude he was saving me the effort. At least this way I could save my own energy for the task ahead: getting seven or eight people safely through that damned portal.

We reached the intersection splitting the main thoroughfare we had been walking along from the narrow, silent avenue leading to the temple. Charlie left the cobblestones to duck into an even narrower gangway between a boarded-up former furniture store and a thriving-so-much-it-was-already-closed-for-the-night pawnshop. The rest of us followed suit.

"Something wrong?" I murmured, once all four of us huddled inside the gangway.

Charlie hesitated before shaking his head slowly. "Not wrong, exactly. Just interesting. I know you're not strong in earth magic, but tap into the area and tell me what you think."

Trusting his instincts, I complied without question, although it took me a few moments to pick up on what he'd noticed right away. Normally, vast pools of magic layered the ground beneath our feet, waiting for practitioners to call upon and channel them in whatever manner they could. Each magic user had personal stores of energy to call upon, but those would fade quickly if not replenished from some external source. The Underbelly had been founded in this area of Boston not only because mortals had mostly abandoned it during the Great War, but because an exceptionally high number of magical reservoirs rested beneath.

Reservoirs that, at least in the immediate vicinity I could sense, currently measured at dangerously low levels. We would be able to channel magic to fuel our abilities, if needed, but not for very long. My body tensed. I couldn't think of too many—okay, any—natural causes for such a major power depletion in such a large area, not so late at night or without some very apparent, very large magical ritual going on.

Mac's eyes zeroed in on my face. "Trouble?"

My turn to hesitate. "Not anything obvious, but the magical reservoirs around here are really low."

His frown was apparent even in the abysmal lighting cast from a faraway streetlamp. "Low enough to present a problem getting where we need to go?"

"It shouldn't be, not with everyone's personal reserves to draw upon if needed, plus whatever is available inside the temple. No, *that's* not what has me concerned."

"Then what—"

Durra's irritatingly familiar voice responded before I could. "If none of us have depleted the area's magic, then who—or what—has?"

We four whirled to see Durra lead Laurell and Patricia between the walls of our temporary hideaway. Funny how, respecting her mother as I now did, Durra *still* hadn't grown on me any. Okay, maybe not so much *funny* as logical considering everything she'd done to me—orders or not. Still, just having three Furies added to our number made a small measure of inner tension evaporate. No matter how much I trusted the others to kick ass and take names, they simply weren't Furies. Not even Mac—not yet. Mom might have taught him a lot, but some abilities and knowledge came only upon swearing the oaths.

Oaths I very much hoped he would be allowed to someday take.

"My question exactly." I made quick introductions before getting back to the immediate concern. "This temple is the only one for at least a block radius. Is there some sort of Underworld convention going on that I don't know about?"

I addressed my question mostly to Sahana because— Hey! Death magic!—and she tilted her head in consideration. "Not that *I've* heard."

Which pretty much meant *hell no*.

Charlie piped back up, "Should we find some other temple portal to—"

If only life were that easy. "We can't. It has to be a portal directly into *his* territory."

Durra shifted her weight from one foot to the other. "It makes little sense to speculate on the cause for the depleted reservoirs. Either it has nothing to do with the temple—and by extension us—or the priests have likely used the power to fortify the temple's defenses, and we'll simply have to adapt. As you said, we have no other choice."

I hated it when Durra was right even if she *was* agreeing with me. "If all else fails, and trouble ensues, all I have to do is assume—" I looked from Durra to Laurell and Patricia and arched a questioning brow. When Durra nodded, I continued, "—Nemesis form, and the priests will have no option but to let us pass. Extra defenses or not, both arcane *and* immortal law dictate that portals are to be open to Nemeses at all times."

Everyone else relaxed . . . everyone except Durra and me, who had the greatest understanding of what we might be up against. I'd had a sudden newsflash on just *what* the Anubian priests might have used that large amount of magic on and was willing to bet Durra had, too: summoning Anubis himself from the Underworld to the mortal realm, something that would require a hell of a lot of juice. Especially if, like the members of the Triad, he *had* made the power jump from lesser god to greater.

In which case, we were likely about to get our asses kicked in all ways figurative and literal—and I was the only one who couldn't be killed. Meaning everyone else's lives depended upon me. No pressure or anything.

CHAPTER EIGHT

ENTERING TEMPLE ANUPU WAS A SIMPLE enough task—a matter of walking up to the front doors and stepping into a dimly lit but pretty vestibule. Polished hardwood floors made it difficult to sneak in quietly, but we hadn't really been going for stealth. The walls might have been a generic beige color, but vertical stripes made up of brilliant Egyptian hieroglyphics saved them from being a total snoozefest. A wide hallway led left and right, each branch ending in a staircase, one heading up, one down. And another set of double doors, this time featuring a stained-glass depiction of Mr. Jackal-Faced himself, stood opposite the entryway. As usual, he stared out of a black-cowled robe, his true face shrouded behind a golden jackal mask with only neon yellow eyes—nearly identical to a Hound's except for the stark silver light rimming them—visible.

The telltale tingle of magical wards washed over my skin upon crossing the threshold, but no hint of blaring sirens heralded our arrival. I was almost disappointed. My companions shadowed me into the entryway and spread out to each side. The mercs—Charlie and Mac—and we Furies cataloged our immediate surroundings for potential threats and escape routes while Sahana admired the elaborately designed walls. Not that one could blame her—they *were* pretty impressive, other than the whole beige thing.

"Several people touched by Death magic are approaching," she murmured, showing that Sahana was no less observant than the professional killers in the group—the big reason I'd been so eager to involve someone who was neither Fury, merc, nor, technically, a police officer. *Nobody* knew Death magic better than a Bhairavi Raga except, *maybe*, a Death Lord.

I nodded but kept my expression serene. Just because most temples kept their doors unlocked for weary worshippers at all times didn't mean they turned a blind eye to potential thieves or troublemakers—or surprise visits from what amounted to a veritable arcane task force. Not too surprising that the newcomers emerged from below: a trio of black-robed priests—and one priestess—who wore lots of gold jewelry, including a neckpiece from which dangled oversized jackals and woven gold belts, also featuring jackals. Their expressions appeared as unruffled as my own even when faced by our intimidating entourage. Too bad I couldn't just challenge them to a game of poker over a bottle of Jack. From the look of things, they would give me a run for my money.

One of the priests allowed an unconvincing smile to touch his lips as they stopped several feet away. His eyes moved straight to me, still in mortal form, although wearing slacks and a sleeveless blouse that clearly displayed my usual (thanks to magic) red snake tats. These days, my own mortal form was as easily recognized by arcanes as my Fury getup. "Chief Holloway. I am Khenti-Manu. To what do we owe this unexpected . . . honor?"

The *Khenti* surprised me, since I knew that was a very high-ranking—and rare—title in Anubis's priestly hierarchy. It seemed weird for someone of that level to be working in a relatively obscure temple in the U.S. rather than in Egypt or the Underworld itself. "Good evening, Excellency." A little brown-nosing never hurt. "I apologize for the unorthodox nature of our visit, but I am here in my capacity as Fury rather than Chief Magical Investigator."

Not a single chink appeared in his priestly armor. "I see. How can we be of service, then, Kindly One?"

One of those old-school euphemisms for Furies meant to sweeten us up. Guess *brown-nosing* was a two-way street. "We are carrying out a gods-blessed Mandate, Excellency, and have need of your portal to the Underworld."

His serenity didn't falter, but I couldn't say the same for Tweedledee and Dum standing to each side; their clenched fists and ugly scowls showed what they thought of *that* request. Not such stellar poker opponents after all.

"I'm afraid that won't be possible, Kindly One. Please forgive me for the impertinence."

Huh. Outright refusal *had* been a possibility, but I hadn't really thought it a likely one. It made no sense for Anubis to paint a bigger target on his back by issuing a blanket order to *all* his priests in the mortal realm to deny passage to Furies traveling to the Underworld.

Unless . . . unless he hadn't; say, for instance, he'd some-how known exactly *who* the Triad would select as Nem-esis and had only instructed *this* temple to block portal access to *this* Fury. That would also explain why such a high-ranking priest had been sent to pull duty *there.* Apparently Anubis had a damned good spy among either the Megaeras or the *Gens Immortalis* to obtain that information so quickly.

The urge to shift to Nemesis mode and set to smiting was hard to resist, especially when Rage suddenly tinged my vision gray, but as long as I had the slightest chance of making it through that portal with my secret intact, I would damned well keep trying.

I blinked several times to clear my messed-up eye-sight. "Forgive me, Excellency, but I'm not sure I under-stand. Are you actually refusing portal passage to a Fury on active duty?"

"Of course not." Gods, but he would make a master poker player. The uninflected voice; the neutral expres-sion; the lack of any giveaway *tells.* "I'm afraid that our portal has been malfunctioning for the past several days and thus is quite useless."

I just bet it is. Still, I had to give him props for com-ing up with a cover story that would both give no offense and effectively dissuade most Furies from pressing fur-ther. Too bad for him I wasn't *most Furies.*

"Fortunately for you, Durra here is an expert on repairing malfunctioning portals." And lucky for *me,* she managed a mean poker face of her own. "You won't mind if we take a look at it now." Very deliberately *not* a question. If he refused this time, he'd be openly defy-ing the Sisterhood and, by extension, the immortals themselves. Anubis wouldn't want to risk that yet, not when he hadn't declared open warfare or himself to be a greater god.

A bead of sweat appeared above Mr. Cool's upper lip. I almost felt sorry for him. "How fortunate indeed. What a generous offer. Please, follow us to the portal room." Tweedledee and Dum appeared no less annoyed than before but didn't gainsay their spokesman.

Durra touched my arm, and we let everyone precede us before falling into step at the back of the line. "Why would you tell them I'm an expert in portal magic, Marissa? They're going to notice when I fail to repair it."

Weird how she kept her voice actually respectful; maybe because of my newfound divinity? "Because I'm pretty sure that it's just a ruse meant to send us packing without suspicion. Unfortunately for them, I was born suspicious. I'd stake my life—okay, *your* life since I can't die right now—that their portal is working just fine."

"Logical, I suppose. But what if they're just leading us into a trap?"

"I don't think that's an *if* so much as a foregone conclusion."

"You don't seem overly concerned. Is it because we have Nemeses—a Nemesis—on our side?"

"That—" I acknowledged, "—plus I know good and well thanks to Scott that this temple numbers, at most, six priests and ten acolytes. Even without a Nemesis, we're more than a match for them. Besides, I really don't think it will come to that. They'll try and stall us while getting a message to the Big Guy, but I have no intention of being stalled."

"And what if the *Big Guy* is already waiting in the portal room?"

I let a fierce grin twist my lips. "Then I'll have no

problem kicking his ass, Nemesis-style. There's a reason the Triad itself appoints Nemeses." I would be able
to tap into their power on a limited basis when facing my
quarry. Otherwise, mere demigoddesses would never be
able to drag in unwilling—and unkillable—deities to
face justice.

She fell silent, and I focused on our descent down two
flights of candlelit stairs, electric candles in a nod to
modern technology and standards of cleanliness. That
many wax candles dripping onto the stone stairway
would have made the temple's liability insurance sky-
rocket. The stairs spilled out into another hallway, this
one lined with several doors and leading farther than its
aboveground counterpart. The priests stopped halfway
down the hall in front of a plain oak door. Not the one I
would have guessed to mark the portal to hell when
compared to some of the more ornate doors along the
corridor, but that was undoubtedly the point. Tweedledee and Dum reacted to something said (or unsaid) by
their superior and slipped through the doorway while he
allowed the door to click shut. Khenti-Manu turned to
us—or specifically, once I caught up, to me.

"The others have gone to turn on the lights."

Yeah right, and I really *was* a Kindly One.

My companions readied themselves for a good ole-
fashioned brawl without obviously doing so; I just knew
most of them way too well not to notice. Fury eyes
glowed an even brighter green; Mac's eyes took on a distinct gleam of their own; Charlie flexed impressive
biceps when he clenched his fists; and even Sahana
seemed to brace herself. Khenti-Manu appeared oblivi-
ous, but he hadn't seemed a complete moron up to this

point, so I didn't count on it. He knew we were expecting a fight and was trying that whole stalling tactic.

I shouldered my way past the others—surprised to see Durra keep pace as if she actually cared for my safety—and placed my hand not so subtly upon the door. "Most of us can see just fine in the dark if needs must."

Another solitary bead of sweat bubbled up, this one on his forehead. He picked up on the *hint* and pushed the door open without protest.

Tweedledee and Dum stood on the far side of a subterranean room nothing like the polished entrance or hallways we had passed through. *This* chamber had been roughly hewn out of solid rock, with only a poured-concrete floor to indicate man's touch. Esoteric symbols—including the one for Anubis along with the Egyptian ankh—had been etched onto the floor with gold paint: actual twenty-four-karat gold, I was willing to bet. Mr. Jackal-Faced seemed to go in for flash and dazzle worse than any glitter-happy eight-year-old. To give Khenti-Manu bonus points for honesty, a bank of electric switches *did* rest along the wall where his subordinates were standing. On the other hand, the room's distinct lack of furniture, summoning circle, or—most importantly—anything resembling a potential portal detracted from his integrity score.

"Where's the portal?"

He motioned to a tapestry featuring Anubis in all his canine-headed glory just past the other priests. "This is merely the antechamber."

Ah, the tapestry apparently hid another doorway, leading deeper into the earth itself. Oh joy, Anubis enjoyed catering to stereotypes as much as he did the shock-and-awe routine. Where else would one find a portal to hell than inside an actual cave?

Khenti-Manu cleared his throat. "I'll have to ask your—associates to wait here while you two"—he waved to Durra and me—"inspect the portal."

Well, never let it be said he didn't have balls of steel. "You can ask that, Excellency, but I fear we cannot oblige the request. We will *all* be passing through that portal. Tonight."

The sharp scent of perspiration caught my attention, and I noticed several damp areas peppering his robe. Ah, so those two drops of sweat had been the only *visible* signs of his burgeoning fear. He started to blubber some sort of argument, but I strode toward the tapestry, followed closely by everyone else.

"When I said *tonight*, what I meant was *now*. Your Excellency."

None of the three Anubians were foolish enough to interfere when I yanked aside the tapestry-turned-curtain and stepped into the narrow tunnel revealed. *Shit!* While not technically claustrophobic—Furies simply couldn't afford to be—small, subterranean enclosed spaces and I did not particularly get along. For that moment, however, I pulled up my big-girl pants and stalked along the rocky corridor as if it didn't bother me in the least. Reaching the far side and stepping into a huge dank cave, I discovered something that *did* bother me very much. The sight of my lover, Scott, Mac's wife Elliana, and several other Murphy Shadowhounds standing between us and the oversized mirror marking a portal on the opposite side of the cavern, full-out bodyguard style. Proving yet again that Anubis was more than willing to play dirty.

* * *

MY BREATH CAUGHT AT THE UNEXPECTED image of familiar shoulder-length red hair, golden eyes, and deeply burnished skin covered by black cargo pants, a matching T-shirt, and combat boots. Weapons covered every spare inch of his mercenary getup: short but deadly swords sheathed at his waist, knives in various leg and arm straps, crossbow (now *that* was new) hanging from his back. I was willing to bet the accompanying arrows were spell-worked silver—just about the only thing capable of killing Furies—and could guess whose idea *they* had been.

Scott appeared every bit as shocked to see me step into the portal room as I was to find him guarding it. Had any doubts remained that Anubis knew I was gunning for him, they would have shriveled up and died. He knew, all right, knew and was prepared to hit me where it hurt. Like he thought it would stop me. *It won't, right?* my guilty conscience questioned. Of *course* it wouldn't . . . Scott would just step aside once I explained, and everything would be all hunky-dory.

Cause life *so* often worked out that way.

He looked like he wanted to rush over to me, but his sense of duty made him maintain his post despite the obvious emotional turmoil waging inside. "Riss, what are *you* doing here?"

I took the opportunity to peruse the room's occupants quickly but didn't see any signs of Sean, who I'd started to think might have been the one responsible for hiring the Shadowhounds to do Anubis's dirty work. It wouldn't have been a big shock if I'd learned he'd been working for the Big Guy this whole time rather than being held hostage by brainwashed Sidhe. I was getting used to being stabbed in the back when least expected.

My gaze settled back on Scott, and I shook my head the way he'd done to me the other night in front of Serise. He took my hint and fell silent.

My allies crowded behind me, and I stepped forward, stopping just in front of the black pentagram etched onto the smooth granite floor, smoothed using copious amounts of magic since no natural weathering could account for its perfect flatness. Scott, Elliana, and a half dozen of their relatives, along with the remaining Anubian priests and most of their acolytes, fanned out between the pentagram and quiescent portal, which wouldn't remain so for long if I had my way.

Khenti-Manu and his shadows stepped around us, stopped at the far edge of the pentagram, and turned to face me. Tweedledumb and Dumber wore stupid little smirks while *His Excellency* still sweated like a pig. Guess we now knew *which* Anubian priest had hired them for their latest bodyguard assignment.

"What the f—um, *what* is going on here, Excellency?"

He licked his lips—probably to clear any lingering hint of perspiration—and raised a placating hand. "Please, Kindly One, we do not want this to come to blows, but we are prepared to defend our Lord's territory. To the death, if need be."

Easy enough to make that sacrifice when one's personal deity was a Death Lord. "You say you do not *want* bloodshed, and yet you have the *audacity* to hire my lover and sister-in-law to stand between me and my duty?"

The priest flinched as violently as Scott and the Shadowhounds—who had by now clearly recognized

Mac and me. Ah, I was willing to bet Anubis hadn't shared *that* information with his Underbelly spokesman. Typical.

"Please, Kindly One, we're merely acting upon our orders—"

"Orders that you very well *know* violate every single precept laid down by arcane as well as divine law. *No* arcane is to stand between a Fury and her gods-Mandated quarry. And yet you stand here ready to flout that very law?"

Scott's eyes took on an anguished glow, and he opened his mouth to speak, but *His Excellency* beat him to the proverbial punch. "We flout no laws, Kindly One. The portal truly is malfunctioning." Helped along, no doubt, by the excessive amounts of magic these damned Anubians had channeled at their lord's command for this very purpose. It looked like Mr. Jackal-Faced had planned for every eventuality when he took an educated guess—or was told by spies—that I would be chosen as one of the Nemeses to bring him down. Oh wait, I was willing to bet he *hadn't* counted on my employing the unexpected ace up my sleeve—Sahana.

Since pretense now seemed pointless—and I wanted every bit of authority I could muster—I shed mortal form the way Amphisbaena discarded unwanted skin, blinking from blue-eyed blonde to black-clad Nemesis, complete with ebon-scaled serpents and charcoal-colored wings. Durra sensed my shift just quickly enough to step out of wing-clobbering range. My transformation to Nemesis seemed to blindside His Excellency and company, along with Scott, making me wonder what the hell kind of game Anubis was play—

That's it! He wants this whole debacle to delay me,

wants me to waste time negotiating and working things out so he can block us from his realm. He really *should* have learned not to count on my being so boringly predictable. I mean, *really*, what kind of Fury did he think I was?

I stopped wasting time and turned to Sahana rather than the priests, who would have *seemed* the only ones capable of opening the portal for us. "Sahi, would you mind terribly?"

Her sudden feline smile made me proud. "Not at all, Nemesis."

That title was *so* much better than empty euphemisms.

The Anubians shared confused looks while I motioned to my companions, who steadily advanced until the three priests stepped off the pentagram entirely, only to merge into the still-reeling line of priests and Shadowhounds. Scott was the only one with courage enough to step toward where I took my place blocking our adversaries from Sahana, who now stood at the northern point of the pentagram. "Riss, please, what's going on?"

It took every ounce of willpower not to melt at his bewildered, pleading voice. *Gods-damned Anubis!* "Anubian Warhound, do you hold loyal to the Sisterhood of Furies and the Triad of immortals?"

He flinched as if physically struck. "Ris—" Then, realizing the seriousness of the situation, stiffened his stance and steeled his expression. "Of course I do, Tisi— Nemesis."

"Blasphemy!" Tweedledum screeched. "We True Believers owe allegiance to Lord Anubis alone!"

Elliana *accidentally* planted an elbow into the priest's jiggling midsection. "Oops."

I kept my voice ice-cold. "Do you really, Warhound? Even if that means going *against* your personal deity's orders? The Triad believes he has committed treason against them—and so do I." My heart wanted to shatter into tiny pieces at the way he looked at me when I used that tone and those words. Necessary evil, but heart-piercing all the same, especially considering there were no guarantees he'd forgive me later.

My eyes moved from him to all the Shadowhounds. I was pretty sure he and Elliana would make the right choice, but the others weren't sleeping with allies-turned-*enemies*.

Magic roared into the pentagram at my back; magic flavored most heavily with the clichéd but appropriate solid black of Death, magic ringing with a thousand discordant notes of Raga song that originated with and poured itself into Sahana's spell. That realization had the Anubians breaking past their reluctance to actually take up arms against a Nemesis. They hadn't believed any of us would be physically capable of activating the summoning circle. The game had suddenly changed.

Guilt tugged hard on my heartstrings as I saw warring emotions play out among the Hounds in what felt like an eternity but was more like seconds. Horror, denial, acceptance, anguish, regret, and finally, determination. I braced myself to discover *what* shape that determination would take. My body sagged when the Shadowhounds turned on their brother Anubians and shoved them away from both the pentagram and now-glowing mirror. They were outnumbered by priests and acolytes, so my companions—minus Sahana and me—dove into the fray. The acolytes were barely nuisances—knowing too little Death magic to prove any true threat.

Charlie and several of the Shadowhounds soon had them cowering on the far side of the cavern, leaving the bulk of our forces to stave off the much more experienced, deadly priests.

Durra and Scott squared off against *His Excellency*. My breath caught again, and Rage burst unexpectedly, demanding that I leap forward to defend my mate—something I *would not do.* Sparks of black energy danced in the air, skittering from Sahana and the pentagram into the mirror, which pulsed with silver in addition to obsidian light. The portal was opening—despite the wards the Anubians had likely cast to block off Fury magic, never anticipating I'd bring a Death magic practitioner of my own. If I had jumped into the fight then, as instinct screamed for me to do, I would have left Sahana vulnerable.

I bit down on that Fury instinct to *fight* and maintained my position between Sahana and the portal. Every couple of moments I glanced behind to make sure no Anubian reinforcements had popped in from the tunnel, but most of my attention focused on the black-and-silver energy writhing around and *into* the otherwise innocuous mirror. Sahana's Raga song reached a fever pitch, then *pop!* The link between mortal realm and Underworld snapped into place.

I checked on Sahana and knew from her haggard expression that she wouldn't be able to maintain the portal for long. My gaze flicked to the fight still ongoing, and unease washed over me. No way would we be able to subdue *all* the priests in time for everyone to make it safely through, which meant some were going to *have* to be left behind. Stubbornness flared, and I considered wading into the fray to end it quicker, but the over-whelming sense of *Mandate* drove that urge away.

"Quickly! Whoever can, into the portal NOW!"

Durra and Scott didn't hesitate; she distracted Khenti-Manu, and Scott knocked him halfway across the cavern. Then my uneasy Megaera ally and my Warhound lover leaped into the portal in a few quick strides and vanished. Mac and Elliana—who had fallen into their usual pattern of fighting back-to-back—disabled their opponents long enough to follow suit. The remaining Shadowhounds redoubled their efforts to keep the Anubians off our backs, but I could tell it wouldn't be enough—and so could Laurell and Patricia. They aborted their started run toward the portal and gave in more deeply to Rage's burning insanity to help make up for decreased numbers.

I wouldn't waste their sacrifice, either. "Charlie!" He responded to my call and swooped the still-chanting Sahana into his arms as if we'd planned it. They disappeared in a flood of silver-and-black lightning. I saluted Laurell and Patricia before jumping into the mirror—and a world of agonizing pain.

CHAPTER NINE

TRAVELING THROUGH A PORTAL WAS *NEVER* a pleasant experience—how could having your molecules magically zapped out of and back into existence ever be termed such a thing?—but none of my prior voyages could have prepared me for the maelstrom now tearing every fiber of my being apart before s—l—o—w—l—y smashing them back into place. I screamed—or tried to anyway—but my voice fell into formless darkness that had no end; until suddenly it did.

I stumbled out of a mirror several times larger than the one I'd leaped into, only to promptly fall to my knees retching onto the rough stone floor. By the sounds around me, I knew the others had been hit just as hard—except for Charlie, who moved to check on me, and Sahana, who waited for me to barrel out of the portal before she, too, fell to the ground. She was wiped out from working such an insane amount of magic, however, rather than suffering from the sudden urge to empty a week's worth of meals like the rest of us, including Scott, Durra, Mac, and Elliana.

Charlie touched my shoulder. "You okay, Riss?"

"Peachy," I managed to choke out before another paroxysm had me doubling over again. He waited for it to pass, eagle eyes scanning our surroundings for dangers the rest of us were currently unable to give a crap about.

Happily (at least for me), I seemed the first to recover despite being the last through the portal. "Jesus, Mary, and Joseph, as my sister-in-law would say. No *wonder* nobody travels to the Underworld in physical form unless they abso-fucking-lutely *have* to. That was *way* worse than dying and being revived." Weird that it had hurt so damned much considering I was now a full demigoddess; but that could be because I didn't know how to use all my new abilities yet.

Charlie glanced at Sahana, and the two shared a brief snickering jag before he turned back to me. "I don't want to seem insensitive since I obviously hit the iron-constitution jackpot, but we need to get moving like five minutes ago."

I pushed to my feet, gritting my teeth at the lingering nausea and forcing myself to smile grimly. "You *are* an insensitive, lucky-ass SOB, but you're also right."

He grinned and moved to help Sahana stand. Either sheer determination had worked, or my body finally recovered: I no longer felt like my insides had been sliced, diced, and Super-Glued back together. I started to move from the foot of the portal to examine our surroundings when magic flared behind me—a shitload of pure, unadulterated Death magic. The hair on my neck rose, and I zeroed in on Sahana, who shook her head wildly.

"Fuck!" I muttered, and whirled. That sheer amount of concentrated magic gave me a pretty good idea of who—or rather what—was trying to link up to our current location. A Death Lord. Three guesses which was most the most likely culprit.

"Can you stop it?" I threw over my shoulder as I stepped up to the pulsating mirror.

"Sorry, but no."

The exhaustion in her voice told *why* she couldn't. *Guess I'll get the chance to test my Nemesis skills in the Underworld a lot sooner than I—* Inspiration struck a split second before I did, sending my booted foot back and forward with way more strength then necessary. The immediate section of mirror I kicked split into myriad pieces, which rained against my bare skin and onto the ground. A dozen shards stung my skin, but I ignored them to kick another section of mirror, then another. Death magic struggled to manifest a large enough link for its maker to travel through; struggled and failed as my foot stayed inches ahead of it. Finally I ran out of mirror to smash, and so, too, did the magic fade away.

Or, at least I *thought* it did. What actually happened was that the Death magic that had made it through the aborted portal zapped into me when it couldn't be channeled as intended. That didn't seem so bad considering my temporary imperviousness to death, until the magic recognized the same thing and shot straight toward the nearest living being. Charlie, the lucky-ass SOB who'd nobly put his body between Sahana and the portal and was about to die a very painful death.

His luck kicked in again in the form of someone I'd

once more underestimated. Sahana—all five feet nothing of her petite frame—barreled into Charlie with just
enough force to move him so that the Death energy hit
her instead of him. And, unlike me, she was very much
able to properly channel it.

Her already dark eyes took on that freaky obsidian
hue they got when she worked Death magic, this time
becoming so dark her pupils blended in well enough
they seemed to disappear. She began humming in dis-
parate tones that should have clashed but somehow
merged into a not-unpleasant melody. Her music absorbed the splashes of Death magic flooding into her
although I couldn't have said what she did with it. Asking would have just been rude.

The excitement of shattering glass and ricocheting
Death magic hastened everyone else's recovery, as evidenced by their staggering over as quickly as unsteady legs
could manage, weapons drawn and fur figuratively (and
not so figuratively on the part of the Hounds) bristled.

"Everyone okay?" Scott addressed the question to all
of us, but his gaze focused solely on me. While seeing
him safe was a relief, the pain clearly evident in his eyes
was not. Could anyone blame him? He'd just violated the
direct orders of his personal deity, a crime punishable by
agonizing death if (gods send it not be *when*) Anubis
caught up with him.

I bared my teeth at that thought. First, Jackal-Faced
had to get through me. Besides which, the Triad's decree
superseded any given by an individual god. Scott had
absolutely made the right choice; but I knew that
wouldn't make it any easier on him. I only hoped our
relationship would be able to recover from the blow I'd
been forced to deal it.

Mac, Elliana, and Durra indicated they were in mostly good shape, a sentiment soon echoed by Charlie and Sahana. She seemed to actually mean that and, looking her over with enhanced Nemesis vision, for once I believed her. Normally Sahana was the type to insist she was *just fine* even if she were bleeding out all over the place, but that infusion of ill-gotten Death energy had apparently been just what the witch doctor ordered. She noticed my skeptical inspection and gave a toothy grin. "I mean it, Riss. I've never felt better."

"Okay, then. I'm going to second Charlie's recommendation that we get the he—heck out of here."

Durra's lips curved in an unusually demure smile. It was almost like she'd had a personality transplant. "Motion thirded. Where to?"

Good question, one I'd been contemplating in the back of my head since I'd been tasked with making this journey. I had to find proof that Anubis had broken immortal law, but it wasn't like I could just walk up to his Underworld followers and ask them to *pretty please* rat their lord out. That meant we had to use more roundabout methods, which was why I had wanted to make use of Liana's extensive knowledge of Ancient Egyptian lore to discover a viable strategy for accomplishing my goals.

"The Hall of Two Truths."

Those of us not well versed in Egyptian mythology showed little reaction. Durra, Scott, and Elliana on the other hand . . .

"Are you *out of your mind*?" Elliana, never one to miss an opportunity to criticize me, unconsciously touched Mac's hand for comfort. That's how much what I said freaked her out.

Scott muttered something that sounded suspiciously like, "I'm beginning to wonder."

Durra frowned but didn't dismiss me as criminally insane. "You mean to face the Feather?"

I nodded. Charlie snorted. "A feather doesn't sound that bad."

Elliana turned her scowl from me to him. "The Feather of Ma'at, which is the Egyptian version of an individual's Judgment Day. And the minute she goes to invoke the Scales, the exact freaking god we just pissed off will show up immediately to oversee the weighing of her heart. Even *if* Riss manages to pass the test, Ma'at won't be able to protect us from Anubis afterward."

"Oh." I attempted to keep my voice casual. "It's not *my* heart she's going to weigh." Durra's widened eyes indicated she had already caught on. Still, I spoke the rest for everyone else's benefit. "I'm going to demand what is the right of any Fury in the Hall of Two Truths—that the heart of my quarry be measured instead of my own."

Elliana's mouth made like Durra's eyes, and Scott let out an indrawn breath. "Insane—or freaking brilliant. Anubis won't know what's going on until it's too late."

"Precisely. The Feather will confirm whether or not Anubis has turned traitor against his fellow immortals." I gave a sweet smile. "And now, if you do not mind, this *lunatic* would like to hit the road—*before* Anubis uses the nearest portal and backtracks to kick our asses."

Not too surprisingly, *that* prospect lit a fire under their . . . rear ends.

WE HIKED OUT OF THE DISMAL CAVERN HOUSING the shattered portal and found ourselves in yet another dimly lit subterranean room. Okay, this one could more accurately be termed a tunnel since it steadily narrowed from where it jutted onto the portal room until becoming a corridor barely wide enough for three of us to pass side by side. We kept to single file for the most part, with me insisting on taking up point while Scott just as adamantly brought up our rear. I hoped that wasn't because he was just *that* pissed off at what love for me had made him do.

Though to be fair, he probably would have made the same choice if another Fury had been the Nemesis putting that *do-or-die* choice in front of him. Probably.

I forced my attention onto my immediate surroundings. Humanity has this image that the Underworld is some vast underground pit filled with perpetual doom and gloom, but that's not entirely true. Portions of it *do* conform to that stereotype—like the portal room we'd stumbled into after fleeing Temple Anupu. Other areas could have been picked up and plunked down into the mortal realm with none the wiser. Each Death Lord's territory corresponded for the most part to the flavor of hell envisioned by the early followers of his or her particular mythos.

Which was how we wound up trading the dank underground cavern housing the shattered portal for . . . another dank underground cavern. Duat, the Egyptian version of the Underworld, consisted of a series of interconnected chambers beneath the earth that wasn't too far off from what most mortals pictured. Unlike what mundanes tended to imagine, however, Duat's landscape teemed with geographical features as plentiful as those found on the mortal realm: fields, meadows, rivers, lakes, islands, and mountains, just to name a few. Of course, there were supposedly also fantastical lakes of fire, walls composed of living iron, and Technicolor trees to save the place from total mundanity. Not that we'd come across any of those yet.

Durra matched her pace to mine at the front of the group. "I didn't want to gainsay you in front of the others—" *Since when does* she *care about making me look good in front of people?* I guess since we became the only two Furies along for the ride. "But are you sure this is a wise idea?"

Ah, now *there* was the Doubting Durra I was used to. "I'd say more like it's my *only* idea at the moment. We lost any chance of stealth we might have had, and Anubis is going to send every single one of his dead and undead minions to hunt us down if he hasn't already."

"True, but if proving a deity is guilty of a crime were a simple enough matter of invoking the Scales and Feather, why doesn't the Triad do that every time? Why go to the trouble of involving Nemeses at all or conducting an actual trial?"

I barely managed to hold back an eye roll. "A *simple enough matter*? First of all, the Scales and Feather can only be invoked by one who was actually born a mortal—meaning the only ones who haven't actually died and can successfully accomplish that are, for the most part, Furies. Second of all, Ma'at will only allow the weighing of hearts to be done for those with either Egyptian blood or true believers of the Egyptian mythos."

"Then how—"

"I may look as pasty pale as they come, but there *is* Egyptian blood in my heritage. Plus, I'm going to actually invoke the Scales to weigh *Anubis's* heart, and it doesn't get much more Egyptian than him."

She frowned. "But if the Scales only work on those born mortals—"

"I didn't say they only *worked* on those groups, I said the Scales could only be *invoked by* them. Deities *can* have their hearts balanced against Ma'at's Feather. Yet another glaring loophole in immortal law, though one that is rarely taken advantage of, which brings me to the other reason your calling this a *simple enough matter* is so laughable. If it really *were* that easy, don't you think we would hear of its happening more often?"

"Well, yes, but—"

"And yet we haven't. Because typically the only ones who can *find* the Hall of Two Truths are spirits who have actually died. Those who travel there in living form have to do it the hard way: making it safely through Duat until they reach its heart, where the Hall is reputed to reside. Even *if* we make it through everything Anubis is going to throw at us and find the Hall, we'll then have to prove we're worthy to step before Ma'at."

"Won't just our—your—being a Nemesis prove your worth?"

I snorted. "If *only* it were that easy. And again, assuming we *do* pass whatever tests she throws at us, she's going to demand a price in exchange."

"What sort of price?"

"Not sure, but it will most likely suck and be way worse than we can imagine. Asking Ma'at to weigh a fellow deity's heart is no small thing to ask."

"So then—"

A soft rumble was the only warning before the ground gave way beneath our feet, and we went pitching forward at a crazily steep angle. "Stay back!" I shouted for the benefit of those behind us. My body banged against rock outcropping after outcropping as I tumbled for what seemed several minutes but couldn't have been more than thirty seconds, at most.

Instinct had me leaping to my feet the moment my uncontrollable descent ended. I summoned Nemesis and Nike into living form and peered into the inky blackness of our new surroundings. The fragrance of lush vegetation hung in the air, and I could just make out the shape of tropical leaves swaying in response to the magical breeze generated from my partial transformation. Goose bumps pricked my flesh as a sense of something *wrong* swept over me. I couldn't *see* or *hear* danger nearby but, gods, could I *feel* it.

I beat back the urge to call Durra's name; she was a big girl and would have to take care of herself while I stalked whatever seemed to be stalking us. That had been no innocent fall back there: Earth magic had flared just before we took that unexpected tumble. The wild thought that Charlie might have betrayed us lasted a bare millisecond before I discarded it. No way would he ever do such a thing. I'd sooner believe it of Scott. All right, maybe not the greatest analogy considering my beloved *had* just turned traitor against his personal god . . .

Not as though he had a choice, all things considered, Nike pointed out reasonably.

Too true.

Behind you! Nemesis launched herself away from my body as she mentally screeched that warning. I twisted and saw her coils strike against a solid, man-shaped object—or rather, as evidenced by the voice that proceeded to curse her out, woman-shaped object.

At first I assumed Durra had made the mistake of

sneaking up on us, but then I realized two things. One: The woman currently wrestling with one-half of my Amphisbaena pair had the washed-out look of a *shade*, those souls waiting in the Underworld for their own meeting with Ma'at, after which they'd either be reborn, condemned to suffering in a particularly harsh area of the Underworld, or rewarded by moving on to their specific religion's idea of heaven. Two: While the woman wore a dingy version of a Fury's red leather, her serpents were every bit as crimson as my own rather than Durra's emerald green.

And then the woman succeeded in thrusting Nemesis away from herself, giving me a clear glimpse of her face and inspiring a third, far more shocking realization. This was no random Fury's shade: It was that of my psycho former mentor, Stacia.

CHAPTER TEN

WONDER WHY HER SERPENTS REVERTED TO Tisiphone red rather than Elder silver? I rolled my eyes when I realized how ridiculous that random thought was. What difference did *that* make now? Finding myself face-to-face with the bitch who'd betrayed not just me but the entire Sisterhood was wrong on every level. Forget the personal baggage between us that could have filled in the gaping crevice Durra and I had been magically shoved into. How the *hell* had Stacia's shade popped up here in the territory claimed by Anubis? The souls of deceased Furies went on to a special area by virtue of the fact they swore allegiance to no specific— *Holy shit! Stacia was working for him all along.*

Makes sense, Nike grudgingly agreed.

But—why?

Before either of us could puzzle that out, Stacia sent

me one panicked expression of recognition—as if she were surprised to see me and had been drawn there against her will—and vanished into thin air. I cursed and leaped forward, scooping up Nemesis with one hand. Stacia's making like Houdini wouldn't have surprised me had she still been alive, considering the phenomenal cosmic travel powers that came with the Elder schtick. But, as far as I knew, shades trapped in the Underworld didn't retain their magical abilities once dead . . . Otherwise, *nothing* would have kept many of them from flitting back to the living world whenever they so desired.

Rustling in underbrush to the left had me crouching in a defensive pose. I squinted, grateful to find that my vision had adjusted to the lack of light, just in time to see Durra creep into the clearing where I had—for several tense seconds—confronted Stacia's not-so-dearly-departed spirit.

I strode forward so she could see me. "Are you all—"

She frantically waved for me to get down, but it was too late. Several heavily armed shades—all wearing flashy gold armor and jackal-headed helmets—poured into the clearing from two dozen feet away. I realized belatedly that Stacia hadn't been the one to thrust us into this hasty ambush—earth magic had never been her strength any more than it was mine.

Adrenaline and Rage surged, and so did I. My body hurled several feet into the air and a single wing beat thrust me straight at the nearest Anubian. Arrogant certainty that no mere shade could stand up to a Nemesis was soon proven wrong when he didn't immediately fall beneath me. Death magic tingled, and the unwritten truth that shades could not channel magic was ripped to shreds. *This one* surely could.

Unfortunately for him, Death magic did nothing to me but tickle. I let not-quite-sane laughter pass my lips—often good for intimidating the crap out of opponents—shoved aside foolish pride, and gave in to the Rage-fueled battle lust taking me over.

He seemed just as surprised by my immunity to his spell as I had been by his failure to fall to the ground in the face of my Nemesis awesomeness. That element of surprise gave me a slight edge. I danced in around the wicked-looking axe serving as his backup weapon and kicked at the hand wielding the axe. It flew across the clearing, landing upon hard-packed earth with a clang difficult to hear among the sudden shouts and curses ringing out around us. I felt like I'd stumbled into some fractured version of *The Twilight Zone*, one where shades could wield magic as well as the living, fight with as much fiery passion, and give battle-hardened Furies (one a Nemesis) the fight of their lives. Because once the shade recovered from that momentary lapse, that's exactly what he did.

He blocked the second kick I aimed at his vital parts, then tried to grab my foot while it was midair. I jerked my hands forward and blocked his attempt, planting my foot firmly on the ground and trading blow for blow with him over the next few moments. Sweat stung my eyes by the time I managed to sneak through his guard again and snap his neck with inhuman strength. Thankfully, his oddly solid form wavered, then disappeared, presumably popping back to whatever starting zone newly dead spirits went to in this place. Another bizarre realization that shades could be killed a second time, but damned good to know.

I whipped my gaze to Durra and saw her surprisingly faring as well as I. She had her own opponent down on the ground and crushed his windpipe beneath her boot as I watched. That shade, too, vanished.

A second shade appeared to take his place, and I noticed something else—each waited to challenge the two of us to single combat, either because it was some Underworld rule I didn't know about (doubtful) or because it gave them the advantage of being fresh to the fight while progressively wearing us down (more likely). I turned to face yet another shade and fell into a rhythm of dodge, strike, parry, and strike again. The enemy tactic of wearing us down didn't seem to work as well as they expected: on my part because I had the increased stamina and strength of a demigoddess, and on Durra's probably because she was just a cursed ornery bitch, not to mention a natural-born killer. A trait I could admire in a battle partner in a way I couldn't my former attempted assassin.

Nemesis and Nike saved me from my own momentary lapse, launching themselves from my body to attack the shade who had jumped forward to replace my fallen foe. Trusting them to handle her quite nicely without my help, I took the initiative to attack yet another shade waiting in the wings. He let out a rather pathetic yelp and went down more like I'd expected the first guy to drop. The two remaining Anubians abandoned the single-combat idea and came at me in unison, and I just let out another berserker's laugh. The laugh gave them momentary pause, which I used to my benefit by feigning a lunge toward one, then flapping my wings and leaping instead upon the other. Either I was getting used to my newfound Nemesis abilities or I'd just surprised him that much, because snapping his neck came ridiculously easy this time.

I whirled to meet the remaining shade's attack only to find it never came. Instead, Durra had downed her second opponent before turning upon the sole survivor (when Nemesis and Nike snaked their way up to my waist I correctly assumed they had taken theirs out already). The other Fury fought with a fierce intensity that rivaled my own, something that had me frowning. *Is it just me, or does she seem to fight just as well in Fury form as I do in Nemesis form?* Durra moved in for the killing blow, and sudden realization had me dash between my sister Fury and her intended target. She hissed at me as angrily as her Amphisbaena, and I raised my hand in a placating gesture. "We should question her first." Rage continued seething in her expression until she fought it down and gave a grudging nod.

The shade didn't wait for her acquiescence before trying to flee. I say *trying* because, hey, I had wings, and she didn't. The shade snarled when I knocked into her from above and sent her to her knees. I landed and cocked an eyebrow. "Going somewhere?"

Her snarl turned to an angry hiss reminiscent of Durra's, and her faded eyes temporarily glowed brighter green. My left eyebrow shot up to join the other. *Holy hells. What is one of* Bast's *children doing in Duat?* Anubis and Bast hated each other with *way* more than a passion—the primary motivation for the racial hatred between the shape-shifting Warhounds and Bastai, AKA Cats. Also the biggest reason the wedding between Harper (a Cat) and Scott's cousin/Elliana's brother Penn had caused such a fervent uproar among the Belly's arcane elite.

Where did you *think* the stereotypical image of cats hating dogs came from?

I pasted a saccharine smile on my face and stroked each serpent twined around my waist. "We've already proven your manifestations can be killed here. Shall we find out how toxic Amphisbaena venom proves as well?"

"Do as you will, Fury. My lord rewards loyalty as highly as he punishes betrayal." Her face contorted into an even uglier expression, and she spat at my feet. "Which your bastard lover will soon discover."

That had me giving a hiss of my own and stomping down on her abdomen, harder than intended because of the whole Nemesis thing. *Really.* "Oops, my foot slipped. The same way my beauties are about to slip poison into your veins." They obligingly went all cobraesque with their hoods and spat venom onto her cheek. She squealed and wiped it off—only to wind up with the acidic substance eating away at her hand *and* face. *Idiot.* I might have felt sorry for her under other circumstances.

"Aw, does that hurt? It's only gonna get worse here in a minute."

Durra stepped up beside me and glanced down with disdain. "I suggest you tell us what we want to hear to save yourself agony, Cat. Who knows how long your manifestation will survive as the venom destroys it from the inside out?"

Raised voices and stones skittering down from above hinted that our companions had finally found a safe path down the ravine and would soon join us. "Funny you mention my hot-as-hell boyfriend since that's who's about to join in the fun. I bet he'll find the idea of *your* treacherous ass calling *him* a traitor hilarious. At least *he* is following divine law rather than throwing in with an immortal thug. When the Triad catches up to your boss, you'll be in for worse than anything *I* can do to you. Sure hope Jackal-Faced paid you more than thirty silver pieces to go all Judas on Bast. Come to think of it, the Triad will probably just give you to *her* as punishment."

Durra chuckled in a distinctly menacing manner. "What do you want to wager she condemns her to eternally having her tongue sliced out so she can choke on catnip?"

I had to give Durra points for style. Not only had she given a nod to my recent serial-killer case, she'd managed to break through the Cat spirit's defiance. *Nothing* disrespected—or terrified—a Cat more than the reverse of the coup-counting they had pulled on Hounds for millennia in ancient Egypt (and sometimes beyond).

My lips curved upward when I leaned forward, and she pushed as far from me as possible without moving from her sprawled position. "You're between a rock and a hard place here, Kitty Cat. You know I'm a Nemesis, so know this also: I don't care whatever line of horseshit Anubis has fed you or what rewards he promised to entice you into switching teams. The Triad is onto him and has set loose *several* Nemeses after his ass. He's going down hard, and the only question I have for you is: Are you *really* willing to do down with him? *He* can't die, but *you* can be killed over and over and over again until the immortals tire of playing with you and destroy your soul entirely." The only threat even harsher than the coup-counting thing. "Or . . ."

She leaped upon my words as the lifeline they represented. "Or?"

"*Or* you tell us what we need to know, and I personally assure that you face Ma'at's Feather *before* the Triad or Bast can step in—meaning your soul moves on rather than being endlessly tormented."

"W-will you swear to that as a Fury?"

"As a Fury and by my position as Nemesis. *If* you repent and help us now."

With a typically feline display of self-interest, she nodded. "What do you want to know?"

"Is Anubis amassing an army to conduct war against the Triad?"

She licked her lips. "N-no."

"You don't sound so sure of yourself. That makes me less inclined to believe you. You do *not* want me to think you are lying to us."

"I'm not!" she rushed to reassure me. "It's just—*yes*, he is amassing an army; but no, not to wage war against the Triad."

"Then for what purpose?"

Another hesitation. "I'm not entirely sure."

Durra let out an incredulous sound.

"Truly, *I do not know*. He only discusses such things with the Khenti-priests and his lover."

That had my eyes and mouth widening. Ancient Egyptian mythology spoke of Anubis being married to the goddess Anput; but—like the original Nemesis—she had never been a true separate being, more a feminine aspect taken on by Anubis occasionally over the millennia. Fury gossip held that Anubis contented himself with one-night stands with lesser immortals and arcanes rather than forming a more permanent union. The buzz said he considered himself too good to do more than screw around with anything less than a greater immortal; the Catch-22 was that none of *them* would be willing to marry a lesser god . . .

My breath whooshed out explosively. *Jeez. Us. That could explain why he's pulling this power play* now. *Whichever Deity he's fooling around with won't take it to the next figurative level unless he makes it to the next* literal *level.* For a moment, I just shook my head. Would someone *really* go to all this trouble—cause *this* much pain and betrayal (not to mention death and civil war)—over a simple *love affair*? Then I thought of the lengths Scott and I had been willing to go to for each other over the past few years, up to and including him forsaking his personal god at my request. That thought led to memories of what Victor's crazy ass had done because of green-eyed envy when Harper loved a Hound more than a fellow Cat and the fact he'd been willing to drug me with magical GHB when he transferred his obsession with his ex onto me. My headshake turned to a grim nod. Oh yeah, people did crazy shit for love—or facsimiles thereof—all the time, immortals as often as others. We *were* made in our Creators' images.

Durra's gaze focused on my face as these realizations struck in rapid succession. She gave a questioning tilt of her head. I nodded toward the shade and mouthed *Later.*

I glanced back to the Cat and assumed a carefully blank expression. She had actually let slip something bigger than she knew, not that I had to tell *her* that. "So basically you can't give me any useful information I didn't already know, certainly nothing worth sticking my neck as a Nemesis out for."

Desperation lit her shade's eyes a slightly more brilliant sheen a second time. "No, that's not true! I can give you plenty! Anubis has—he's got two Fury shades working for him. Surely *that* is something you didn't already know."

Surprise twinged inside but not so much that I showed it on the outside. Having already spotted Stacia on the Underworld prowl and knowing that he had living Furies working for him in the Palladium, it wasn't a particularly big shock to discover he had another already dead sister on his side as well.

The Cat shook her head and corrected herself. "He *had* two Fury shades working for him, but . . . rumor has it one of them was the first he chose to reward with New Life. She hasn't been seen in Duat in several weeks."

Durra asked the obvious before I could. "New Life?"

The shade met our skeptical expressions with very nearly a smirk. "Yes. Those who serve our lord most faithfully are promised a way to . . . circumvent Ma'at's Feather in order to live again."

Whoa. That was just crazy talk. *Every* individual's soul had to face some sort of divine balancing act— Ma'at's Feather, St. Peter's Book, judgment by once-mortal King Minos for many of the ancient Greek persuasion—before they could either move on to some iteration of heaven *or* be sent back to earth to try again and get it right. By *get it right*, I mean become a better person or, in the worst cases, suffer some of the same torment their last incarnation brought upon others to reap a little karmic payback intended to teach the soul humility for yet another incarnation. Hell as the fire-and-brimstone types thought of it was reserved only for the worst-of-the-worst souls who never learned a damned thing after umpteen chances to become less . . . well, evil was a simplistic way to put it, but yes. Some souls were made of pure evil when you got right down to it. Even then, though, if they *finally* had some sort of epiphany while suffering through damnation, that torment could be ended if they *truly* repented and asked for another go at this crazy thing called life.

So, long story short, what this all boiled down to was the fact that there was a set routine to things that didn't vary, even from mythos to mythos. Souls couldn't be reborn without being weighed. Anubis couldn't conduct that balancing act himself, and even if he could, he was a *Death* Lord, not a Creator. He couldn't just *give* someone a new bod . . .

Suddenly a horrible thought clicked inside my mind. An Anubian (blech) Fury rumored to have received New Life in the precisely right time frame added to the fact that Anubis could *not* manufacture new bodies in the earthly realm added to the knowledge that something had gone horribly wrong with my grandmother when she awakened from her coma could really only suggest one logical conclusion.

New Life didn't mean reincarnation in the traditional sense. It meant that, somehow, Anubis had discovered the means to do the unthinkable: help shades loyal to him steal the bodies of others. Nan wasn't just being manipulated magically. She was suffering through her own *Invasion of a Body Snatcher. But, if that really is true, how does the whole thing work? Is she trapped inside her own body at the mercy of the invading spirit or has she been displaced entirely? And if she has, where is her spirit now? Can she be safely restored—or is she now as good as dead?*

This time I couldn't keep emotion off my face or out of my voice. "Son of a *bitch*!" I growled just in time for everyone else—led by Scott—to scramble into the clearing. Seeing my lover's face had me thinking about his blackhearted, Jackal-Faced god having the *balls* to screw around with something so sacrosanct as other people's souls, and *that* had me cursing again for good measure. *"Son of a bitch!"*

CHAPTER ELEVEN

SCOTT AND MAC, NOT SURPRISINGLY, ZEROED in on me right away and took up places between the unknown shade and me, a case of the train having already left the station, but it wasn't worth pointing that out to them. No matter how liberal, that overprotective gene lurks inside lovers and brothers the arcane world over. Everyone else fanned out behind Durra and me, but nobody said a word. Apparently they'd heard enough of the interrogation while approaching not to want to jeopardize my authority with the Kitty Cat.

I folded my arms across my chest. "Well, I think you can safely assume the Triad is going to put an end to whatever New Life old Jackal-Faced is promising his faithful servants." Both the Cat and Scott clenched their teeth and fists, something that had me clenching my own. When Scott finally got me alone after this was all over, would we even still *have* a relationship to salvage? "I, on the other hand, *always* keep my promises. If you stay out of my way while I carry out my duties, I will invoke Ma'at on your behalf as promised. If, however, I discover you have betrayed me in any way . . ."

She swallowed with a visible shudder. "I—understand." Her face took on a determined expression. "My decision is made, and you were right to remind me of my duty to the Triad of immortals. I don't know how *he* ever convinced me otherwise."

Pretty words, but I sure couldn't take them at face value. Nothing guaranteed she wouldn't tear off as soon as my back was turned and go straight to Anubis to rat us out, which naturally led to the dilemma of what I should do with her in the meantime. If I killed her like the other shades, that would just give her the chance to double-cross us that much sooner when she rematerialized wherever it was Anubian shades materialized. If I *didn't*, though, she might very well follow us with the sole purpose of summoning Anubis directly to our ultimate destination: the Hall of Two Truths. Which meant I needed an option number three . . .

My lips curled into a self-satisfied smirk when inspiration hit. "I assume the unhealthiest place for you to be right now is wherever *he* is if he finds out what you've just told me."

The Cat blanched. "I—oh—gods."

Obviously she thought as far ahead as most other felines—which was to say not very. "Would you be willing to seek out the Fury shades you mentioned? See if you can find either of them and, if so, get word to me."

She blinked. "I—yes, I could do that. But how would I—"

"Don't worry, I have that part covered."

Nemesis and Nike suddenly clued in to my thoughts—and the former didn't like them at all. *Nuh-uh. No way. Not a chance.* Easy to see which of the pair paid more attention to mortal slang.

I expected Nike to be just as pessimistic, but she surprised me—and her sister. *I agree with Marissa. It's the perfect opportunity. Not only can you ensure she doesn't betray us, think of how it will simplify matters if you do find one of the Fury shades.*

That slightly took the wind out of my sails since I'd been prepared for a knock-down, drag-out. *Ah—um—exactly. If the Cat does find evidence Anubis has Fury shades in Duat, that proves he must have sworn them to himself when they were alive. We can take that proof to the Triad without needing to risk invoking the Feather against him.* Because, contrary to the front I put on, I wasn't 100 percent certain that plan was going to work out quite the way I intended.

All eyes remained focused on me during that internal debate. Nike succeeded where I failed in convincing Nemesis. I relaxed when she silently capitulated and turned to the Cat with what was meant to be a reassuring smile. The fact that she backed away several steps said I had failed miserably on the comforting front. Big surprise.

Try not to scare her any more than you have *to.* I held my hand out to the Cat, and Nemesis wound her way to the end of my arm. Realization flickered in the Cat's eyes, and she appeared torn between fascination and revulsion. "She won't hurt you. Not unless you try to betray us. In either event, she'll be able to get word to my other serpent immediately, and through her, to me."

Nemesis could no more project a reassuring air than I could, but she managed not to hiss, spit, or flick her tongue while she snaked from my arm onto the Cat's trembling limb. "Relax. She is as intelligent as any of us—if not more so—and she can understand anything you say. But mark this: If *anything* happens to her and she loses contact with us, I will hunt you down on the spot and bring the full wrath of Bast and the Triad upon you. Now go."

"But, what if someone else—"

I snarled, and she stumbled back a few steps before turning to flee like a bat out of—you know. Nemesis chuckled inside my mind before her presence slowly faded away. She'd be able to communicate easily with Nike from a distance thanks to their magical bond as twins born from the blood of their dying mother, but all I'd be able to get were vague emotions as usual, if even that.

All will be well. Nike managed a maternal air far better than I ever could, but still . . . I worried.

I've never been separated from either of you. Not since I Fledged. I didn't even know it was possible until now.

Rarely done, but very possible. Now focus, silly child.

She was right. One problem might have been solved for the moment, but a dozen more waited in the wings, starting with the one turning to stare me in the face.

Scott scowled and stepped close enough to kiss—although that seemed to be the last thing on his mind right about then. "What the hell was *that*?"

Durra sidled closer, becoming an oddly supportive presence at my side. The Apocalypse couldn't be far behind.

I arched a brow. "Which part? Where magic-wielding shades—something that should be *impossible*, by the way—culled Durra and me from the rest of you, and we kicked their asses, or the part where I recruited one of said shades to the good side?"

My revelation *we* hadn't been behind the separation seemed to take the edge off the fight in him. Of course, that still left a whole lot of fight. "What were you *thinking* to trust her enough to send her off that way? What if she runs straight to—to *him*?"

Poor guy couldn't even say *his* name. Not that I could blame Scott—not for *that*. For not trusting me, however . . .

"Did you *miss* the part where I sent Nemesis to keep tabs on her?" When he opened his mouth, I just glared him down. "If I *had* just killed her, she would have materialized wherever Anubians do that in Duat and told them exactly what she told us. This way, we have a chance of keeping her *away* from *him*, at least for a time. You may not have heard everything, but he *does* have Fury shades working for him. I saw one before the attack."

Durra's breath caught, and she touched my arm. "Who?" Her fears were obvious: that it might be a fellow Megaera. If only . . .

"St—" I cleared my throat and tried again. "Stacia Demetriou. My mentor."

"Your *former* mentor!" Mac exclaimed out of loyalty. He had just as much reason to hate the bitch as I did. She had been the mastermind behind abducting our mother, engineering Mac's birth, and brainwashing him throughout the formative years of his life. Thankfully, he'd broken through that due to his own innate goodness, intelligence, and a little help from Mom.

"Former mentor," I allowed with a tiny smile. "She appeared just as shocked to see me as vice versa, so I don't think that was part of the plan. The Cat"—I probably should have bothered to get her name before sending her off—"claimed Anubis has two shades working for him, and I have a pretty good guess who the other one is."

Durra frowned. "You don't think your *grandmother*—"

I shook my head fervently. "No, *she* would never betray us like that. Her sister, on the other hand . . ."

Her eyes widened, but then she nodded slowly. "We need to get word to your mother and my d— mine, as well. If Anubis has found a way to help shades take on New Life by possessing the bodies of full-grown arcanes, they should be forewarned." She shuddered in most un-Durra-like fashion.

My sentiments precisely.

Scott drew my attention again. "Okay, so *he* knows you're here, and you have the Cat searching for your *former* mentor. We need to keep moving before his next patrol finds us."

"Good point." I tapped my fingers against my pants and tried to *think*. Where could we send word to Mom that wouldn't take us too far out of our way to the Hall of Two Truths? There was really only one method of communicating with those in another realm from the Underworld—the same way we came in: via mirror. Since I'd shattered *that* one, we had to find another, though *not* the one Anubis had most likely used to send that patrol in after us. Granted, my knowledge of Duat's layout was limited to my last, extremely abbreviated visit and what I'd researched before making that crazy-ass trip, but there simply *weren't* that many portal-worthy mirrors down there. Especially considering that Anubis had cut off access to a lot of the Otherrealms from Duat.

But that doesn't mean they do not function from this *side,* Nike pointed out.

My eyes widened. *True!*

Okay, so Ala's position as an African Death Lord (a gender-neutral title) meant her realm would lie physically close to Anubis's (also an African Death Lord) in the Underworld. This also meant it would take less magical energy to contact her from here. She could, in turn, pass word on from us to Mom, and the reverse. Now I just had to figure out *where* to find a mirror . . .

"I can't believe I'm about to say this, but I know where we need to go." Oops. Obviously I'd said that last bit out loud (a bad habit of mine) since Elliana volunteered that little tidbit.

Mac gave a nod as if to say *of course* his wife knew *that.* I, not so convinced, pursed my lips. "And how do you know that?"

She bared her teeth in an expression that most definitely *wasn't* a smile. "Because I am—I *was*—one of *his* handmaidens."

That pronouncement had me wincing as nausea twisted my stomach. Elliana and I had enjoyed a toleratehate relationship as long as I could remember, though things had improved a lot over the past few months thanks to Mac. Never would I have guessed in a million years that she would *ever* choose loyalty to me over a duty as sacred as serving as a god's handmaiden. Handmaidens tended to be as tight-lipped about their positions as Fury classes were about their Primes. It was mostly a ceremonial title in life that granted a few extra

powers such as—apparently—the ability to sense magical artifacts tied to the god being served. Most handmaidens didn't really do much to serve their deities
directly until death—at which point they joined an elite
group of guardians in the Underworld. Chances were
that, now, Elliana would never get the chance to perform
that particular duty.

As if she sensed my thoughts, she rolled her eyes and
stomped across the clearing. "Don't flatter yourself,
Riss; I did this for Mac—and the Triad. *I* know my
responsibilities even if *he* has chosen to forsake them."

I let out the breath I hadn't realized I'd been holding
and absentmindedly caressed the single serpent twining
herself along my upper arm. *That* would take getting
used to. "All right, then, let's get a move on. The sooner
we get word to Mom, the sooner we can finish what we
started."

Or so I had to believe. Anything else spelled
disaster—not just for us, but for the entire arcane world.

ELLIANA LED US FROM THE CLEARING,
through a mundane-seeming forest, and into a bizarre
neon blue desert landscape without missing a beat. Mac
and Durra trailed a few feet behind her while Scott,
Charlie, and I brought up the rear, keeping watchful
eyes out for any sign of pursuit. So far, however, so good.
Other than the blasted blue sand, which kept churning
up beneath our feet and flying into eyes and mouths.

Scott and Ellie soon showed us the trick for ripping
up articles of clothing to cover our mouths, but the eyes
were another matter entirely. We *had* to be able to see,
after all. Eventually I worked out the timing for blinking

or completely shutting my eyes at the most opportune moments, but that didn't make me hate every single trudging step forward one iota less. Even the novelty of looking across Technicolor sand dunes quickly wore off under the blistering sun (don't ask me *how* a subterranean place like the Underworld even *has* a sun) baking our ill-protected heads and backs.

Just when I gave serious consideration to sending everyone else home and flying to the Hall of Two Truths, Elliana let out a sound of triumph and waded over, then down a particularly steep mound of sand. We eagerly followed after, though Charlie (thanks to his earth affinity) soon outpaced Scott and me. The damned Giant didn't look or sound the least bit winded or sunburned, either. *Bastard.*

Topping the rise and seeing a veritable oasis spread out before me inspired a burst of speed. Scott shot a boyish grin my way, and for a moment, I could forget we were slogging our way through hell on a quest to bring down his personal lord and savior. *Former* savior.

I tightened my lips and plowed down the hill and into the line of palm trees swaying in the breeze blowing off the small-but-pristine pool of water at the center of the oasis. My feet left behind unnatural blue sand to step upon ordinary green grass, and I gave a smile every bit as childlike as Scott's. Palm trees blocking out the harsh sun; a cool wind washing over my parboiled skin; decadent green grass beneath my low-heeled boots—how could I *not* smile? At least until I caught sight of the army waiting for us.

Okay, so *army* was a slight exaggeration. A dozen Anubians garbed in flowing black robes covered in golden hieroglyphics appeared from the opposite line of trees and took up place between us and the crystal-clear pond. The very *mirror* I was willing to bet Elliana had been leading us to. *Son of a . . .*

A dozen or a thousand, they outnumbered us, and I was willing to bet were just as capable of channeling magic as the first patrol had been. That thought had me peering at them more closely. *This* group bore no weapons and something about their robes seemed off, different from those of any of the Anubians I'd thus far seen. And that's when it socked me in the gut: These *weren't* Anubians. Their robes featured elaborate falcons rather than jackals.

Elliana waited for me to step up beside her and murmured out of the corner of her mouth. "These are *not* the handmaiden shades I expected we might have to fight through."

Durra nodded, gaze sharply focused upon the group blocking us from our goal. "They look like members of a rival death cult. That language isn't *quite* Egyptian, but it's damned close—"

My breath sucked in. "By all the gods and goddesses, they're Imseti's priests." The missing priests mentioned by the Triad, to be precise.

Imseti was indeed another Death Lord, although he was more influential among arcanes than the minor funerary role Ancient Egyptians credited him with, and more accurately, an amalgam of the Four Sons of Horus, who were associated with the body's vital organs and believed to reconstitute bodies for the dead, as opposed to the one son who shared his name. He bore little love for Mr. Jackal-Faced; by which I mean *loathed* him with a passion. Funny how that could be said for most deities— except for those minor ones Anubis had suckered into pledging allegiance to him. Finding a dozen of Imseti's

followers here in Duat could mean only one thing:
Anubis must have had the balls to imprison all twelve
priests when Imseti sent them here to investigate the
portal closures. As we were quickly discovering, there
apparently weren't many things Anubis wasn't willing
to do in the name of *love*.

The others tensed when I stepped forward, but I
waved them off and strode forward half the distance
between us and the pond. Likewise, a masculine figure
broke away from their line and approached me in the
middle. The closer he drew, the more convinced I
became that I'd been right to trust my instincts. This was
definitely no priest of Anubis's.

The gold-on-black robe was the only resemblance.
This man's skin wasn't the burnished bronze of Scott's
or even the deeper brown of his pure-blooded Egyptian
mother's, but the deepest shade of obsidian. His equally
dark hair fell past his waist in thick dreadlocks that
made me think of my serpents, but only briefly and only
because they bounced fluidly as he walked. When he
drew up a few feet away and regarded me with dark,
unblinking eyes, that fancy faded.

"We have been waiting for you, Nemesis." His voice
rang with a musical lilt way stronger than Durra's *or* her
mother's, bringing to mind a deeper part of Africa than
northern Egypt or even Nigeria, where I was beginning
to believe the Megaera hailed from.

I forced away my sense of insignificance—I came
from my own long and distinguished line, and by gods,
I was a *Nemesis* and would damned well *act* like one.
"Greetings to you, Priest of Imseti. This is a long way
from his realm. How is it that you come to be here at *all*,
much less are waiting for me?"

He bowed deeply at the touch of suspicion in my voice. "Peace, Nemesis, we mean you no harm. My name is Mijai; I am the senior of our priests, who have been imprisoned in this part of Duat against our will and against that of our patron Imseti as well. It was only when the foul Jackal left to send out forces against you that we were able to escape and make our way here."

If the past few months had taught me anything, it was that things that seemed too good to be true usually *were*, in one way if not the other. "And you knew to wait for us here *how*?"

Mijai motioned and another black-robed figure, this one feminine, hurried forward. "Because I am a Seer, Nemesis. Once we broke free from our collars, I was able to divine your most likely course."

Scott and Elliana gave Cat-like hisses at that revelation. Anubis had designed the hated collars that could enslave one arcane to another's will millennia ago and allowed them to be used against his own children. One reason they so rarely went against his wishes . . .

I acknowledged the Seer with a nod but kept my attention on the first priest. They obviously wanted something from me, and I was still trying to decide whether or not to trust them. Their story made perfect sense, but that didn't make it *true*. Something else my lovely *former* mentor had taught me. "If you divined that as you claim, then you undoubtedly saw my purpose for coming here."

Mijai motioned to the Seer again, who spoke up. "Yes, you plan to open a portal to send word to another Nemesis of your progress here in Duat. I could not see more than that, of course, as you are on a gods-blessed Mandate, but I *could* see that we can trust you to help us."

I shifted my weight slightly, ready should this devolve into an unexpected ambush. "And why should I take time from that gods-blessed Mandate to help you?"

Mijai spoke this time. "Because we can prove that which you may already suspect: The Jackal-god has been transmuting Anubian shades into the bodies of unsuspecting souls. Or rather, I should say he has been forcing *us* to do that very thing, since *once* only our lord had that power."

Nausea churned inside my stomach again, but Scott asked the inevitable question before I could, "What do you mean *once* only he had that power?"

The Seer spat upon the ground at her feet. "Anubian priests used their vile collars to force us to first transmute their chosen souls, then to teach several of *them* how to do the same. We dragged the process out as long as we could and made sure we failed more than we succeeded, but the more they experimented, the more success they had. Now, they need us no longer— which is why we took the chance to escape when we could."

Her partner nodded. "We likely would have survived little longer. At my best guess, the Jackal-god would have transmuted Anubians into *our* bodies before sending us back to our earthly temple since he couldn't simply kill us."

My lips twisted. "You would have just warned your lord what his enemy was up to."

He nodded. "Exactly so. The Jackal-god is setting his sights higher and higher; for what exact purpose we cannot say, but it can bode no good for the other deities, including our own. We risked coming here to pledge ourselves as proof that Anubis is violating immortal law but also because we rescued another being held captive by him, another who most desperately wishes to speak with you."

A third figure stepped forward, lowering the hood of her robe to reveal that, unlike the others, she possessed the dull coloring of a shade's Underworld manifestation. My gaze took in her red hair, blue eyes, and familiar face as surprise flooded over me. This woman was no stranger although she was someone I hadn't seen—not truly—in over two long decades.

"Gods, Riss my lass, it is *so* good to see you!" She held her arms out, and those two decades faded away. I threw myself into her arms with none of my earlier hesitation. *This* was the woman I'd missed for so long: my grandmother, Maeve.

CHAPTER TWELVE

HAVING HER ARMS WRAP AROUND ME FELT like coming home, more so even than when Mom had miraculously walked back into my life, mostly because Nan had taken a sabbatical from the Sisterhood that first decade of my life to raise me while Dad held down his prealcohol nine-to-five, and Mom did her thing as an active Fury. Don't get me wrong—Mom had been an amazing mother in the short twelve years I had her, but she'd never been the homemade-cookies and bread-fresh-from-the-oven type like *her* mother had been.

Then reality intruded, and I pushed away to regard her in horror. Grayscale coloring and snakes in tattoo form pointed to the ugly truth my brain had initially tried to ignore. She was, without a doubt, a full-on shade. Meaning she could only be . . .

"But—but how did you *die*? You seemed fine a few

hours ago. Unless . . . that wasn't you at all." Gods, had that not been her in the hospice all those years? "We all thought *you* killed *Medea*!"

Her lips twisted grimly. "I killed her Harpy ass all right; but she made a pact with the devil beforehand. When her body died, she managed to throw her spirit inside mine. I've spent the last twenty damned years fighting that bitch for control."

Gone was every ounce of the former sisterly affection that had sent Maeve hunting to put Medea out of her misery. Though after two decades of a living nightmare, who could blame her? "So, wait. If you didn't die, then why—"

"Am I trapped in this hellhole as a shade?" She folded her arms with a distinctly crabby expression. "It was the damnedest thing a few months ago. We were lying in that hospital bed the same as usual when something— changed. Felt like yet another spirit wormed its way inside my body, and nothing I did made a lick of difference. They'd quiet down now and again, and I'd feel like maybe I might finally get the strength to wake all the way up, but then—the devil himself stepped in."

"Anubis." I'd done the math, and nothing else added up. Stacia wouldn't have bothered visiting Nan for all those years if she hadn't known good and well her lover was inside her enemy's physical shell. They'd obviously made whatever pact they had with Anubis prior to Nan's attacking Medea, and Stacia had probably been trying to help oust Nan completely during her visits—with no luck. *Her* bargain with Satan—er, Anubis—had then kicked in when I killed *her* crazy butt several months ago, allowing her to bolster her lover's spiritual strength until they finally wrested control from Nan right before my serial-killer case kicked into high gear. They'd forced Nan out of her own body, and Anubis had held her hostage here since her body still lived, and he couldn't risk Nan's shade ratting him out to the powers that be.

I let out a breath. "Medea has your body in the Palladium. Meaning you're not truly dead, and we still have a chance to restore you."

She gave me an approving smile. "That's my grandbaby!"

Durra cleared her throat. "I hate to be the wet blanket—" *Sure*, she did. "But that's not going to be as easy as you make it sound. First of all, Maeve's shade can't just hop from here to there through a portal like the rest of us. Secondly, Medea isn't going to hand the body over without a fight."

Proving I did indeed come from her bloodline, Nan's smile only widened. "Oh, I hope not!"

Durra's eyes glinted with an emerald sheen Nan's shade couldn't quite manage, but our Megaeru sister didn't crack an answering smile. "Third, we'll need someone to help pull a transmutation in reverse. Assuming that's even possible?"

Mijai tilted his head in consideration. "Honestly, we've never tried it in reverse. Our lord designed it as a spell to be used only against traitors, who would instantly face Reckoning once a loyal shade took over their body and they met our lord in the Underworld. Theoretically, it *should* be possible . . . but we'll need both the original shade and her body in still living form. And it will need to happen here since we cannot guarantee your grandmother's safety as a shade elsewhere."

"Guess that means you're coming with us to the Hall of Two Truths, Nan."

Mijai blinked at that announcement. "You mean to invoke the Feather? But against wh—" His eyes widened, and fierce pleasure swept across his features. "Anubis. You mean to call Ma'at's Feather down upon him."

Well, guess *that* cat was out of the bag. "Indeed I do. Providing we make it there before *he* makes it to us." I narrowed my eyes in calculation. "Your Seer claimed I could help you, but now I'm thinking it will be the opposite. We'll need at least one of your number with us to restore my grandmother to her rightful place once we lure Medea here with her body." Something I was willing to bet would be pretty easy once Nemesis and the Cat tracked down Stacia's shade wherever it was hiding in Duat. "Any others of your number who can help us reach the Hall safely would be *more* than welcome. The Triad would owe both you and your lord a tremendous debt of gratitude." Sweetening the pot never hurt anything.

His nostrils flared as he considered. I found it *more* reassuring that he didn't just blindly pledge his companions to the cause. With the exception of Nan—kind of— the rest of us were still very much alive and breathing, meaning we stood to lose everything we knew on earth if we were killed there. Okay, and excepting me, since I still had just under forty-eight hours of true immortality remaining.

He glanced at the Seer beside him, who nodded. "I can't divine much under these circumstances and without my tools, but I do know that our lord approves. But—you and me only. The others *he* has need of."

Well, not as good as I had hoped, but far better than nothing; and if things were shaping up down there the way they seemed to be, Imseti was only smart to marshal his forces—in case I failed, and Anubis got his gods-bedamned war.

"Okay, we need to make this snappy, then, before Jackal-Faced senses the portal and tries to intervene. Here's the plan: Sahana will put us into touch with Ala so we can get word to my mother and the Megaera. Once we do, Sahana will convert the scrying portal to one for traveling, and you can send your people through. It will be way easier for them to get back to earth from Ala's territory than from here. As far as I know, She's on good terms with your patron . . ." Mijai and the Seer nodded. "Then let's get this show on the road!"

Everyone burst into action; the Imsetians clearing a path for Sahana, Durra, and me to inch as close to the pool as we could come without actually toppling inside. Grass gave way to smooth white pebbles that encircled the water's perimeter. I almost felt guilty for disturbing the precise rock pattern someone had taken great pains to lay out, but then I remembered they'd been handmaidens of the Jackal-Faced prick, and guilt pretty much evaporated. Sahana crouched at the water's edge and began chanting, using some of that erstwhile Death energy she'd claimed from the aborted portal earlier to begin linking the pool's perfect reflecting surface with an answering mirror in Ala's realm.

Ripples swirled across the pool with steadily increasing frequency until, all at once, that magical link *clicked* into place. Black-and-silver light flowed across the now-still waters and stretched toward Sahana as if the combined Death and immortal magic had a mind of its own. *Stranger things have happened,* I reminded myself, then stepped forward when a familiar face appeared in the water. Ala.

She frowned when she recognized me and gestured to someone behind her. "Clear the room!" Footsteps against stone heralded several someones complying with her order before she spoke again. "Have you succeeded already?"

If only! "Not entirely, Your Grace, although circumstances indicate we are very near that point. As I'm sure you can tell, I have journeyed to Duat in Nemesis form and found proof that Anubis has at least two Fury shades in his service—which means he must have sworn them to himself *before* their deaths. Additionally, I found the missing priests you mentioned. Anubis imprisoned them when they came to investigate the missing portals, and he forced them to transmute souls loyal to him into the bodies of still-living arcanes." I motioned, and Nan stepped up beside me. "Including the body of Maeve Holloway, my grandmother. Her sister, Medea, now possesses control of her body although two of Imseti's priests have promised to restore her should that prove possible."

Ala's silver-rimmed eyes flashed with growing anger at each revelation. "He *dares* not only to swear Furies to his service, but also commit sacrilege against other deities? Abducts their priests; forces souls out of their rightful bodies so he can replace them with—with Anubian filth?" She spat into the mirror—which was fortunately not yet rigged up for physical travel.

"There's more, Your Grace. I interrogated one of his shades, and she claimed that he isn't planning a coup against the Triad; rather, it appears he seeks to consolidate more power so he can make the leap from lesser god to greater."

"If not to overthrow the Triad, then for what purpose?"

I cleared my throat and decided there really wasn't a *delicate* way to put the truth. "To become powerful enough to attract the full-time interest of his—ah, lover."

Funny how distinctly unsurprised she appeared in comparison to some of the previous revelations. I had to wonder what sorts of things *she* had done in the name of love—or Kamanu had done for her. Somehow it just seemed wrong that immortals would be as driven by base instincts as we mere mortals and arcanes, but I wasn't exactly willing to take up residence in glass houses anytime soon.

Several tense moments passed before she spoke again. "No matter the reason, he has clearly violated not just one, but several immortal laws. Have you shared this news with anyone else?"

I shook my head. "We're trying to keep as low a profile as possible. Your territory seemed the easiest to reach with this news. I was hoping you could help us pass word on to my mother in the Palladium as well. She needs to know about my grandmother's sister so she can better be prepared to apprehend her."

"You may tell her about your grandmother, but it seems unwise to spread anything else via portal until you have concrete proof. Something you now have less than forty-eight hours to accomplish."

Hearing her say it out loud like that made me want to break out in hives, so I did the only thing I could: ignore the obvious jibe. "May these priests have safe passage through your territory as well?"

Her eyes snapped with fire, but the smile that spread across her face indicated my audacity amused rather than annoyed her. "How could I refuse priests who serve another Death Lord loyal to the Triad? Send them through once you speak with your mother. And obtain that proof quickly, Nemesis, lest we lose your services just when you were proving yourself useful."

Wow, did she really just compliment *me?*

Don't let it go to your head. You could still crash and burn ingloriously. Trust Nike to keep me humble.

Ala's image disappeared, and black-and-silver light washed across the pool's still waters once more. Mom's surprised face stared out at me several moments later, flanked on one side by Adesina and Ekaterina on the other. Odd, only Mom wore Nemesis form; Adesina stood in red leather uniform with typical green serpent tattoos on each arm. I made the logical assumption that Mom's wearing Nemesis form in front of our favorite Tisiphone to hate meant she'd decided she could be trusted. Ironic when *she* numbered on the very short list of Furies to Be Trusted.

I didn't waste time with pleasantries, simply filling them in on an accelerated version of what had gone down since I'd seen them last. Mom's eyes shone with triumph when I stepped aside to reveal Nan's shade standing behind me.

"I *knew* that wasn't you!"

Nan gave her a smile every bit as approving as the one she'd earlier beamed my way. "Of course you did."

They refrained from indulging in a more sentimental greeting, but the way their eyes drank in the sight of each other spoke volumes. I couldn't hold back a smile. Ekaterina, on the other hand, suffered from nothing so plebeian as *sentimentality.* "We plan to meet with certain sisters of the Alecto persuasion later today."

I took that to mean they'd been able to make contact with the Alecto Prime as the Triad had instructed.

"Perfect. Hopefully there's a logical explanation for why *she* stopped answering the Triad's summons."

The Moerae's twisted lips indicated she highly doubted that but didn't care enough to argue the point out loud. Typical. She hated being gainsaid even more than—well, me. "To make matters worse, we also suspect that an imposter is posing as our own Prime, which explains why *she* fell out of contact with the Triad."

Sorrow washed over me at that thought. Our Prime was one of the most respected—and eldest—Furies in the Sisterhood. For an imposter to be successfully masquerading as her could mean only one thing. She was dead.

Mom leaned forward suddenly. The portal couldn't transport her body in its current form, but it *did* magnify her face as if she'd pressed it directly against a camera lens. "I thought you should know that I contacted Serise to ask if she might be willing to safeguard Cori again until we can bring her back to swear to the Sisterhood." The plan had been for her and Adesina to exchange their hostages when they first returned to the Palladium, then send Cori somewhere safe. "Or rather I should say, *tried* to contact her."

I frowned. "Well, she *is* drawing near to her delivery time. Maybe she went to an Oracl—"

Mom shook her head with migraine-inducing force. "No. I spoke with her new second, who indicated Serise simply vanished a few hours ago. Zoline was concerned enough to share that her Queen made arrangements with Gianna and Eugenie to help with the delivery and told me neither had heard from Serise today. Besides which, she left Rinda behind."

That news had my mouth drawing into a very large *O* shape. Rinda was another modern-day miracle who unfortunately owed her existence to my psycho former mentor: the world's first biologically *born* Harpy. Harpies were generally only created when a Fury gave into Rage and lost every single one of her marbles, slaughtering her Amphisbaena and turning into an unrecognizable version of her former self. Cats feared having their tongues cut out and replaced with catnip; a Fury's worst nightmare was Turning Harpy.

The Harpies prized Rinda even more than any other race treasured its young—*especially* Serise, who loved her infant daughter dearly, inasmuch as a Harpy was capable of love. She would *never* have abandoned Rinda willingly; no more than I would abandon Rinda's half sister, Olivia, who shared the same unknown Hound father as the Harpy child.

Realization had my blood going cold. The timing once again worked too perfectly. "They snatched her and probably brought her here."

Mom's gaze sharpened. "To Duat? But why would they bring *her* there?"

I gave her a sardonic eyebrow raise. "Have you forgotten how very hard Stacia worked to become Queen of the Harpies? Now that her lover has a new body, she's going to want one of her own."

Nan let out a vicious curse. "If this Serise is the new Harpy Queen"—Calaeno had held that distinction before Nan slipped into her coma, until Stacia had mowed her down in cold blood—"you're absolutely right. She'd make the perfect transmutation victim for that bitch. From everything I've seen, Anubis's priests find it easier to force souls out of their rightful bodies here in his realm, which is why it took them so long to knock me out of *mine* in the living realms."

Mom nodded. "Logical. We can assume that Stacia's first decree as Harpy Queen will be to throw in with Medea and *her* sycophants to further whatever scheme Anubis is working on. It would be a *disaster.*"

Yeah, like I didn't have enough pressure already. Speaking of which, my unfulfilled Mandate chose that moment to send bursts of pain radiating throughout my body. Mom's suddenly gritted teeth mirrored my own grunt although Adesina's serene image on the other end of the portal indicated she had a higher pain tolerance than either of us.

Durra let out a vexed noise that sounded almost pained and stomped her foot. "We need to *act* rather than gossiping foolishly. Time to send the priests through and get *on* with the rest of our mission."

Unexpected outburst aside, she had a point, especially considering that the longer we kept the portal open, the greater the chance that Anubis would commandeer our link so he could send his forces through. "I doubt we'll get another chance to contact you before we reach the Hall."

Mom nodded. "Good luck and be careful." She didn't need to remind me that the successful completion of our joint Mandate now fell mostly upon my leather-clad shoulders. We both knew that and knew also that I would do everything in my power to see it through. For all my faults—which were legion—I never gave up once I'd made a vow. Anubis was *so* going down, even if I had to die trying, which might very well happen if I couldn't invoke the Feather before my quickly ticking hours ran out.

I gestured to Sahana, who worked her mojo (with Ala's help) to transform the speaking portal into one fit for travel. Mijai and the Seer arranged their group into an orderly line that began filing into the pool-turned-portal. The tension gripping my body faded a little more each time another black-robed figure took the plunge, which was, of course, when all hell broke loose. There was little warning. One moment a priest stepped toward the portal, and the next he collapsed into churning water with a high-pitched scream. Black-and-silver energy rolled across the pond as our portal collapsed and a new one began to form. The priest's cries choked off suddenly, signaling an end to his suffering, which was confirmed when a dull-colored figure stepped away from the underwater corpse. His shade, prevented from materializing where it should by Anubis's foul magic.

A magic that would shortly turn on the rest of us, too. *Shit!* No way I could destroy *this* portal the way I had the previous. It wasn't an actual mirror I could shatter. "Kill the portal!" I screamed to Sahana while at the same time shoving the two remaining priests back toward their superiors.

"I'm trying to!" she yelled back. "Whoever's running it is *way* stronger than I."

Anubis, then. My heart dropped to the bottom of my feet. The people around me were *so* screwed once this new portal snapped into place. *I* had nothing to worry about—other than the horror of watching every person around me be cut down one after another since Anubis would be smart enough not to mess around this time. He'd send wave after wave of attackers through the—

Waves! That's it.

"Everyone into the pool. Splash around as much as you can."

Mijai shot me an incredulous look. "Are you insane? That thing just *killed* one of us!"

Scott and Sahana caught on right away, leaping forward along with me and splashing for all they were worth. Elliana turned on the Imsetians and started pushing them into the water. "She's right! Disturb the water's surface enough, and the portal won't be able to solidify."

At that pronouncement, everyone else jumped in and spread out, kicking and churning the water for all they were worth. We looked ridiculous, but more importantly, it worked. As much black-and-silver energy that poured along the pool's surface, it still could *not* get a solid enough grip for the portal to form. Not that Anubis gave up right away or for the next ten minutes, during which time Sahana siphoned off his stray Death magic so it couldn't hurt anyone else. By the time he *did* give up, our kicks and splashes were much more halfhearted and clumsy—though no less effective. Finally, magic dissipated and we could take a breather, all still standing *inside* the pool, except for the newborn shade, who wandered around us with a lost look on his face. Poor bastard.

"He'll try again when he thinks we've let our guard down." Elliana, as matter-of-fact as always. And, as a *former* Anubian handmaiden, *she* would know.

"Of course he will," Durra said with a scowl. "But we can't just splash around forever. He'll send reinforcements to another portal and overland the slower way."

Slower than traveling straight to *this* portal, but not slow enough. Rage burned the back of my throat when I faced the inevitable. Someone was going to have to stay behind to churn the waters long enough for the rest to get away—and it couldn't be me. Despite my imperviousness to death, I was also the only indispensable member of our group. I *could not* fall into Anubis's hands—he might not be able to kill me yet, but he could keep me away from the Hall of Two Truths until my time expired and he *could* do me in. Or worse, do to me what he'd helped Medea do to Nan.

I shuddered. *Over my dead body.* Such a stupid thought under the circumstances, but it steadied my resolve.

I opened my mouth to ask for volunteers but Mijai beat me to the punch. "We three will stay while the rest of you make for the Hall."

The Seer clenched her fists. "You mean the *four* of us."

He shook his head with a resolute expression. "No, Jeserit, you will go on with them. They'll need you to restore any transmuted souls along the way."

"But you can do that just as well as I. Better! *I'll* stay."

"No, I forbid it. You may be able to divine something for the Nemesis when she needs it most. Now go, and that's an order."

Tears welled at the corners of the Seer's eyes, but she stopped arguing. These two were obviously more to each other than fellow priests. I wanted to offer to stay in Mijai's place but knew I couldn't. *Gods damn you thrice over, Anubis.*

Nan patted me awkwardly on the arm and stepped toward the center of the pond. "Three of you will not be enough to cover the entire pond. I'll stay as well."

The newborn shade jumped at the chance for something to do and leaped into the water next to her. "As will I."

I shook my head as firmly as Mijai. "No, Nan, you

can't. We need you with us so we can restore you when we find Medea. We can't risk—"

She gave me a decidedly *grandmother* look, one that suggested she'd like nothing better than to turn me over her knee if I didn't behave. *Been there, done that.* "I *can* risk it and I *will*. Besides, what's Anubis going to do? Kill me? Wait, no, I'm already a shade. He can capture me again, but then you'll just rescue me once you invoke the Feather against him. Now stop being stupid, Riss, my lass, and *go.*"

Gods damn it, but she was right. The pond might have been small, but not *that* small. Three people would never be able to keep the water's surface moving. Three people and two shades, on the other hand, just might.

Scott's hand settled upon my shoulder, giving me the strength to do what had to be done. I reached forward to hug Nan, then turned to Mijai. "Thank you. May Imseti guard you and yours and—see you safely home." Home in this case likely being the afterlife. Anubis wouldn't *need* to keep them alive anymore.

He nodded brusquely. "Gods speed and good luck, Nemesis." Then he added in a more emotional tone, "Please keep my wife safe."

Tears pricked *my* eyes at that choked plea. No wonder they'd argued over who would be the one to go—and live. My gaze flew to Scott, and we shared a wordless look. Would we be willing to make such a sacrifice to save others? He'd given up his patron deity out of love for me, but would he be able to walk away from me to carry on with our mission? More importantly, would I be willing to do the same were the roles reversed?

Nike gamely tried to reassure me. *It won't come to that.*

Of course it won't, I echoed automatically, though deep inside I didn't believe that. Having had to give up the man I loved most in the world once, I knew it all-too-surely *could* happen again. What scared me was the fact I truly didn't know what I would do if faced with that awful choice. Once, my mission—whatever it was— would have been my number one priority. Now? I wasn't so sure . . .

CHAPTER THIRTEEN

WALKING AWAY FROM MY GRANDMOTHER'S shade wasn't the hardest thing I'd ever done, but it came close. It did help to remind myself what she had pointed out: Anubis *couldn't* kill her again, especially considering she wasn't technically dead. While her body lived, Nan was safe. Well, in a manner of speaking.

We hotfooted it away from the oasis and back into the neon blue desert. The sun was sinking into the horizon way faster than it would have on earth, which made it easier to travel quickly since we weren't sweating out every ounce of the water we'd replenished before leaving the pond. About an hour into our twilight jaunt, Nike let out a hiss and tightened her body around my upper arm. *Nemesis says she and the Cat have infiltrated Anubis's stronghold unseen.* She gave another hiss, this one very much in disgust. *They have managed to track down your bitch former mentor, who seems to be ordering other Anubian shades around.*

Amusement at her snarky—though accurate—designation of Stacia soon faded, to be replaced by a sudden flash of insight. We wouldn't have a better opportunity to discover if Stacia really *was* planning to steal the Harpy Queen's body. *Ask them to look for a pregnant woman with white hair, yellow-green eyes, and pale skin. Stick skinny except for the prego belly.*

So you really do *think Stacia is behind Serise's disappearance?*

Is my former *mentor a psychotic bitch?*

Mental laughter was the only response to *that* rhetorical question. Seconds later, she spoke again. *Nemesis says they haven't seen any pregnant women but that the Cat is willing to check the areas where they might secure such a prisoner.*

Good. Make sure they let us know right away if they see her.

Done. Nemesis confirms that Anubis does *have a lover among the greater gods; the buzz among his followers is that the lover is someone powerful married to an equally strong Deity. Oh! She says that a number of shades and priests just jumped into a portal in a hurry.* No need to guess where *they* might be headed . . .

Scott's voice suddenly murmured into my ear. "You planning to set up camp already?"

I started, then flushed when I realized my steps had slowed to a near stop. "No, Nemesis was giving Nike an update. Stacia is *definitely* involved in this whole mess, and they're going to see if they can find any trace of Serise. Apparently Anubis just sent a hunting party through a portal—which means we need to put as much distance between us as—"

"Riss! Do you feel that?"

Sahana's panicked tone had me augmenting my senses and shooting my gaze to the west, from where a humongous burst of Death magic had flared. She and I shared a grim glance and began urging the others to step up the pace. Nobody was dumb enough to protest, but Scott did arch a curious brow. "There must be a portal within a mile or two of here." *That* statement had everyone moving even faster than before. Too much was at stake to give up.

At first it seemed like we might manage to stay ahead of any trouble as the seconds turned into minutes, then over an hour without any further signs of pursuit. I had just started to breathe a little easier when Sahana let out a hiss and slammed into Scott, knocking him to the ground just as a deadly spear of magic lanced through the air. Sparks of Death energy rained against my arm, enough to have me growling at Scott's near brush with death. No time to thank Sahana for intervening, time only to shift into full Fury form, leap into the air, and *hunt*. "Run!" I screamed over my shoulder as Durra and Mac launched themselves after me. "We'll slow them down and catch up. It's our only chance!" Fortunately, most people assumed that Mac's Sidhe blood allowed him to imitate my own Fury form—something the typical half-blooded Sidhe could *not* do, but everyone assumed the genetic manipulation performed by the scientists allowed him the ability to use full-on glamourie. A misapprehension we took every advantage of.

Our airborne trio topped a nearby sand dune, only to see a group of Anubian priests working more Death magic, surrounded by a miniature army of shades. What had ice forming into a frigid lump in my belly, however, were the four immortals letting out battle cries and rushing toward us, steely resolve on their faces and murder in their silver-rimmed eyes.

I let out a roar of my own, made all the more impressive by my extra boost of Nemesis power. Durra and Mac echoed my hundred-decibel cry with none-too-shabby shrieks of their own, and we swooped upon our divine enemies. Magic responded to my call, knocking into the four immortals with the impact of a tornado, sending them flying every which way and blue sand swirling angrily, giving us a slight edge as we attacked the sprawling figures ferociously. Durra and Mac were wise enough to dart in and out, making as many on-the-fly swipes as they could and getting back out of reach before their targets could really retaliate. Both channeled as much Rage and magic as they dared, eyes glowing with the same furious emerald green as mine.

My hands were full harrying two of the immortals, since I knew my partners would barely be able to stand up to one divine opponent each, much less two. Death magic swirled around us, and it took every ounce of flying skill we possessed to avoid it—Durra and Mac because it would kill them and me because I *wanted* the priests to waste as much magic on fruitless attacks as they could be goaded into squandering. We were vastly outnumbered, and our only hope was to delay our attackers as long as possible so the others could make good their escape. Then we would have to fly faster than *any* bat out of hell.

It helped that Anubis must have given the order to capture *me* as priority number one because they focused their efforts on that rather than stopping to wonder where the rest of our party had disappeared to. The shades and priests also couldn't fly, so were limited to throwing spell after spell into the air against us. The immortals could likely have manifested wings to come after us, which was precisely the reason that we concentrated most of our efforts on keeping them off balance.

Minutes passed in a painful blur, and I knew that Durra and Mac wouldn't be able to keep this up much longer—not and still be able to make a madcap flight away. I racked my brain for a plan of action, but no flash of insight ignited other than making a kamikaze stand here while everyone else got away since I couldn't be killed. While I would have no problem making such a sacrifice, that plan would only lead to ultimate failure since only *I* could invoke the Feather against Anubis. Letting his minions capture me would give him *exactly* what he wanted. My gaze jumped from my opponents to my baby brother, who bore many cuts and bruises and whose wings were looking much the worse for wear. He gamely fought on, but exhaustion etched itself onto every line of his face, and I knew he couldn't hold out much longer.

Gods, no, I can't *lose him now!*

But it was quickly looking like I had no other option, as his enemy let loose a sudden burst of magic (*not* Death energy, thankfully) that Mac was a fraction too slow to dodge. He plummeted toward the ground, and my heart sank along with him, certain he was falling to his death—but Durra moved with inhuman speed to catch him under the elbows and zoom away. Knowing she had risked her own life to save his bumped her up a few notches in my book, and I focused on doing what

I could to cover their retreat. Unfortunately, once I was the sole target available, it looked like I was going to give Anubis that chance to open up his best Chianti after all. All four immortals turned their attention to me and started channeling magic—most likely so they could make like birds—until something unexpected happened. An explosion of silver-touched earth magic went off like a bomb beneath the Anubians' feet, and the sand swallowed them all whole.

My mouth dropped open in shock, and I shot a glance behind me, catching sight of a haggard-looking Charlie, his eyes rimmed in silver showing that he'd *somehow* tapped into divine magic in order to pull off that mind-blowing spell. I knew it wouldn't hold our enemies forever—especially not the immortals—but it just might manage to buy us enough time to get away. There'd be time later to wonder how he had pulled off the minor miracle. I landed next to him, and we took off running; no way could I leave him behind when he had risked his ass to save mine. Fortunately, whatever extra power he was channeling granted him augmented speed and stamina, which meant we rapidly left the Anubian sink-hole behind and caught up with everyone else before they had gone more than a few miles.

We might have managed a last-minute escape from the overwhelming odds sent against us, but Anubis was by no means willing to admit defeat, which he proved by turning Duat's very environment against us. Despite the fact I *knew* we kept moving in the same direction, we found ourselves coming across footsteps we had previously made in the sand, meaning we were somehow managing to walk in circles. We paused long enough for Jeserit to try scrying the whereabouts of the Hall of Two

Truths, only to fail miserably—an undoubted defense mechanism meant to keep the unworthy from tracking it down. An eerie dark purple mist descended upon us not too long after, making it even more difficult for us to catch our bearings. At that rate we'd make it to the Hall of Two Truths right around the time I became eligible as a Fury Elder.

And seeing as how we didn't have forty years to wander around the desert like that Moses guy, I had to come up with a better plan for finding the Hall of Two Truths ASAP. I could have run a tracer spell if only I had the blood of Ma'at or one of her guardians, but that wasn't exactly an ingredient one could run down to the corner mart to pick up. Even if Duat had *had* a corner mart . . . No, all I had to work with were a couple Warhounds, a sister Fury, a half-Fury-half-Sidhe hybrid, a Death-touched Raga, an earth-friendly Giant, and an unfamiliar Seer who owed allegiance to a Death Lord I didn't know very . . . well . . .

I froze halfway up a sand dune, causing a domino effect of bodies piling one into another and curses flying into the evening air. Not that I took much notice, I was too busy thinking over Mijai's words when he insisted his wife be the one to come with us. *You may be able to divine something when the Nemesis needs it most . . .* Considering the insistent Mandate burning a hole in the back of my brain, that Serise and her unborn child were being held prisoner by my crazy *former* mentor and her power-hungry, lovesick god, the fact that other people's lives depended upon my *not* screwing up, and—the kicker—I had *no* idea where we were going, it seemed safe to say that *this* would be the time I needed help the most.

Durra opened her mouth to bitch, but my wild-eyed

gaze shut her up. I waded through the stupid sand and stopped in front of Jeserit. Her eyes were red, and her cheeks bore dirt-stained tear tracks—something that sent guilt shooting inside again, but I forced that aside. None of us had time for tender emotions just then. We had a *job* to do. Time—as always—to grieve later. Besides, her husband might not even be dead. Anubis might have just let him go . . .

Yeah, I didn't really believe that, either.

"Jeserit, I hate to ask this of you, but I have to. We've been walking out here for hours, and if I don't miss my guess, we've just been wandering in circles. Your husband had faith in your abilities and—and he somehow *knew* it would come down to this. He *knew* I would need *you* to help me find my way to the Hall of Two Truths. Please—is there any way for you to try scrying again? I know you can't divine the Hall's exact whereabouts, but what about—what about something more general, like the best direction for us to travel in?"

Jeserit's eyes flashed with pain at the first mention of her husband, but resolve replaced it. She clenched her teeth and nodded. "He's right, and so are you. I won't let his sacrifice be in vain. But this time . . . this time I need the proper tools, or as close as we can get in this blasted wasteland."

I let out the breath I'd been holding and nodded eagerly. "Yes, surely between us we can come up with what you need. Just let us know."

The others gathered around us and soon echoed my words. Jeserit became more determined with each voice that spoke and began rattling off the items she needed. "A ceremonial dagger—the bastards took mine when they ambushed us."

Scott produced a stainless steel knife from a boot sheath. "I've not even used this yet, so you should be able to bless it for ceremonial use. I know it's not pretty but—"

"No, that's perfect!" Jeserit snatched the blade and sheathed it at her belt. "We'll need something to use to make a pentagram on the ground."

My hand whipped into a utility pouch at my waist, and I drew out a pack of cheap but functional chalk. "Check! Never leave home without it." Not since the one time I failed to bring some, and it nearly got me killed.

She nodded and glanced around our surroundings with a frown. "I really need a *flat* surface in order to make this work."

Something that might be easier said than done. We hadn't seen a completely flat patch of land since leaving the oasis a good three or four hours earlier . . . The ground began rumbling beneath our feet, and we all went into attack mode, surrounding Jeserit and waiting for the coming ambush—all except for Charlie, who simply walked to the foot of our sand dune and made some wild gestures. Blue sand smoothed out at his command, packing down into a hard, flat surface a couple of dozen feet in diameter.

"Check!" the earth-friendly (duh!) Giant called out once the ground finished rearranging itself for him.

Sahana offered to sketch out the pentagram upon the hard-packed earth, and I handed her some of the chalk. Jeserit spared a small smile before continuing with her shopping list. "Didn't I see one of you fill a canteen at the pool?"

Elliana and Mac held out utilitarian canteens that had been clipped to their belts. Mercs could be *so* useful to have around, especially anal-retentive ones.

"One of these will do, thanks." She reached beneath the neckline of her robe and pulled out a gold chain, which bore a large, cabochon-cut chunk of rainbow obsidian that must have cost her a pretty penny. "The idiots *did* let me keep my scrying stone, with which a Seer can do far more damage than a mere dagger."

I gave an approving grin at the tone of her voice since it reminded me how often mortals feared my police-issue Sig Sauer more than my innocuous bare hands—which were in actuality way more dangerous, even in only partial Fury form.

Jeserit leveled her gaze upon me. "The last three items must come from you, Nemesis. Since *you* are the one with the gods-blessed Mandate and the one whose needs are most dire, I will need *your* blood, flesh, and hair."

I'd been half expecting that, since some of the spells I used to summon spirits or trace a person's location— very much like scrying—required the same items. Scott helpfully offered another of his many concealed blades (likely unsuitable for ceremonial use due to having been used for violence) so I could cut a lock of hair and scrape off a portion of skin covered with drops of blood. The wound closed over even more quickly than usual thanks to my Nemesis genes, but fortunately not so quickly I couldn't get the flesh and blood first.

Jeserit held out the oversized scrying stone, and I carefully placed my vital essences upon it. She murmured magical phrases, and the hair, flesh, and blood fused together before a spark of black energy flashed, and the obsidian actually *absorbed* the essences, leaving not a visible trace behind.

That seemed easy. Knowing magic the way I did, *too* easy. "That all you need from me?"

"For now. Just wait outside the pentagram with the others. This might take a while." She got a sudden fierce expression. "Whatever happens, I *must not* be interrupted, or I'll have to start all over again."

Good to know. We didn't really have *a while* for her to do this once, much less twice. And considering the fact Anubis had patrols scouring the desert for us, we couldn't count on their *not* showing up at the worst possible moment.

Safer to assume that's exactly *what's going to happen and be prepared,* Nike pointed out, and slithered along my arm to get more comfortable.

Out of the mouths—okay, minds—of snakes . . .

I turned to Scott, only to find him nocking an arrow to his crossbow. "So when did *you* take up archery?"

He laughed at the question I'd blurted out unintentionally. "I don't tell you *every*thing, baby. Have to keep you guessing so you don't get bored."

As if *that* would ever happen in a relationship involving a Fury and a Warhound . . . I was just relieved to find we *could* share a moment of humor in light of all the crap going down. "Can I count on you Shadowhounds and Charlie to cover our perimeter?"

"Consider it done." His glance fell upon Jeserit, setting up shop at the center of Sahana's perfectly sketched pentagram. The muscles in his jaw tightened, and he pulled me to him roughly. My eyes fluttered shut, and I drank in the feminine scent of berry-flavored candy contrasted with the more masculine musks and sandalwoods that comforted my soul because they meant Scott was nearby. He sucked down those candies to stave off his cigarette cravings, the smoking a habit he'd given up for me.

Rather than kissing me as expected, he ran his hands through my hair and murmured sweet Egyptian nothings in my ear. I didn't waste magic translating his mother's tongue, just savored his scent, sound, and most importantly, touch. For this one moment I could forget we were on a desperate quest to stop Anubis before he could bring war to both our world and the immortal, forget that Scott had betrayed Anubis the way Jackal-Faced had betrayed his fellow gods, forget that one of us might well have to make the sacrifice Jeserit had made when she chose to carry on knowing that her husband faced certain death. For now, we were just Scott and Marissa, two people who loved each other, who always had and—I hoped—always would.

I opened *my* eyes to find *his* devouring my face as if he could imprint it onto his memory the way a food connoisseur would a meal. My pulse skittered as emotion welled inside me. "Gods, Scott, I love you."

"I know," he murmured, fisting his fingers in my hair possessively. "As much as I love you. I gave up my god for you, Marissa, and I would do it again, a thousand times over. *This* is love, not whatever emotion is driving—Anubis—to betray immortal law and steal the free will and bodies of those weaker than he. Remember that no matter what happens, but also remember this: Your Mandate *must* come first." I opened my mouth, but he pressed a finger against it. "I know you, Riss, and I saw that silent war waging across your face back in the oasis. Love is important and worth fighting for—worth *dying* for—but true love would never ask someone to sacrifice honor and duty for mere selfishness. You *do* what you have to and let the rest of us do what *we* have to. Even if that means letting go."

Like I'd had to let my grandmother go. Like Jeserit had to let Mijai go. I'd had no choice but to accept Vanessa's passing months earlier, and that had been the most gut-wrenching loss of my life—worse than losing my father, mother, or grandmother. Scott I loved with even more strength, more fire and passion, and I couldn't imagine living life without him again. But, if push came to shove, could I honor our love and his request and fight on if I had to?

"I—I will."

Scott pressed a frenzied kiss against my lips before pushing away, "I knew you'd make the right choice."

He turned and began organizing Charlie, Elle, and Mac to spread out and form a protective layer in the distance. *Funny,* I thought with a bemused expression. *How did he know that when I wasn't sure of it myself?*

Because, Nike interjected with that maternal air she pulled off so well, *he loves you for who and what you are, and he sees you the way Nemesis and I do. Strong enough to do what needs doing even when it hurts. That's why we chose you, why* he *chose you.*

Gods, but her matter-of-fact certainty humbled me in a way nothing else had. To hear that she and Nemesis had actually *chosen* me as their Fury—something I always figured had just been some sort of cosmic crapshoot—explained why I'd always felt such a deep kinship with them even when I couldn't understand them verbally. Hearing Nike confirm something I'd always known but never really *gotten* on a visceral level, that Scott had *chosen* me, made me narrow my eyes and figuratively gird my loins. Our love was amazing and worth fighting for, but Scott was right. Shirking one's sacred duties out of selfishness only dishonored that love. Something I *would not do.*

Unlike Mr. Jackal-Faced pain-in-my-ass.

"This is *so* on!" I muttered with a feline smile that would have done Harper proud. "And your immortal ass is going down!" Even if that meant I lost mine in the process, or worse—Scott lost his.

SAHANA FROWNED WHEN I APPROACHED THE spot where she and Durra were keeping watch over Jeserit, who had apparently used the canteen's contents to bless her ceremonial dagger, offer up some of her blood as a sacrifice, and bathe the scrying stone in both water and blood. She sat chanting magical phrases while twirling the gold chain over the soggy sand beneath the stone.

"I know I'm not a merc, Marissa, but I'm just as deadly as the others. I can pull my weight!"

"I know, Sahi, and you're probably *deadlier* than the others, which is why I want you here with Durra and me. We're the last line of defense."

Annoyance faded, and she nodded thoughtfully. "You think they're coming?"

"I *know* they're coming. The only question is when they'll catch up."

Durra nodded next to me. "Since Anubis has been playing his games with us, he's probably herding us somewhere we'll be easier to find. That's what I would have done."

I couldn't resist shooting her a sardonic expression. "Yeah, you *are* pretty good at forcing people into unexpected ambushes." She didn't have the grace to flush, merely returned my sarcasm with an angelic (ha) smile.

Jeserit's voice rose a few decibels, hinting that we

were making her task more difficult with our chatter, so I motioned for the others to spread out around the pentagram's edge. The sun had long since disappeared, but twin moons out of some science-fiction novel vied for supremacy in Duat's night sky, providing enough illumination to make our lives easier. Unfortunately, that fact would aid our pursuers as well.

For the first hour of Jeserit's divination ritual, though, we neither saw nor heard any sign of pursuit. The Seer's voice rose and fell in varying volumes until it grew hoarse, meaning *quiet* became the default setting. I paced my third of the pentagram's perimeter, gaze sweeping the area around us. Every once in a while I climbed a sand dune so I could see farther into the distance. I caught an occasional glimpse of Scott and Elliana stalking the night in Hound form several hundred feet away. I never really saw Charlie or Mac—Charlie presumably because he had some earth-magic form of camouflage and as a part-Fury, part-Sidhe, I figured Mac would be even better able to blend in with his surroundings than I was.

Another monotonous half hour ticked by. Nike grew as on edge as I, moving from one arm to my waist to the other arm, and back again. Despite our vigilance—or perhaps *because* of it—the expected attack never materialized. Instead, Jeserit's voice rose one final time in a triumphant shout, and magic flared inside the pentagram in a burst of shimmering silver light before pouring *into* her scrying stone and fading away.

Jeserit flopped onto her back and convulsed several times. The three of us panicked and ran forward, each smudging a portion of the chalk outline to render the magical circle harmless since Jeserit's collapse meant she hadn't been able to properly banish it. Sahana managed to reach Jeserit first by virtue of being the closest when she fell. Not a bad thing, since the same gifts that allowed Sahana to bring Death could also allow her to sometimes chase it away.

She felt for a pulse and let out a relieved sigh when she found one. "Just backlash, it looks like."

I heaved a sign of my own and zeroed in on the scrying stone, still dangling from the Seer's fingers. It glowed with a distinct blue energy it hadn't possessed before, a light that reminded me very much of the physical manifestation of Fury magic. *Most likely from your life essences,* Nike hypothesized. *If she succeeded in divining the best path for you to take to fulfill your Mandate, the stone should now show the way.* Made sense to me, even if it was a little unsettling to see an inanimate object giving off the same glow that a Fury working magic would.

Sahana began shaking Jeserit gently in an effort to revive her. I grabbed the discarded canteen and shook it. Empty. *Of course!* I shifted to full Nemesis form, beating my wings and jumping upward. "Be right back. Mac has more water." Which was more than I could say for myself. Since I didn't *have* to eat or drink, I hadn't even thought to pack something so mundane, not even for the nonimmortals around me. Then again, the optimist in me had envisioned our foray here being a more straightforward dine-and-dash type of affair than the slog it had actually become.

I allowed myself to enjoy the wind dancing along my skin as I flew in the direction I'd last seen Mac head in. Just when I started to worry that some ill had befallen him, magic tingled below, and he popped into view. My eyes widened because whoa! That had been the closest thing to true invisibility I'd ever seen. Other than a slight blurriness as he materialized, Mac had been virtually undetectable against the blue sand dune he'd been standing upon.

He hurried forward when I landed. "Everything okay?"

I nodded, gesturing to the spot where he had just been. "You never told me you could actually go freaking invisible!"

He shrugged. "You never asked. Besides, I just assumed all Furies could."

My brows furrowed. "No, not like that. We do a mean magical camo that makes just about everyone overlook us, but not even close to what you just did. It must come as much from your Sidhe genes as your Fury."

"Maybe. I never bothered talking too much to the Sidhe Stacia's cronies captured. Half had been so brainwashed they wouldn't say *boo* without her permission, and the other half spat every time I came anywhere near their cells. They considered me one-half abomination, one-half traitor for cooperating with her."

Hard for me to consider someone else who had been raised believing Stacia an authority figure to be trusted only to find out the exact opposite was true any kind of traitor. Especially not when he'd had the courage to break through her mental programming and rescue our mother from the nightmare in which she'd been trapped for two long decades.

"Jescrit finished her divination but passed out. Sahi's trying to wake her up, but she's gonna be thirsty when she does."

He nodded. "Backlash is a bitch. I'll get it to her while you gather the others."

At my nod, he began the shift to Fury form—or his modified version. Rainbow-scaled serpent tats burst across his skin, but they'd not yet come to life that I'd ever seen. I was hoping they would once he swore to the Sisterhood. His red hair shaded to charcoal, and his eyes became glowing green orbs the same as mine, and massive, dark-colored wings unfurled at his back. His clothing stayed the same black cargo pants and tee, however.

I waved, and we launched into the air in different directions. Finding Scott and Elliana proved easy enough, and I sent them hurtling toward our temporary camp in Hound form. Charlie, however, was as difficult to track down as Mac had been. He'd also gone farther afield than anyone else, thanks to his ground-eating strides. In the end, *he* found *me*, appearing unexpectedly from behind and snatching a loose feather off one of my wings. Instinct had me spinning and lashing out with wicked sharp talons, but he'd been smart enough to leap back the instant he plucked the feather.

He guffawed at the outrage on my face and wisely took several more steps back. "Sorry, darlin', but I couldn't resist. It's flipping boring out here. Jeserit discover where we need to go yet?"

I gave a grudging nod and took off walking in the direction Mac had taken. *Would serve him right if I left his Giant ass to walk alone!* Nike agreed with my sentiment, but we both knew neither of us would make good on that threat. Charlie fell in step beside me soon enough—ridiculously long legs of his—and cleared his throat a couple of times. We made it another minute or two before he started clearing his throat again, over and over like he really *had* swallowed a frog. It was so very un-Charlie-like that I stopped and turned to stare. "You swallow some sand or something?"

He started guiltily and drew to a stop across from me. Another annoying throat clear before he finally spoke up. "I've got something I've been wanting to talk to you about."

His voice sounded so suspicious, it had me folding arms across chest and Nike tightening her grip around my waist. "Am I going to want to kick your ass when you do? Because it's only fair for me to point out that we're in the middle of nowhere, and there's no one here to pull me off you."

Charlie winced because he knew I was only half joking. I'd gone at him once before when he'd made a very bad joke at my—or rather, Vanessa's—expense years before. He hadn't meant his comment the way I took it, but Rage had kicked in before I could stop it, and luckily someone else had been there to keep me from killing him. I liked to think I wouldn't have taken it that far, but I'd been younger and even more susceptible to Rage then . . .

"I hope you won't, but there's never any telling with Furies, now is there? Look, it's not something we've been intentionally hiding from you." *We?* I liked the sound of that even less. "But we didn't want to share details with *anyone* until we were sure of each other's feelings."

I blinked, and burgeoning Rage at the thought of another betrayal coming on vanished. My brain switched tracks and tried to think of *who* Charlie could be talking about. I'd suspected he might have a lover when I'd shown up at his apartment unannounced but hadn't tried to guess who it could be. That list was longer than you might imagine, because Charlie was known to play for both teams. He was an equal opportunist when it came to love and had a long trail of ex-girlfriends and boy-friends to prove it. Oh, there weren't a lot of them *be-cause* he was bisexual—Ekaterina was the next thing to celibate, and she was also—but because he was Charlie. He loved as hard as he worked and played, with lots of enthusiasm and energy and without fear of putting him-self out there.

So who among my friends had he most likely hooked up with on the sly? As far as I knew, he and Sahana had only just met when I introduced them. Same thing with Durra—and if she *had* been the one, I really *would* have kicked his ass. Hmm . . . maybe one of Scott's relatives? We'd all worked closely together bringing Stacia's ass down. Kiara was a safe no-go since she only dated wom-en; none of Scott's brothers were into guys although a couple of his male cousins *were* . . . None Charlie had worked with, though, as far as I knew. Then I remem-bered how Charlie had valiantly assisted a battered-looking Amaya out of Stacia's mad-scientist compound the night we had assaulted it, and I grinned. They wouldn't be the first couple to bond after a rescue scen-ario, for sure.

"You sly dog, you. Congratulations!"

His turn to blink. "Wait—you don't mind if she and I . . ."

She? Ha! I guessed right. "Now why would I mind? I think that's just great. Scott might be another story, but I'll work on him for you."

He frowned and tilted his head. "Why on earth would *Scott* mind that I'm seeing your partner?"

My ears started buzzing, and I had to try to several

times before I managed to take a full breath of air. "My p-p-partner? You're seeing . . . you're seeing *Trinity*?" The last part emerged as a louder-than-intended roar.

Charlie gulped and edged a few feet away. "Yeah, who'd *you* think . . . Oh. His oldest sister? The one we saved. Amaya?" At my fierce nod, he gave another wince. "No, she's just not my type. Way too much of a tomboy."

Which was just *rich*, considering that he had no problems being attracted to actual *boys*. "Son of a . . . I knew you were open to love, Charlie, but I never knew you went for *mundanes*."

He stopped edging backward and scowled at the tone in my voice. "What the hell, Riss? You *work* with mundanes; your lover is the *son* of a mundane. I never figured you for a bigot."

I glared and gestured rudely. "I'm *not* a bigot, no more than any other arcane. Less than most, since I *started out* mortal. But you're a merc—just like Scott's dad—and you both are used to our world."

"And your partner isn't? She works with you on arcane cases, for gods' sake. She held her own with me in that compound, Riss, and that's a fact. I didn't have to slow down for her even once." He shook his head. "Trinity told me you used to coddle her like a child, but she claimed you were over that. Said you respect her skills and—"

"I *do* respect her skills. Very much! It's just . . ." My voice trailed off, and I tried to figure just what *it* was. Why *should* I mind if Charlie and Trinity, two consenting adults, became involved? I hadn't minded one bit when she used her feminine wiles on Pennington Banoub's brother, Tariq. She'd even gone on a few dates with him, and that hadn't bothered me one bit. She dated a lot, though she hadn't gotten serious with any one person since I'd been working with her . . . and *that* was it exactly.

Whoa . . . I'm jealous. Jealous she's committed enough to someone, and he's pretty much asking for my blessing. And a little hurt that she *wasn't the one to tell me.*

I opened my mouth to tell him the same thing when something odd occurred. Panic flashed in his eyes, and his body twitched several times. He raised both hands and shook them vigorously, as if trying to shake off something sticky, which was when Nike and I had the same thought and kicked into gear. I flapped my wings and surged forward, knocking the giant to the ground so I could straddle his still-twitching body. Nike slithered from my waist to his neck, where she remained calmly, tongue flicking in and out but venom remaining safely inside.

Charlie's convulsions stopped, and his eyes opened, eyes that had become rimmed with glowing silver. I gasped at the visible confirmation of what I'd already guessed: Someone had transmuted into Charlie's body, and that *someone* had to be a deity. The obvious guess would have been Anubis, but that just didn't feel right. If Anubis were going to do something as crazy as switching souls with another being himself, it sure as hell wouldn't be with a lowly arcane. It would be with another, more powerful immortal.

Silver light flickered, and I swore I saw *Charlie* looking out of his own eyes, begging for help. The silver glow solidified, indicating the immortal had reasserted control. Rage had talons bursting from my fingers, and I pressed them to the Giant's chest, directly above his pounding heart.

"Who the hell are *you*, and *what* are you doing inside this Giant? Try anything stupid, and I won't hesitate to rip his heart out." A bluff, but the immortal wouldn't know that. I had a reputation—and so did Nemeses.

Charlie's lips moved, but the voice that emerged echoed with some indefinable quality that screamed *other* as loudly as the silver-rimmed eyes. "Peace, Nemesis, I mean neither you nor the Giant harm. This is the only way I could speak with you here, and that only because some of my followers are in this realm for me to draw strength from."

"Imseti?" He nodded. Inner tension released, but only slightly. This *could* be a trick. "Why didn't you just take over *Jeserit's* body?"

"Because helping her break through the block that prevented her from completing that divination nearly killed her as it was. You need her to guide you to your destination so I daren't risk killing her myself."

Fair enough; and that explained the silver explosion of magic when she finally succeeded in her divination spell. "Why did you feel the need to risk contacting me at all? And—wait. You said you have *several* followers still here." My pulse quickened, and I couldn't hold back the surge of hope that flooded me. "Does that mean Mijai and the others are still alive?"

Compassion lit in those eerie eyes staring out at me from Charlie's face, which gave me my answer before he spoke. "They *were* living when I crossed over into this part of Duat after Ala and the priests you sent to her contacted me; but I underestimated Anubis. He used my link with Mijai to lure me through that portal, then killed all three of them before . . ."

His voice trailed off, and compassion was replaced by revulsion and—terror. Seeing terror on the (borrowed) face of a deity who could *not* be killed had anxiety twisting my own insides into knots. Goose bumps pricked my flesh when my subconscious mind put the pieces together and my conscious picked up on it.

"Before—before he forced you out of your body and transmuted into it?"

"You have it half-right." He clenched his—Charlie's— fists, and bitterness chased away the other emotions. "He indeed forced me out of my body, something that should be *impossible,* but *he* was not the one to take over my physical form. Instead, he—through one of his high-ranking priests—gave it to one of his pet followers. An arcane."

He spat the last two words, and his revolted terror suddenly made perfect sense. The thought that a god—even a lesser one—could be expelled from his physical body was bad enough. Learning that a nonimmortal had been transmuted into his place nearly had me turning tail then and there. If a full-fledged *god* could be evicted from his body, what chance did a mere *temporary* demigoddess have? Scott and the others wouldn't even have a snowball's chance in hell. But if we didn't stop Anubis immediately, where would it all end? If he and his priests already had the power (thanks to blood sacrifice) and skills (thanks to stealing the knowledge) to oust immortals and take over *their* power and skills, nothing would stop him from rolling over the Triad, then, all other immortals.

Which was very likely the plan. Other than a few minor losses, it would be a relatively bloodless coup. And Anubis would get around the conundrum of not being able to kill his enemies by transmuting them instead, giving their bodies to those loyal to him. Like Stacia, Medea, and all his other shades itching to return to the living world, one way or another.

My eyes narrowed as another thought occurred to me. "I found out that he has a lover among the greater gods, one who has a spouse with a great deal of power. Someone who might make a perfect transmutation victim for a lesser god hoping for an easy promotion. And considering that you were ambushed only *after* Ala contacted you, and her spouse is about as powerful as they come . . ."

Imseti's horrified gaze met my own. "You think *she* is Anubis's lover and plans to help him take over her own husband's body? But—that would give them a majority on the Triad. They could do *anything* they wanted without anyone the wiser until it was too late to stop them."

I nodded grimly. "Exactly."

His silver-rimmed eyes went blurry for a moment. "I hate to think such a thing of her, but she *did* contact me the moment the portal was taken over by Anubis and supposedly *helped* me regain enough control to go and aid my followers—which was precisely when I was ambushed." Something that must have happened long after the rest of us rushed away from the oasis. Exhaustion suddenly washed over Charlie's face. "I fear your friend is taking exception to my *borrowing* his body. Not that I can blame him, considering. I came to ask you to restore me to my rightful form if you can, to warn the other Deities if you cannot. Either way, you will be rewarded."

My gaze grew fierce. "I will restore you if I can because it's the right thing to do. The same reason I will avenge your followers' murders if the chance arises. They didn't deserve what befell them."

"Without my corporeal form, my ability to assist you will likely be limited. But rest assured I will shadow you as long as possible and do whatever I can."

As he'd helped with Jeserit's divination, his offer was something that was not to be taken lightly. His abilities might be limited from a deity's point of view just then, but that by no means made his assistance insignificant. And at this point, I would *so* take what I could. He was gone before I could respond, something heralded by Charlie's beginning to twitch beneath me again. I scooped up Nike and jumped to my feet, watching as Charlie slowly returned to himself. His eyes fluttered for a good thirty seconds, at which point they shot open, and he lurched to a sitting position.

"I—whuh—what just happened?" A shudder, this one purely reactionary, racked his body one more time. "I feel like shit. How'd I end up down here?"

Since time was at an ever-growing premium, I helped him stand and filled him in as we walked back to the others. He bounced from ticked off at being used without permission to understanding *why* Imseti had resorted to treating him the way Anubis had treated Imseti, to equally determined that Jackal-Faced had to be stopped at any costs.

Funny how I no longer thought that sacrificing the lives of others—even Scott's—would be nearly as difficult as I'd earlier imagined . . .

CHAPTER FOURTEEN

JESCRIT WAS AWAKE AND ALERT—AND REHY-
drated, thanks to Mac—by the time we made it back. I
gave everyone else a CliffsNotes version of what had
taken so long, leaving off Imseti's confirmation that Mijai
was indeed dead. What Jescrit had to do was hard enough
given the uncertainty over her husband's fate; we couldn't
afford for grief to debilitate her if she learned the truth
now. A cold and practical decision, but one that had to be
made. Guess Nike and Nemesis were right after all . . .

You are not *a coldhearted bitch for doing what has to
be done,* Nike chided my dark turn of thought. *And we
can't afford for* you *to go into self-pity mode.*

Touché. And too true.

During my absence, Durra and Elliana had dutifully
erased every trace of our time there, starting with the
worse-for-wear pentagram and ending by wiping away

as many of our footprints as they could manage. Charlie
summoned the energy to put the land back into order
while Sahana and I did what we could to bolster Jeserit's
flagging strength. Since neither of us were true healers,
we couldn't do much; but every little bit helped. Sahana
pulled a neat little trick out of her Raga bag: She sought
out every instance of cellular *death* in Jeserit's body and
flushed them away, restoring quite a lot of the Seer's
energy lost during her harrowing divination. I then stepped in to siphon some of the residual magic pooled beneath us and funneled it into Jeserit's flesh and bones,
much as I had for Cori not so long ago to give her
increased speed and vitality. Jeserit wouldn't be setting
major land-speed records anytime soon, but her body
would be able to do more with the energy Sahana had
given her than would otherwise be possible.

The two Hounds volunteered to trail behind our
group to scout for signs of pursuit, an offer I gladly
accepted. Durra and I stepped to each side of Jeserit, not
yet putting our arms around her shoulders, but there for
her to lean on if that became necessary. Mac, Sahana,
and Charlie fell into place behind us, and I nodded.
"We're ready when you are."

Jeserit raised the scrying stone in the air, uttered a few
unintelligible words, and twirled the gold chain several
times. On its third pass, the stone flared with sapphire
energy and stood on end, pointing clearly to the east: the
same direction Charlie and I had just come from. He and
I exchanged rueful glances, then we started walking.

The difference between our earlier random blundering
around and the new situation became evident early on.
Once we passed the point where I'd come upon Charlie, we didn't find ourselves stumbling upon tracks we'd

already made in the sand. We also weren't plagued with random bursts of thick fog or disorientation, either. Jeserit and Imseti sure could cast a *mean* divination. We made more progress in twenty minutes than we had in all the hours before. Night-drenched desert quickly gave way to unexpected bog land replete with hair-curling humidity and wildlife, things the blue sand had been devoid of.

We didn't come across any signs of *sentient* life, merely gigantic, ungainly (and orange) frogs, dragon-flies the size of small bats, and dull tan crocodiles that were way more timid than their earthly counterparts. We never got closer than a few dozen feet to any of the crocs, something I couldn't say I minded. Snakes were one thing, crocodiles quite another.

On the plus side, the bog didn't try to suck us into quicksand or drive us mad with heat exhaustion and dehydration like the desert. On the minus side, mosqui-toes as big as my fist started going for as much blood as possible—and those SOBs *hurt*. I would have *killed* for a can of supernatural *Off!* but finally, we broke free of the malodorous marsh and stumbled into comparable paradise: a landscape of low-lying mountains that was neither hot nor cold, wet nor dry, with dozens upon doz-ens of caves dotting the surrounding hillsides.

We paused at the mouth of an ice-cold, mountain-fed stream to refill our canteens and allow Jeserit to take a much-needed breather. She looked up from the rushing water she'd been staring at in the moments since every-one else decided to forage for something to eat. The last thing we needed was to face any new threats with most of our party weak from hunger.

"Mijai is dead, isn't he?"

The guilty expression flashing across my face gave

me away; no sense in denying it—not that I was willing
to outright *lie* anyway. "I—I'm sorry, Jeserit, but yes, he
is. The three of them gave their lives defending your
god." Okay, so technically Anubis's priests had slaugh-
tered them to gain enough Death magic to kick Imseti
out of his body, but that was playing semantics. They
very much *had* given their lives for Imseti and deserved
to be honored accordingly.

Tears shone in Jeserit's eyes, but she didn't allow
them to fall. "I—think I felt it when they fell, sometime
during the divination, but I didn't want to admit it. It was
like . . . if I could just do that damned spell right, maybe
I'd find out I was wrong. Maybe—maybe the scrying
stone would lead us back to Mijai, and we could finish
this together. Gods, I sound so stupid, don't I?"

I hesitantly reached out and touched her shoulder
when she didn't recoil. "Not at all, Jeserit. I—just a few
months ago, I lost the Fury who was like a sister to me.
We were close before either of us Fledged, and watching
her die knowing that I failed to save her was like losing
a piece of my soul."

She shuddered, and one of the tears managed to break
free, trickling down her pale cheek before slipping to the
ground, where it would soon be absorbed into the nearby
stream: The gods-bedamned circle of life.

"That's it exactly." Her hands went to her belly and
cradled it exactly the way Serise did hers. I held my
breath. "I hadn't even gotten the chance to tell him . . .
tell him we'd finally been blessed with the baby we'd
wanted for so long. I think he guessed, though, and *that*
was the real reason he insisted I go with you when he
is—was—a hundred times more powerful than I. I

wasn't thinking straight when I offered to stay. It's still so strange to think . . ."

Son of a . . . I gritted my teeth. So not only did I have to worry about saving *one* pregnant woman, I had *two* to think about. Annoyance flared. Surely Imseti had figured *that* out when he helped with the divination, if he hadn't known already . . . Most likely he had but hadn't wanted to betray her trust until she chose to share the news. *Unlike certain* other *betrayal-happy gods I could name.*

I forced myself to speak softly. "You're right, he probably *did* guess. I've noticed a lot of husbands pick up on that even before their wives do. It's obvious he loved you both very much." Several more tears shadowed the first, and all I could do was rub her shoulder softly. There were no other words I could offer, certainly nothing that would bring back the father of her child. That seemed to be all she needed in that moment. Soon her tears dried, and she pushed to her feet with resolve glinting in her eyes.

"I'm going to guide you to the Hall, both because it's the right thing to do and to honor my husband's memory. I hope you'll understand that my first priority must then become seeing my child to safety. He—or she—is all I have left of *him.*"

A wistful smile crossed my face as I stood. "I understand and would have insisted myself, now that I know." I couldn't help but wonder if Scott and I would ever reach that stage. He had made it clear he wanted children, and part of me would love to see mini-Scotts running all over the place. The other part, however, wondered just how fair it would be to have children when one parent worked as a soldier-for-hire and the other was *two* times a cop. Look at Mijai and Jeserit—they'd been innocuous-enough priests caught in the cross fire of a power struggle among immortals—and one parent was dead, and the other might soon be. Their child would be, at best, fatherless and, at worst, not even born before moving on to the underworld. Scott and I were *paid* to put our lives on the line on a regular basis. There would be no semiretired Nan to raise our children like Mom had had, not to mention a mundane father who *didn't* regularly risk life and limb.

Unless . . . unless there will *be a Nan to depend upon. You forgot to ask Imseti if he'd seen her shade, you idiot!*

Before I could criticize myself *too* severely, Scott and Elliana bounded up, big canine grins on their snouts after they each dropped a sizeable green rabbit at my feet. *Okay,* those *must have been a bitch to track in the grass . . .* I made a face—more for the unnatural color than the bloodstained condition of their offerings. Yeah, I'm an unabashed carnivore.

"Good Hounds," I remarked dryly because they seemed to expect praise for their mad hunting skills; then I pointed to the frigid stream. "Now wash that blood off." They whined unhappily, but when I bared my teeth, they scampered off to obey. Fury trumped Hound on the alpha-meter, at least when they were in animal form.

I turned my attention to the M&M-colored hares and frowned. Okay, so I was a meat eater, but I'd never claimed to be a hunter or trapper. Jeserit took pity and apparently had more practical knowledge than I; she borrowed the blade Scott had given me earlier and went to work skinning the rabbits. Seemed fair, really, considering that she needed to eat, and I didn't.

By the time a cleaned-up Scott and Elliana returned in human form, so had the others, and Jeserit had the makings for a decent supper of rabbit garnished with bizarre but nonpoisonous (they had me taste to be sure) vegetables and a dozen eggs stolen from the nests of a bird that sounded like a cross between a pink flamingo and a piranha on steroids. *I* wouldn't have wanted to eat any of it, but everyone else seemed to manage just fine. Then again, it *had been* nearly an entire day since they'd eaten, a day complete with forced marches in subpar conditions and multiple deadly fights to cap it off.

Feeling full and refreshed, the others insisted we could keep pushing on, which had me secretly grateful. The Mandate's ticking deadline throbbed in the back of my brain, never letting me forget that time was running short. Durra seemed to share my sense of urgency— she'd barely touched her portion of food and coaxed the others on to greater speeds when any of them seemed to slow down. Then again, it *was* in her mother's best interests for us to beat that stupid deadline—something I was beginning to believe Ala had imposed to increase *our* chance of failure and her lover's chance for success.

Jeserit's trusty scrying stone led us on an unerringly eastern path for another hour, up and down fortunately low, easy-to-climb *mountains* more like the Ozarks than the Rockies. She paused at the foot of another overgrown hill to consult the stone once more, doing the usual spiel of lifting the chain, chanting mumbo jumbo, and twirling the stone above the ground; only this time nothing happened. Jeserit frowned and repeated the whole process but with the same disappointing results.

My heart sank. "What's wrong?"

She pursed her lips and kept spinning the stone's

chain. "Well, either someone's blocking the magic, or we're nearly there."

I knew which option *I* would prefer. "And how do we tell which?"

"I keep doing this until the damn thing works again— or we're ambushed." My expression must have been suitably dark because she shrugged. "Divination is not an exact science under the best of circumstances, Nemesis, but I'm leaning toward the theory that the Hall must be—" The scrying stone suddenly burst into incandescent blue mixed with silver and pointed directly below, something that appeared puzzling since there were no cave entrances to be found where we currently stood. Jeserit cursed and tried once more, only for the stone to flare with even more silver light and point to the exact same spot.

I huffed out a breath. "It seems both Imseti and the stone insist the path for our destination lies below." I turned to arch a brow at Charlie. "Think you could check to see if we're missing something?"

He nodded, face appearing much less haggard than when he'd had to rearrange the earth several hours earlier. The rest of us stayed out of Charlie's way as he paced around the spot where Jeserit had been standing, channeled earth every so often, then widened his search area by a few feet at a time. Frustration had just started to etch his face when the ground trembled, and he let out a satisfied call. "Here!" We hurried over and found him gesturing to—an innocuous rock wall carved into the nearest hillside. Charlie frowned when we started at it in puzzlement, then he caught on to the problem. He murmured something in Latin and stepped *into* the wall.

I rubbed my eyes, but reality didn't bend. Still the same rock wall standing a few feet away, blocking our path, but then Charlie reappeared, and *I* figured out what was going on. "Illusion spell?"

He nodded with a grin. "Pretty good one, too. I tried erasing it, but apparently it only worked for me. Here, I'll mark it so everyone can see." A few swipes of the heavy axe he always carried sent several chunks of stone flying and outlined a vaguely rectangular shape in the wall, large enough for two of Charlie to pass through side by side.

"So what's on the other side?"

"An underground tunnel pretty much like the one we popped into."

Of *course* it couldn't have been a three-ring circus or a gigantic castle perched on picturesque Scottish moors. No, we were stuck with more subterranean enclosed spaces.

I insisted on taking point position and the initial leap of faith through Charlie's rock doorway. Okay, not so much a leap as a stumble, but it got the job done. Magic teased my skin as I crossed the cavern's threshold. My left foot caught on a crack, and I not so gracefully found my balance before falling flat on my face. Once steady, I moved away from the entrance and surveyed my surroundings. Dull gray floors pocked with miniature fissures and stone rubble, matching walls that also boasted glowing purple lichen, and dank air that inspired gooseflesh. Although strange, the lichen provided sufficient illumination that I was able to avoid any other near tumbles while waiting for the others to file in. Their spectral glow also allowed me to see clearly the tall, dark, and handsome god who stepped out of a nearby tunnel.

Not Anubis, but that didn't mean a damned thing considering the sheer number of lesser immortals he had at his beck and call. Retreat seemed the wisest course of action, especially since the others were taking their own sweet time coming through. My back slammed against a barrier that shouldn't have been there, and the deity's hands gesturing wildly told me *why* no one had followed me in. He'd blocked them.

Option Number Two it is then.

Nike hissed in agreement as I surged forward, talons front and center, intending to demonstrate just how well a demigoddess measured up to a lesser god, but then something unexpected happened. Silver light flared over the deity's head and flickered furiously, shaping into an octagon that very much resembled a stop sign. The whole thing reminded me very much of when Imseti had taken over Charlie's body to speak with me, and I froze. Could this be Imseti's hijacked body under the navigation of a mere arcane?

The light dissipated when I broke off my attack, hands still lifted but mind racing to consider my options. Could I help Imseti oust the interloper somehow? A full-blown god by my side just about then would be worth his weight in platinum. The shade we kicked out could then be sent back in figurative pieces as a warning to his Jackal-Faced gang leader and—

The imposter god's face shimmered and transformed into a visage familiar to me, someone I'd regarded fondly until innocent puppy love blossomed into uncomfortable sexual advances and resentment toward the man I loved; someone neither of us had seen since the day renegade Sidhe clones had—so we all believed—abducted him.

Scott's baby brother Sean shot me a devastatingly devilish grin. "Honey, I'm home."

CHAPTER FIFTEEN

THE SENSE OF SHOCK—AND BETRAYAL—HAD me gasping for breath. "*What* the hell are you doing in Duat?"

"It's good to see you, too, Riss. Shouldn't you be happy to see me? Heard you've been looking for me high and—most especially low." He chuckled at the stupid pun: calm, collected, and—damn him—sexy as sin, *sin* being the most operative word. He wore much the same getup as he had the last time I'd seen him: tight blue jeans, white sleeveless shirt, and way too much confidence for someone as young as he. Then again, if Imseti and appearances could be believed, he *had* helped Anubis take over another god's physical form . . .

I forced my eyes to meet his. He looked like he'd grown up a lot in the past several months, which pissed me off considering how hard we'd been looking for him, and he hadn't bothered to let us know he was alive and apparently quite well. I gritted my teeth and tried to keep my voice neutral. I needed to stall him until I figured out how loyal to Anubis he really was, or the others managed to break through his spell. "Of course, *we've* been searching for you high and low. Nobody kidnaps one of *our* own and gets away with it."

Despite my stressing the words *we've* and *our*, he seemed to turn that into *me*, *myself*, and *I*. "Oh yeah, my Fury's lost none of her edge."

Something in his now freaky, silver-rimmed eyes had me narrowing my own. "The Sidhe didn't kidnap you outside that facility, did they?" Gears started turning in my brain as I began putting unwanted pieces together. His repeated attempts to seduce me—clumsily but enthusiastically—whenever Scott wasn't around; the times it seemed like someone inside the Murphy compound was feeding information to the assassins Stacia sent to drive me into Turning Harpy; the Sidhe who escaped from Stacia's secret laboratory when we freed Amaya and the others, only to find out they'd hijacked Sean along with his getaway car. We'd originally assumed they needed a driver and held on to him as a hostage just in case. But now . . .

"It was you."

"What was me, love?"

I let the *love* slide. "Feeding information to the enemy. There *was* a traitor in the family." Jesus. I couldn't take a step without tripping over yet another one. Sweet, baby-faced Sean—the Murphy nobody would ever suspect. Not even me.

"Ah, love, you wound me. I don't consider myself a traitor, merely a man seeking his place in the world, out of the shadow of his *big brother*." He spat the last two words as if they tasted bitter.

Rage stirred quietly. "You *do* realize you nearly got us killed several times over?"

His tone became affectionate. "I would *never* do anything to hurt you, Marissa. Everything I've done, I've done for you. Nothing I told them would have hurt you or the ones you love. Well"—his voice grew hard—"I didn't know you'd show up with Scott that day at Faneuil Hall."

The hair along the back of my neck rose. That day at Faneuil Hall, the day Scott's friend Harper lost one of her lives to a Sidhe clone impersonating Scott. It made much more sense to hear that Sean had set the mad scientists to try to capture her that day since they'd attacked her before my electronically tracked ass had shown up with Scott.

"Sean, what the hell do you want?"

He sighed. "So single-minded in purpose. Just one of the things I love about you. Gods, I hope my little girl takes after you."

His little girl? Sean didn't have . . . a . . . daughter. Nausea burned a hole in my stomach when a sickening thought occurred to me. We'd never figured out just *where* Vanessa's captors had gotten the Hound DNA they'd spliced with Fury and Sidhe when they impregnated her.

"You—you *raped* my best friend? *You* did that to her?" Nausea faded as Rage sent metaphysical sparks dancing along my skin. Nike spat venom toward him. My hands curled, and I was halfway toward Sean before conscious thought caught up and I forced myself to go very, very still. I couldn't rip Scott's baby brother limb from limb because he currently had control of a deity's body, meaning he *couldn't* be killed. Besides which, love for Scott dictated I find out if he could be swayed to our side *before* I set to maiming.

Sean stayed equally still but stared into my eyes earnestly. "No, gods no, Riss. I'd *never* force myself on any woman, especially not someone you cared about so much. I didn't even know the scientists I volunteered my, um, sample to had Vanessa."

Slowly, I beat the Rage back to a more controllable level. "So, wait, it's okay to help them take Harper, let them take your own freaking *sister*, because *I* didn't care about them?"

He let out a frustrated breath. "They just wanted to know where Scott would be that morning, so when he called me to check in and mentioned Faneuil Hall, I passed that info on to them. Far as I knew they just wanted to take samples from him and Harper and let them go. And I would *never* have helped them if I'd known about Amaya. She's my big sis." Affection laced his words, an affection he used to show for Scott. I wondered what the hell had happened to change his feelings for his brother so drastically. It couldn't just be that his boyhood crush on me had grown into something much darker.

"Okay, so let's take a step back." He didn't seem in a rush to attack, and the others appeared just as unhurried in breaking through his blocking spell. "Are you saying you had no clue that these—scientists—you were working for were behind all the arcane abductions the past few years?"

He shook his head emphatically. "I may have been . . . naïve . . . by buying into what they told me, but as far as

I knew, the medical experiments I volunteered for were meant to help the less fertile arcane races by crossing their genes with those arcanes who have no such problems, like Hounds and Cats. The whole reason I cooperated with them to begin with was because one of Anubis's priests asked me to. He *did* tell me the scientists had some Sidhe they were using, but that all their Sidhe had been created in the lab from frozen DNA captured during the War."

If by frozen DNA they meant the several dozen Sidhe they held in captivity over the decades following the Peace Accord, until one by one those last Trueborn Sidhe became too dangerous to hold against their will any longer. Stacia's mortal pawns— the scientists who apparently recruited Sean to their cause—had successfully bred full-blooded Sidhe children off their more independent-minded parents, then started an illegal cloning project where they crossbred and genetically manipulated other arcane races with Sidhe DNA. All in an attempt to breed their own supernaturally enhanced army so they could subjugate the arcanes they viewed as enemy infiltrators. Of course, Stacia had planned to double-cross them, claim the army for her own, and divide and conquer the mortals instead.

Yeah, arcanes could be just as bad as the average Jerry Springer guest.

"So how did you find out about"—I only shuddered on the inside—"your little girl, then?"

His gaze softened, "When I saw you holding her outside the compound, I just knew she had to be mine. Once your brother and Vanessa's sister adopted Olivia, there was no doubt. She is *mine*. Just like you should be."

Okay, so one step forward with him, two steps back.

I clenched my fists and turned the full force of a Rage-fueled scowl his way, glowing green eyes and all. "Since you seem determined not to pick up on my subtle and even not-so-subtle hints, let me say this straight up. I am not now, nor will I ever be, *yours*. I am my own, and I am in love with Scott. You know, your brother. Where's that Warhound loyalty I'm always hearing about?"

"I'm plenty loyal to those who matter. Like my Lord Anubis. Like, just as importantly, *you*. And I didn't risk pissing Anubis off just to see you again. I came to warn you."

I ran a hand along Nike's scales and attempted to funnel off the remaining dregs of Rage. Hearing that he was willing to anger his deity in order to pass along a warning indicated he might not be completely lost to us. "Oh yeah?"

"Yeah. I know you came to Duat as Nemesis obviously." He gestured to my black leather and serpent. "And Anubis knows you're headed to the Hall. He's waiting for you, and you don't stand a chance against him. He's also taken out insurance that you won't *want* to stand against him even if you could."

Well, *that* lack of confidence in my abilities stung a little, especially coming from someone who usually acted like I'd hung the moon. "Forgive me if I don't exactly rush to take advice from one of his lapdogs, especially one who seems so willing to betray his family by allowing them all to believe him *missing* or *dead* all this time. Your mother has been worried out of her mind for you."

His fists clenched, but he merely nodded. "Fair enough, I should have let at least Mom know I'm all right, but she of all people would understand what I'm doing for our lord."

I couldn't hold back a laugh. "What?" My gesture to *his* body was contemptuous. "Helping him abduct the bodies of his law-abiding opponents, kicking them out of their rightful bodies and breaking a dozen immortal precepts in the process? Yeah, I'm sure she'd be *real* proud."

"You don't under—"

Rage flooded my body, and I strode forward, putting my face right into his. "I understand right versus wrong, good versus evil; and, honey, you're *definitely* playing for Team Evil right now. Pretty it up any way you see fit, but it comes down to this: Anubis has murdered innocents with magic and broken more than one immortal law. *I* have been chosen to act as Nemesis in bringing him to justice, and I *will not rest* until that has been done. His power-hungry ass is going down, and so help me gods, Sean, if you stand in my way, I will take *your* pretty little ass down right along with him."

"Please calm down, Riss; I'm not here to challenge you. I just want your safety." His right hand dipped inside his pocket and fiddled with something. "I want safety for you both."

I tensed. "What's that inside your pocket?" He gave a casual shrug, and Rage stirred again. I let it change my eyes to silver-rimmed, Rage-enhanced green. "You don't want to fuck around with me right now, Sean. Trust me on that. Now, take it out slowly."

He did as I asked, withdrawing his hand one careful inch at a time.

I kept my body loose and ready—for a weapon, his wallet, loose change—anything but what actually emerged. A wrinkled but perfectly clear picture showing two of the people I loved most: Cori and her adopted

sister, Olivia, biological daughter to not only Vanessa,
but apparently the cocky young man standing in front of
me. Cori lay on a blanket outside the family home in
Salem helping her infant sister sit up, both girls all sun-
shine and smiles and in perfect focus. Sean had to have
gotten fairly up close and personal to take the picture.
The fact he let me see this meant something critical: He
wanted me to know that he—and thus Anubis—could
get close to his daughter anytime he wanted.

A growl passed my lips, and I danced the hair-trigger
edge separating Fury from Harpy, wanting nothing more
in that moment than to go ballistic on his ass. Scott's
baby brother or not; capable of being saved from Anubis's
brainwashing or not; having risked his own safety to
come and warn me or not. He *dared* show that picture to
me when I was already keyed up? He *had* to know the
Fury in me would see it as a threat and react accordingly.
Young Sean might be, but he was not stupid.

Or was he? The light in his eyes grew bolder,
almost . . . excited. Yes, that was it exactly. He *wanted* to
see me all hot and bothered. Judging by the way his
breath came in quicker pants and he licked his lips, seeing me like this was getting *him* hot and bothered in
another way entirely. My gaze made the inevitable drop
downward and discovered proof positive that Sean was
turned on in a big way. Rage burned even hotter, but I
fought it back—or at least, I tried.

My hand snapped up and back so fast the slap to his
cheek rang out before I consciously realized what I was
doing. Blood flooded to the spot I'd hit, revealing the
bright red outline of fingers. Sean grabbed my hands and
squeezed, but not in vengeance. He used his superior
strength as a full-blown immortal to try to force my arms

around him in an unwanted embrace. Magic responded to my call and washed along my skin, granting me enough strength to yank my hands away from his. Sean's wince when newly formed talons pierced his skin made me smile. The bastard deserved so much worse.

"Final warning, puppy boy. Hijacked immortal powers or not, stay *away* from me *and* mine. If you *ever* dare touch me without permission again, I'll forget my promise to spare you for your family's sake." I dug my claws into his skin a little deeper. "Fuck with my nieces or me one more time, and I'll see you tortured in the afterlife as well, which won't be too hard once the Triad takes down your Jackal-Assed god and finds out what *you've* done in his name."

He choked out a protest, but I lashed out with my dominant foot and kicked for all I was worth. He hit the rock with a sharp *thunk*, head cracking against solid stone soon after his back did, and he went out like a light. His expression was comically surprised as his silver-rimmed eyes fluttered shut, and he slid to the ground in a heap. Useful to know that immortals *could* be knocked out if one applied sufficient force.

Nike slithered along my arms, forked tongue flicking in Sean's direction. I caressed the serpent while I wrestled Rage back to manageable levels.

Are you sure *we can't just kill him now?*

Laughter burst out without my intending it, and I patted her again. *I'm sure. Besides, we* can't *kill him while he's still possessing Imseti's body.*

Oh yeah. She sounded disappointed. *What are you going to do with him, then? He'll just go back to Anubis when he wakes up. And if Scott sees him here like that . . .*

Ugh. *That* would devastate Scott even more than it had me. The others—especially Jeserit—would neither care that Sean was Scott's brother nor want to risk his coming back later to betray us still further. All Jeserit would see is someone who helped Anubis kill her husband and the interloper responsible for ousting her god. Both true, as far as that went, but life was never as black and white as mundanes liked to pretend it was. I *couldn't* kill Sean unless in self-defense: Doing *that* would seal the final nail in the coffin for my relationship with Scott. I might have come to terms with the thought of sacrificing Scott's life if necessary to complete my mission, but damned if I would kill his love for me with my own two hands.

Cursing under my breath all the while, I dragged Sean's inert body behind a rock outcropping a couple of dozen feet away. Once convinced nobody would be able to see him from a distance, I scurried back to the cavern entrance and put my hand out warily—only to have it grabbed and myself hauled outside.

Scott pulled me into his arms and practically squeezed the breath out of me. "Gods damn it, Riss, what were you *doing* in there? You scared us all out of our minds."

I accepted his burst of overprotectiveness gracefully since it reassured me I'd just made the right choice, both to break free of Sean's manipulation and to hide his ill-gotten body until I figured out how to safely switch him and Imseti back. The others crowded in and reassured themselves I was safe. While their concern was flattering, I had no clue how long Sean would be out cold—considering his current immortality, probably not long—and needed to sneak everyone past him like five minutes ago. Especially since he'd been so kind as to confirm we *were* on the right path to the Hall of Two Truths.

"Yes, yes, I'm fine. And that—whatever *that* was— didn't come from me. I was trapped inside the same as you were out here. It could have been some sort of latent defense mechanism"—not a lie, it *could* have been—"but it wore off. I suggest we step through two at a time so no one's trapped alone, and make it snappy. No telling if it will happen again."

Predictably, Scott insisted on going through with me, and *I* insisted we be first. It took every ounce of will-power I could muster to resist glancing at the spot where I'd stashed Sean, but Scott made it easier by hurrying forward to investigate the tunnel from which his brother had originally appeared. We scouted a short way ahead of the others but learned nothing particularly useful other than the fact the DayGlo lichen grew along the tunnel's walls, too. Within minutes we had all congregated inside the tunnel, and Jeserit confirmed our path via the scrying stone, which pointed the way deeper into the earth.

The tunnel remained wide enough for us to proceed in pairs though I itched to order Scott to the rear of the pack even though that was a stupid urge. First of all, nothing said he'd be any safer back there—especially not if Sean caught up to us before we reached our destination. Secondly, I had no chance of convincing him to go, not after that blocking-spell fiasco and not without a better reason than "I'm immortal, and I said so."

I must have snickered out loud because he tilted his head questioningly. "Oh, I was just thinking how I was stupid enough to think cleaning up the Sisterhood's problems would somehow be less stressful than that serial-killer case. And yet, here we are."

He managed a small smile. "Yeah, making our way through another underground tunnel—which creep you out—with several dozen renegade deities and their flunkies on our trail, hoping we can make it to Ma'at's Feather before *they* make it to us. Suddenly hunting down one measly murderer doesn't seem so bad."

One of the things I loved about Scott was his humor in dark situations because it so mirrored my own. If you couldn't laugh in the face of danger—especially when 85 percent of your life *was* danger—then you'd flash and burn out, no longer able to find joy in life and making you that much closer to becoming a bad guy yourself. Or turn into someone like my old *pal*, Tony Zalawski, who took pleasure in other people's pain and fit in perfectly with the drug dealers his new undercover gig with Narcotics pitted him against. There was a difference between laughing *with* the world and laughing *at* it.

I'd prepared myself for another lengthy subterranean voyage through meandering tunnels, so was surprised when we reached a dead end a mere half hour later. The corridor we'd been traversing opened out into a cavern the size of a soccer field, but that was it. No further tunnels to take, no adjoining caverns to explore, just a chamber lined with rocky outcroppings and the interminable glowing lichen.

Panic threatened, but I fought it down. "Jeserit?"

She nodded and raised the scrying stone's chain once more. To my surprise, the stone didn't stay quiet as I'd feared. It lit up with sapphire energy and made like a compass arrow, pointing straight at the far wall, which was all but hidden beneath a lichen infestation. Jeserit let out an annoyed breath and shook her head. "I'm sorry but . . . the divination tells me that our path lies ahead, no matter what our eyes— Wait. Another illusion spell?"

My eyes widened at that suggestion since it was a valid one. I started forward, but Scott laid a hand on my shoulder and turned toward our resident earth expert. "Charlie?"

The Giant trotted forward, stopping a few feet in front of the glowing wall to begin working his mojo. The ground rumbled beneath his feet, but nothing else happened. Charlie clenched his hands, gestured, and chanted loudly, only to wind up with the same result. Nothing. He finally accepted defeat and shrugged in my direction. "Sorry, darlin', not seeing anything there but the radioactive lichen."

Elliana's Hound eyes flashed, and she cursed. "Don't *tell* me we came all this way for nothing!" Mac touched her shoulder and murmured something in her ear that kept her from leaping at the wall as if it were an enemy although, in that moment, it kinda was . . .

My gaze zeroed in on the center of the wall and a patch of lichen that looked a hell of a lot like a deliberate pattern. I frowned and stepped forward. Scott grumbled in protest, but I waved it off. Imseti and Mijai had possessed complete confidence in Jeserit's divination skills, and thus far, I'd seen nothing to indicate that faith was misplaced. Quite the contrary, really, considering Sean's showing up to try to convince me to abandon my Mandate. He'd claimed to be going against Anubis's wishes to warn me that the Jackal-Faced god waited for me outside the Hall to stop me, but what if Anubis had actually put him up to it? What if this was just another trick to throw me off track and get me to give up before I even reached the Hall?

Fat chance of that*!*

I peered more closely at the patch of lichen, and sure enough, it more closely resembled some sort of intentional symbol than a haphazard mishmash of a living organism. Maybe if I stepped back a little . . . No, that didn't put it into any clearer focus, but my hunch grew stronger that something important was missing. If I could just find that vital link, everything would fall into place, like when Jeserit had activated the scrying stone and—

That's it! My pulse accelerated. I drew the borrowed blade, made a few quick slashes, then tossed a hair-and-blood-covered piece of skin onto the lichen patch's center. Silver-and-blue light exploded, and a portion of the lichen similarly flashed with purple opalescence, clearly forming the Egyptian hieroglyph most people—even mundanes—at least recognized, if not understood: the ankh, a stylized loop at the top that twisted into the bottom three-fourths of a cross below, which traditionally translated to mean *eternal life.* Murmurs broke out behind me, but I ignored them. The ankh faded as quickly as it appeared, then writhed before my eyes to form a new symbol: the ankh reversed, which in the arcane world symbolized death, or at least the time a shade spent in the underworld before facing Reckoning and either rebirth, reward, or damnation. One final flare of energy and one more symbol took shape: a simple set of scales, bearing on one end a modified ankh—this one having a heart on the top instead of a loop, symbolizing an individual's soul—and upon the other an elaborate ostrich feather.

Ma'at's Feather and Scales! I let out a hiss matched by Nike, nestled atop my shoulder. I braced myself, but even then wasn't prepared for what happened. The wall before me disappeared—but so did the world around me, including my lover and allies. A shimmering silver-and-blue portal beckoned from just ahead of me. I peered into the inky blackness that lay behind but could see nothing, not even the slightest hint of light or color. Nike wound down to my lower arm, as unsettled as I. I sent a questing tendril of magic, but it faded almost immediately, making me blink in surprise. Panic flared, but I fought it back and did the only thing I could, turned and stepped forward . . .

Magic enveloped me as it had when I stepped through the earlier illusion spell, but this was neither gentle nor dispassionate. Despair and a sense of insignificance flooded into me, threatening to send me to my knees in a crying mess, but I gritted my teeth and reminded myself of everything and everyone I was fighting for. A dispassionate voice echoed inside my head much the way my Amphisbaena finally could: *Turn back now or your life is forfeit!* I realized this was some sort of test and made myself take a second step forward . . .

Despair became an aching desire to flee responsibility, to cast off my duties as Nemesis and return to my normal existence as Boston cop and Chief of the MCU, except that wasn't particularly accurate. *Nothing* about my life was normal, not even my relationship with Scott . . . That disembodied voice whispered inside my head again. *Your lover would never sacrifice so much for you. Just turn around before you lose your soul.* But Scott *had* sacrificed a tremendous amount for me: his relationship with his personal god. That thought made me cry out and push myself another painful inch ahead . . .

Hatred boiled, but it wasn't my own; this came from all directions and burned its way inside, liquid fire making me scream in frustrated Rage. They would *pay* for what they had done, pay with every mortal breath until Duat flooded in a sea of souls. Starting with Scott and Mac and ending with Mom and Nan, images of them each being tortured and killed flashed into my brain, making it impossible to resist the urge to turn and run to their aid. My body started to pivot, but then Nike's fangs nipped my hand, bringing me back to myself. I took a grateful breath and found the strength to take another shaking step . . .

An avalanche of pain forced me to my knees, the inexorable agony sweeping along my every nerve ending much like my initial portal journey into Duat. Tears flooded my eyes, and I screamed for what felt like hours, again and again until my voice went hoarse, cried and screamed but forced myself to endure the pain. *Why do you insist on hurting yourself so? You have but to turn around, and the pain will stop! Wouldn't that be so much easier?* Whoever this mental voice belonged to obviously didn't know me very well. I'd never taken the *easy* route in my life. Eventually I found the sheer determination to stumble to my feet and press another step forward . . .

And found myself standing in the shadow of an honest-to-gods pyramid, one that had been carved from black granite and towered a dizzying height upward that should have been impossible underground, but then I blinked and realized that a million glittering pinpoints in the ceiling were actually stars, and what I'd taken for a ceiling was actually a midnight skyscape blazing with celestial light. My breath caught in my chest, and I could only stare skyward, transfixed.

Then the vocalized version of that unemotional mental

voice claimed my attention. "Long has it been since a Nemesis dared venture into my Hall. Born a mortal, reborn an arcane, then supping the essence of immortals to become one for a fleeting moment. The only time someone who has not yet tasted death but someday *will* may enter my domain—and then only because she feels herself equal to me. Equal to Ma'at, Regulator of the Stars and Seasons, She Who Brings Balance and Sees into the Hearts of All. How dare *you*, Nemesis who shall someday face her own Reckoning, step into my Hall as if you belong here now?"

Did I just call that voice unemotional? Perhaps it began that way, but by the end of that tirade the voice trembled with disdain and loathing and Rage, the same supernatural Rage that fueled a Fury's abilities and gave her the nerve to carry on even in the face of overwhelming odds—and sudden insight told me a world-shaking truth: That similarity was not just figurative, it was literal. I somehow knew the answer she sought.

"Because I *do* belong here by virtue of being one of your daughters, She Who Brings Balance—or as you are called in your Grecian guise, Nyx."

CHAPTER SIXTEEN

AN EAR-PIERCING CHIME RANG OUT, AND MY surroundings vanished once more, only to be replaced by what was obviously the interior of the subterranean pyramid. I stumbled slightly as my mind struggled to catch up. Black granite walls towered overhead, but rich tapestries broke up their stark grandeur, each showing Reckoning scenes from myriad mythologies, all having just one thing in common: immortal beings passing judgment upon mortals or arcanes whose faces looked eerily similar no matter whether African, European, Asian, or Egyptian. Mother Reckoner in all her aspects.

Although, when I looked closer, none of the tapestries near me contained Ma'at in all Her glory. Then footsteps sounded behind me, and I turned, only to find out why that was so. Here in Duat, Mother Reckoner *personified* Ma'at in all Her glory.

She walked in beauty like the night, as a famous poet once claimed, with skin as dark as the granite around us. Her eyes were golden orbs edged in silver that shone more intensely than any star ever could; and she wore a simply cut toga in the fashion of immortals, though hers was an iridescent charcoal that shimmered in the light rather than boring white. The filigree belt wrapped around her waist formed a traditional mythological symbol: a serpent devouring its own tail. The closer she drew, the more awe burned inside me until finally I could stand it no more and threw myself onto the ground. *How* had I dared what I just had, to claim this dazzling being as mother in even a figurative sense? Logic reared its ugly head, too, and doubt only multiplied. Furies did not swear themselves to any one deity, only taking oaths to the *Gens Immortalis* as a whole, then their specific Fury class. Each class might claim its original founder as *nominal* mother, but it wasn't like any of them were literally our ancestors . . .

Nike shot me very amused sensations through our bond, and I blinked. *Or were they?* Had those three original Furies been literal sisters, born from one immortal mother and eventually going on to birth subsequent generations of Furies? Mortal genetic science would have disputed that possibility, but magic and arcane life spans made it an all-too-real possibility.

Apparently my sense of unworthiness showed upon my face. "Rise, daughter, and stop being foolish." That voice had many elements in common with the earlier except it very much trembled with emotion and had a distinctly feminine quality. It also brooked absolutely no argument, and so, I found myself rising without conscious intent. Looking into Ma'at's eyes up close was even more intimidating, but I did my best to obey her command to act like the demigoddess I was. She looked me over from head to toe, her movements drawing attention to the over-sized ostrich feather adorning her midnight-dark hair—hair that shimmered identically to my own.

I let out another deep breath. "You really *are* mother to Furykind."

She smiled a distinctly pleased smile. "Surely you know the alternate story for how the Erinyes came to be, that tells of the goddess Nyx giving birth to them without aid of a father."

"Yes, but—many of mankind's myths are merely that: stories so convoluted by the passing of time, they bear little resemblance to reality."

Her pleasure only increased. "Indeed, but in this particular instance they got it right, at least partially. My three Fury daughters *did* have fathers, each an amazing specimen of his mortal race: Egyptian, Grecian, and what most now refer to as Native American. Alecto, Megaera, and Tisiphone made me extremely proud, as do their many-times-great-grandchildren today, not least of all you, Marissa Eurydice Holloway."

My body shivered involuntarily when she spoke my full name. In her voice it seemed almost magical. "I—I—thank you, Mother."

No matter how impudent it felt to call her that, I could tell how much it pleased her. Then again, it shouldn't have been such a huge surprise; she'd said how rarely Nemeses made the journey to see her in the Underworld, and her duties there meant she probably didn't see much of her birth children, who dwelt in the immortal realms not directly tied to the Underworld. She seemed almost . . . lonely.

And why shouldn't she be? Nike chided. *Haven't you learned how very much we* are *our Creators' children?*

Meaning they felt emotions every bit as much as we did.

Ma'at narrowed her eyes in annoyance when a man wearing a white toga and wielding a golden spear stepped forward but allowed him to murmur into her ear. The look that crossed her face then was way more than annoyed, more like positively pissed off. He finished delivering his message and bowed himself backward, sweat evident upon his brow even though his deity didn't say a single cross word to him. Still, it was *never* fun being the messenger bearing bad news, even less so when delivering that news to an immortal.

Her eyes momentarily flashed emerald green when she turned her gaze in my direction, something that had me gulping nervously. *Like mother, like daughter indeed.*

"My guardians send word that Anubis is at my gates claiming that traitorous followers of his traveled here with you and demanding they be immediately turned over to him."

My own eyes flared with angry light, and I let out the snarl she had kept locked inside. Hey, I was only *partially* immortal. "Over my cold, dead body."

She gave a fierce grin. "Oh, you are *so* much my daughter, Marissa Eurydice. I must ask, however, if he speaks the truth?"

"In a manner of speaking, Mother; two of my companions were once his followers, until they discovered he had broken not one but several divine laws and pledged themselves to my service."

Her lips curved upward again. "I suspected you

planned to invoke the Feather against some quarry, daughter, but I scarcely hoped it would be against my greatest enemy."

My turn for surprise. "I had not heard of such enmity between you. I thought . . ."

"You assumed we two had some sort of alliance because we work together for Egyptian Reckonings?" She gave a fairly admirable approximation of a snort. "Just because I *must* work with him in this guise doesn't mean I've ever enjoyed it—or respected him. Quite the contrary, and he's only grown more insufferable over the past few months though I know not why."

I rolled my eyes. "Probably the influence of his new girlfriend."

Her gaze sharpened. "Oh?" Then she shook her head. "No, time enough to hear the story later. He will not wait long, and I may not be able to stand against him in such a mood, not here in Duat. Now come then, since we must make haste."

I fell into step behind her, pulse skittering since I wasn't entirely sure of her intentions. Also, hearing that she didn't think she could keep Anubis out of her own Hall didn't inspire a whole lot of confidence. Speaking of which . . . "Where *are* my companions if Anubis had to petition you for them. Are they . . . safe?"

She nodded, though her eyes were solemn when she glanced at me over her shoulder. "Yes, since you passed your Trial of Faith, they are now."

My mouth grew suddenly dry. "T-trial? I didn't know . . . you mean if I had *failed* to make it through to the Hall, they would have . . ."

"Perished, as would have you. Well, once your ambrosia wore off. Only a *true* Nemesis may make it through to the Hall of Two Truths in *any* of its guises, and then only if her cause is just."

"But doesn't being selected by the Triad make a Nemesis's cause just by default?"

Her expression turned sardonic as she continued leading me through a dimly lit corridor. "I am the Bringer of Balance, child, no matter whether they who seek to usurp it currently work against those in power or *are* the ones in power."

Her words made a lot of sense, especially considering the point that Nike had just made: Immortals could fall prey to their emotions every bit as much as their children, and when they *did*, entire nations often felt the aftershocks.

We reached the corridor's end and came upon a group of six unsmiling guardians, who stepped aside and opened an enormous door to allow their mistress passage. She led me through the door after leaving strict instructions that *no one* else should be allowed past. I took that to mean not even Anubis and wondered how *they* could be expected to stop him if *she* didn't think she could, but then the truth hit me. The guardians weren't expected to win, only slow him down as much as possible. *That* had me swallowing nervously.

Did I make a huge mistake coming here? What does it matter if I invoke the Feather against Anubis if Ma'at herself can't even keep him out of her own temple?

Then Nike reminded me of the obvious. *Bringing him to justice isn't* her *job—it's yours, with magical assistance from the Triad. The Mother Reckoner's sole duty is to provide the proof the Triad needs to let you finish your job.*

Which was to haul Anubis's ass in front of the Triad

so they could pronounce his sentence for betrayal, not that I really knew what sort of punishment They *could* bring against someone even Their combined might would not be able to kill. And that was assuming they truly *would* be united as a whole. If what I suspected was right, and Ala *had* taken Anubis as Her lover . . .

I resisted the urge to shudder since I needed to appear strong then more than ever. Time enough to deal with *that* later; first things first: nailing Anubis's figurative ass to the wall. Or, in this case, the Hall . . .

Because once I took a good look around, I realized that we'd just stepped into the Hall of Two Truths. It was both plainer and more awe-inspiring than I'd expected. The room truly *was* a hall, stretching out much farther in length than width, with the perennial dais at the opposite end from the entrance. The floor, walls, and ceiling were made of cold white marble, something far more Greco-Roman than Egyptian in nature. My brow furrowed. Perhaps the Hall retained the same basic bones for whatever soul Mother Reckoner was judging, taking on only the barest trappings of the individual's specific religion. The temple outside clearly rested inside Egyptian-flavored Duat; but this Hall was different, tied specifically to Ma'at in *whatever* guise she wore.

I shrugged away my inner musings and continued cataloging in case I needed to beat a hasty retreat later. Nods to Duat's Egyptian heritage appeared in the form of hieroglyphics littering the walls here and there, and a narrow black carpet bearing gold-worked symbols ran along the floor from end to end. Ma'at hurried along that black fabric without outwardly seeming to. I found myself envying her serene demeanor. Then again, of the two of us, she was the only one who would never taste death's touch or have loved ones waiting in the wings who faced the same danger. Easy to pull off the serenity thing under *those* circumstances.

My infinitely-less-graceful feet scurried to keep up with the gliding goddess. Ma'at gestured to the not-unexpected pentagram etched on the floor in front of the raised platform. Oversized mirrors towered above the pentagram to the left and right, their grand scale reminding me of my not-so-pleasant journey into Anubis's realm. Ma'at reclaimed my attention by stepping onto the dais. The moment her second foot touched that platform, silver light flared, flooding the room, then flaring to a painful level before dissipating. When it did, a humongous set of scales identical to those portrayed in modern-day American courtrooms dominated the center of the platform, minus only a blindfolded Lady Justice. Cue Ma'at.

She assumed position behind the Scales, facing me standing on the pentagram. The gold metal making up the framework of the Scales towered even taller than the goddess behind them but had been fashioned so delicately that she could still be seen clearly. The physical Scales themselves sagged equidistantly below the central pillar; waiting only for the metaphysical components they would soon assist their mistress in judging. Cue *me*.

I shifted my weight nervously from one foot to the other and back again, working up my courage. Sure, I knew the *theory* behind what I was about to do, the same way I knew the theory behind having a root canal performed. Didn't mean I was in a rush to go through either . . .

Ma'at drew a slender mallet from somewhere and

lightly struck one Scale, then the other. Musical chimes far more melodious than simple scales should have been capable of producing sounded in the air, making me shudder involuntarily. The chimes struck me to the quick, inspiring a solemn sense of awe unlike anything I'd ever experienced. Seconds later, Ma'at murmured in that unintelligible immortal language I couldn't comprehend even in demigoddess form. Silver and— surprisingly enough—sapphire energy roared to life around me in the precise shape of the pentagram. Okay, cue me for real: once prompted by Ma'at.

"One who stands as Nemesis to the Triad of the *Gens Immortalis* has braved the Trial of the Hall of Two Truths and brings petition to I who stand as Mother Reckoner, currently in my guise as Ma'at, She Who Brings Balance. Tell me, Nemesis, what exactly is it that you petition?"

I forced aside my renewed sense of insignificance to stand straight and tall, in honor of my role as Nemesis if not on my own merits. "I who stand as Nemesis to the Immortal Triad petition She Who Brings Balance by my right to invoke the Feather against he who is my quarry."

Ma'at struck each scale a second time and regarded me expressionlessly. "Against whom would you invoke the Feather?"

"Against Anubis the Jackal-Headed, he who serves as Death Lord over Duat and who has sinned greatly against the *Gens Immortalis* in general and specifically against the Triad I serve." Even if one of their number might have privately disagreed.

She raised those odd musical chimes again, then pulled the ostrich feather from her hair with elaborate hand gestures, moving with fluid grace every bit as lyrical as the Scales' chimes. Before she could set the feather in its appropriate place, however, commotion broke out in the antechamber where we had left her guardians. Fear lit in her eyes, fear that sent my own pulse into overdrive and made me want to shriek at her to hurry the hell up.

Fortunately, she felt that sense of urgency without my verbal prompting and placed the Feather with much less fuss than she'd plucked it from her hair. Magic kept the Scales equally balanced—they wouldn't budge until the mystical representation of Anubis's heart was placed opposite the Feather.

Speaking of the devil . . . a terrifyingly familiar voice screamed on the other side of the Hall's entry door, a voice I hadn't heard in several years and could have gone the rest of my life quite cheerfully without. Screams answered Mr. Jackal-Faced's furious demands, screams of righteous anger and intense agony combined: the guardians giving their lives—and potentially afterlives— to honor their goddess's last request. I gritted my teeth and nodded to that goddess. Their sacrifices—like so many others—must not go in vain.

"Then do so, as is your right, Nemesis of the Triad. Invoke the Feather against Anubis the Jackal-Headed so that We may judge the weight of his sins, heart and soul."

My mouth opened to do just that, but explosive energy concussed at my back, sending me flying into the air and onto the ground just *outside* of the invoked pentagram, something that should *not* have been possible. The star's magical energy should have served as a barrier holding me inside until Ma'at banished it or someone marred the physical representation on the floor. I barely registered that fact since I was busy reeling on my hands and knees from the sheer force of the blow that had sent me sprawling. When I managed to raise my eyes, I caught sight of Ma'at chanting feverishly, hands raised but trembling as much as my body currently shook. *What* on earth—or should I say hell—had her so damned scared?

I somehow found the strength to turn my body enough to look behind me, and my heart plummeted. Anubis strode along the black carpet, body completely shrouded by an elaborately engraved gold-on-black robe, distinctive gold jackal mask glinting from beneath its hood every few steps. *That* wasn't what had me as scared shitless as Ma'at; no, *that* would be the large number of lesser gods and goddesses following in his shadow, several of whom were currently bathed in dark splashes of crimson that could only be the blood of Ma'at's guardians, who had tried—and failed—to give us the time we needed.

Jeez. Us. We are beyond *outnumbered right now.* Nike tried to project calming sensations, but she seemed just as overwhelmed as Ma'at and me. *Even if Scott and the others busted in right now, I don't think we can fight our way out of this . . .*

Anubis stalked inexorably closer, and I couldn't bear to watch, so I focused on his minions, taking stock of faces and symbols on clothing so I could rat them out to the Triad if, by some freaking miracle, I made it out of this. Although pretty much my only hope of *that* was if I made it *back* into the pentagram, reraised the magic Ma'at had summoned, and finished the Invocation—something I was willing to bet Anubis wouldn't just stand back and watch me do.

Ma'at's voice continued chanting, low enough that only I could hear, and I frowned, wondering what she might be trying to—

Harsh sirens clanged all around, sending the hands of every person in the room—save only for Anubis and Ma'at—flying up to cover ears against the incessant shrieking. The Hall itself started shaking, and all four walls faded away, only to be replaced by endless black streaked with shimmering pinpoints of light. My gaze flew back to the dais and saw a no-longer-fearful Ma'at standing there, in her Egyptian guise no more. Now she wore black leather pants and a vest similar to my own, and she glowed with a terrible silver-and-sapphire light. Nyx, primordial Goddess of the Night, Mother of the Furies, and, I was now coming to realize, the Triad's original Nemesis. Not a bad choice to have at one's side in order to make a crazy last stand against impossible numbers, all things considered.

She apparently had loftier goals than I, for she neither made an insane charge against her professed archenemy nor surrendered against what seemed overwhelming numbers. Instead, she started to . . . stall him.

"How *dare* you profane *my* sacred Hall and ceremony, Jackal-Faced traitor? Not to mention slay my guardians inside my very temple?"

Anubis stopped a dozen feet away from the pentagram, which was another dozen feet away from Ma'at—make that Nyx. I huddled halfway between the two full immortals, doing my best *not* to appear like a quivering mass of hysteria while also trying not to draw undue attention. *Gods, I hope she's even better at bluffing than I . . .*

That familiar, deep, almost androgynous voice dripped with derision. "As history has shown, one immortal law stands above all others, Ma'at: Might makes right." Anubis gestured to his minions. "Since I currently have the might, I have every right to enter whoever's temple I so desire, and to slay *any* who stand against me."

Megalomaniac much?

Ma'at-as-Nyx bared her teeth and made a sudden gesture while calling out a brief magical keyword that completed a spell she'd earlier began but left unfinished. The floor rumbled beneath our feet and, just like that, reality shifted, and the pentagram reappeared around me: fully intact and ready for me to use. Anubis let out an angry snarl, but I had already leaped into action. "I invoke Ma'at's Feather against Anubis the Jackal-Headed!" I cried it out once, twice, then thrice, a sacred number across many cultures and religions and, when used by a demigoddess inside an immortal-channeled pentagram, immutable.

Nyx's lips curved into a satisfied smirk, and she slipped into her guise as Ma'at again, her Feather gleaming atop its side of the Scales while she struck the musical chimes three more times. Anubis roared in fury, but he was too late, superior numbers or not. The black-robed, golden-masked immortal was immediately whipped inside the pentagram—against his will—and was pinned at its center by some unseen force. At the same time, a black, vaguely heart-shaped object appeared at the end of the Scale opposite the Feather. That object pulsed with silver-and-black magic much as an actual heart would have beat, but it was merely a magical stand-in, a metaphor for the blackhearted god's soul.

Ma'at chanted another indecipherable magical phrase, and the Scales began tilting wildly, first one way, then the other. Her head jerked back, and she glowed with inner fire, hair snapping in the wind much like a gorgon's serpents would have done. She continued chanting, but her language changed from immortal to ancient Egyptian, one I could actually understand with just a bit of magical effort. I made that effort so I could comprehend her words, which turned out to be a recitation of the good deeds—and correspondingly bad—of the immortal seething just behind me. I could *feel* the rage pouring off him in waves that rivaled a Fury's magic-enhanced anger even though I couldn't see *him*, at least not until I glanced over my shoulder for a glimpse. I allowed a tiny smile to cross my lips. He deserved to suffer way more than that, but at least it was a start. He was forced to stand impotent at the center of the pentagram while Ma'at proclaimed his most notable sins for all to hear. I was surprised that she had to get through a whole lot of good before the bad, but then I shook my head at my own folly. *No one* was all good *or* evil, not even me or, conversely, my psycho former mentor.

My mouth dropped open when I realized that specific person had not come into my mind out of sheer coincidence: Stacia herself had just run into the room, accompanied by the same Anubian priests we had left behind in Boston's Underbelly. All were robed, and several wore deep cowls that concealed their faces; one caught my attention by waddling more than walking.

I forced my eyes away and cursed beneath my breath, with Nike echoing my sentiments mentally. We were trapped, however, forced to remain in the magical circle lest we disrupt Ma'at's spell and free Anubis from his Reckoning. All I could do was hope and pray that Mother Reckoner could hold Anubis's minions off while she finished . . . Scarcely seconds had passed before another group rushed into the Hall of Two Truths, mak-

ing such a commotion I glanced over my shoulder fear-
fully once more, only to catch sight of my grandmother's
shade leading a ragtag band of spectral reinforcements:
the Cat shade being chivvied by my own lovely Nemesis; Mijai and his fellow Imsetian priests who had sacrificed themselves to our greater cause, and—I was
shocked to see—Laurell and Patricia. Shocked because
they were clearly in spiritual form, which meant both
had died, but then appeared in Duat rather than the
realm Furies went to upon death. Unless . . . my pulse
picked up speed. Unless they had actually survived in
the Belly and chosen to travel here in spiritual form the
way I had first journeyed to Duat to confront Anubis. If
that was so, they had shown a tremendous amount of
courage and loyalty. I didn't have enough time to wonder
how they had found us but assumed they'd used some
sort of tracking spell.

Nan and company wasted no time wading in against
Stacia and the Anubians, although one of them—I soon
recognized him as Khenti-Manu—broke free and scurried into the group of immortal flunkies forced to observe
Anubis's Reckoning. No doubt *he* was the "high-ranking
priest" who had done the seemingly impossible: forcibly
transmuting an immortal being *out* of his own body and
an arcane spirit *into* it. Khenti-Manu quickly realized
what I had—that the divine audience members, all
weaker than Ma'at by far, had no choice but to stand as
frozen observers while the forces she enacted played out.
Of course, this bought us only a temporary reprieve.
Once their liege lord's Reckoning ended, I would finally
have the proof I needed to bring him to justice, but he
would then have *me* at his mercy. He and his minions
would attack, and Triad's help or not, there was *no* way

Ma'at and I could stand against so many immortal foes, even if they were all *lesser* gods and goddesses.

My gaze fell upon the twin mirrors hanging on the walls to each side of the pentagram. I let out a hiss of breath as possibilities danced through my mind. Each stood in the direct path of the pentagram's magical overflow, to east and west the way that Ma'at's Scales stood just to the north. This meant that either (or both) could serve double duty as portals, portals to bring in arcane and—hopefully—immortal reinforcements of our own. But first I had to figure out *how*.

Nike wound to my shoulder and nuzzled my neck in excitement. *Nemesis says she can tell your grandmother your plan. Mijai can surely open a portal to Ma'at's temple in Duat.*

Thanks to the fact Anubis had so kindly done *something* to his portion of the Underworld that allowed shades to retain their magical abilities even after death. That meant Ma'at's surviving guardians—and hopefully my *own* group led by Durra and Scott—could leap through to bolster our numbers. Unfortunately, that would *still* leave us outnumbered.

Nike gave me inspiration again. *When Sahana makes it through the first portal,* she *could open the second . . .* But that still left the question of where to send for help. I glanced from the eastern mirror to the western, and my heartbeat skittered again. No way could I risk opening a portal to Ala's realm again. She was likely the one who had gotten Imseti ousted from his body to begin with. As long as there was a chance she *was* Anubis's secret lover, I couldn't involve her unless the rest of the Triad were present to counter her. So where . . . Of course!

Nike, when Sahana does come through, have Maeve send Durra through the second portal to the Palladium for our mothers.

Nike let out an excited hiss. *Three Nemeses and a number of Furies will be more than a match for Anubis and his lesser allies.*

My lips twisted fiercely. *Indeed. And then I can focus on subduing him so that his followers will lose heart and surrender—or Adesina and Mom can fetch the Triad here.* It would be *much* less risky to bring Ala there in the company of Kamanu and Epona, especially *after* we got things here under control. Of course, first we had to pull that feat off.

Pass the plan on to Nemesis, please. I don't care what they have to do—Mijai needs to open that portal to Duat, and Sahana has to open the second to the Palladium. My hands are tied here until Ma'at finishes.

Done! Nike called a moment later. I held my breath while Nan's shades redoubled their efforts, soon succeeding in overpowering the Anubians and sending Mijai under the protection of the three Fury shades around the group of frozen immortals to the western mirror. I couldn't help looking back at Anubis to gauge his reaction and sighed in relief to find him focused solely upon Ma'at as she continued reciting his past deeds, his very *many* past deeds considering how many thousands of years he'd had to accumulate them.

My— okay, thanks to Nike's help, *our*—plan went way more smoothly than expected; Mijai tapped into the pentagram's overflowing pool of energy without disrupting the Reckoning, thanks to the spectral assistance of Imseti, opening a portal to Ma'at's temple in Duat.

Nan leaped through the second the portal solidified. Several tense moments later, she popped back through the portal, followed closely by first Scott (*big* surprise), then Sahana, Durra, and Charlie. *Those* three immediately skirted the pentagram's edge and began the next step at the waiting mirror. Nan and Scott stepped up beside me—remaining outside the pentagram—and narrowed their eyes at Anubis behind me. *He* didn't notice, but it *did* raise my spirits to know they would be at my back to make sure no one took me unaware.

Mac and Ellie soon jumped through the first portal, leading a number of Ma'at's guardians to surround Anubis's lesser gods. My stomach sank because my brother and his wife would be in the second greatest danger after me once Anubis's Reckoning ended, but I gritted my teeth and reminded myself that the danger was theirs to face. I *couldn't* save everyone I loved from facing harm, and thanks to the lessons Trinity and Scott had taught me, I *wouldn't* even if I could.

My body tensed when Ma'at's voice reached a crescendo, and I tuned back in to her actual words. She had reached Anubis's most recent history, which meant his Trial by Feather would soon end, presumably freeing both him and his followers once more. Sweat broke out upon my brow. While we were nowhere *near* as outnumbered as we had been at the start of his Reckoning, our victory—or even survival—was by no means yet assured. I glanced down at Nike. *Pass word on to Durra's Amphisbaena that Anubis will be freed from stasis very shortly. They* must *get that portal up!* She bobbed her head in agreement, all the while sending me comforting thoughts. They didn't really soothe me much, but I *did* appreciate the gesture.

Standing still and waiting for Death to approach had never been a strength of mine. I focused my attention on the robed and masked figure behind me, thinking about the crimes Ma'at cried out that directly impacted my loved ones and me: assisting Nan's sister Medea in stealing control over Nan's body; recruiting, via Medea, a significant number of Furies into his own personal service and inspiring civil war in a formerly united-for-millennia Sisterhood; using Mijai and his peers to lure Imseti to his part of Duat, then murdering the priests to raise enough Death energy to oust Imseti from his body—and giving it to a mere *arcane* merely to prove he could, then sending that arcane who just so *happened* to have an unhealthy obsession with me to persuade *me* to betray my duties and superiors the way he had *his*.

Rage, already running at a low-key buzz beneath the surface, surged to a flood rushing through my veins. I smiled an unpleasant smile and tapped into that riotous flood, allowing it to sweep me up in its grip since—as Nemesis—I didn't have to worry about Turning Harpy. Being able to channel inhuman amounts of Rage—plus tap into the Triad's abilities on a limited basis—were the advantages that would allow me to stand up to Anubis long enough for the cavalry to arrive.

Or so I desperately prayed.

All at once, Ma'at screamed out the greatest of Anubis's crimes as the Scale holding Anubis's heart plunged straight upward: "Plotting to steal the corporeal form of a member of the immortal Triad to pass yourself off as one of them, stealing powers both divine and political that are *not* rightfully yours!"

My lips curved smugly as I stared into Anubis's silver-rimmed, yellow Hound eyes—the only feature I could clearly see through his mask. "Checkmate," I murmured even though he couldn't hear. Ma'at had confirmed *all* the crimes I had suspected; hearing the worst shouted out last made everything that much more dramatic. The universe must have agreed because Sahana *finally* got the second portal up and running. Durra leaped forward at the same time Ma'at's body sagged. The physical representation of Anubis's heart vanished as if it had never appeared, sending the Scale back to its neutral position of Balance. I braced my body, and sure enough, the pentagram's barrier dissolved with one last dramatic flare.

I'd prepared myself as much as possible, but so, it seemed, had Jackal-Faced. He leaped backward the moment the pentagram dissolved, letting out a sharp command, which inspired a flurry of activity among his lesser immortals, who shoved forward another robed figure with an oddly distended belly. My mouth tightened because I sensed who his captive was before a smirking Stacia stepped up to yank off the robe's hood: a heavily pregnant Serise, the figure I'd noticed having such a hard time walking earlier.

I forced a neutral expression, other than the tightened lips, although it wouldn't do much good *anymore*. Stacia knew damned well I had an alliance with the new Harpy Queen, probably knew we'd become something approaching friends, if ever a Fury and Harpy could become such. Still, she *and* her Jackal-Faced prick of a god had another think coming if they thought I would betray the Triad and Sisterhood merely to save Serise— innocent baby or not. If I could sacrifice my lover or baby brother for the cause, an almost friend wouldn't divert me from my duty. I couldn't let it.

Anubis barked out another order, which served to bring Khenti-Manu scurrying to take Serise's other side. Seeing that confirmed one of my fears: Stacia *did* intend to transmute her spirit into Serise's body, cementing her vow to become Harpy Queen one way or another.

Nan and Scott pressed closer to me, and the sounds of skirmishes being fought around the room provided momentary distractions, but I grimly forced those sounds out of my mind. Ma'at and the others would have to make due a while longer.

"Anubis, the Jackal-Headed, you have faced Reckoning by Ma'at's Feather, and your soul has been found wanting. As Nemesis for the Immortal Triad, I am authorized to . . ."

The golden-masked face let out a cruel laugh. "You have made an amusing opponent, Fury, I'll give you that. But *I* have the power of transmutation at my fingertips and fear *no* other being, least of all a weak council incapable of protecting immortals from a supposedly *lesser* god's touch." At my frankly disparaging expression, Anubis gestured. "Perhaps you require a visual demonstration?"

Rage continued pulsing, and I channeled it to make my eyes glow an even more intense emerald green, something I usually didn't consciously enhance, but this was the pissing match to end all pissing matches. "Make as many *demonstrations* as you like, Anubis." His own eyes burned hotter when I used his name alone—something perfectly within my rights as a true demigoddess. "One thing you should have damned well learned by now is that I do *not* respond well to threats."

Stacia piped in from the peanut gallery with a grudging snort. "True as that may be, former pupil of mine, *you* know just as well that *I* do not make *empty* threats; even less does Lord Anubis."

"Oh, I'm sure you both have every intention of hijacking poor Serise's body just the way Anubis ousted Imseti from his—and your crazy-ass girlfriend stole my grandmother's. But what I'm even *more* sure of is this." Death magic stirred behind me from the direction of Sahana's portal, signaling the imminent arrival of the cavalry. "I'm not the only one prepared to fight you with every breath in my Nemesis body."

Anxiety kept that breath bated until several mostly crimson-tattooed figures rushed out of the portal and positioned themselves strategically around *our* side of the Hall. Only when I recognized my mother pushing her way to stand beside me while Durra stepped to my other side did I finally relax that indrawn breath. More figures rushed out of Sahana's portal: another group of Furies—these all Megaeras led by Adesina, once again wearing black rather than red leather although something about her emerald green eyes seemed odd.

I shrugged that thought away and turned a satisfied smile toward Anubis and Stacia, who reacted much to my liking. While neither let outright fear show, they *did* reveal nervousness in clenched fingers, tightened lips, and suddenly expressionless eyes. When yet another group poured out of the portal, this time mostly Alectos, a bead of sweat actually broke out upon Stacia's brow. Interesting how much like the truly alive Anubis's shades acted.

Seeing the blue Amphisbaena upon the arms of a number of our reinforcements was an unexpected but welcome sight. The Triad hadn't been sure whether the

Alecto Prime had sworn herself to Anubis, but their presence now suggested not.

Ma'at's voice rang out before I could make the mistake of taunting my chief opponents. "Anubis the Jackal-Headed, I really *must* insist that you either surrender to these Nemeses to face retribution for your crimes or you and all your minions leave *my* domain at once."

Anubis let out a hiss that sounded more Cat-like than canine. "Oh, you must *insist*, must you? Making an enemy of me is really not wise, Ma'at."

She appeared between him and me as if from thin air. Apparently she was already recovering from the magical drain of Anubis's Reckoning. "*You* made yourself an enemy of mine long before this moment, Anubis. Most especially when you dared to swear my daughters to your own personal service and strike out against fellow immortals." In another seamless shift, she went from toga-wearing Ma'at to leather-clad badass Nyx, making me feel like a knockoff.

Anubis opened his lips—probably to talk some more smack—but Death magic flared sharply behind us before falling away entirely, replaced by the telltale silvery flow of divine energy. I glanced overhead and my heart soared still further. Only one group of immortals would have reason to commandeer the portal linking the Hall of Two Truths with the Palladium at the exact moment we most needed them. I couldn't hold back another smile. We'd gone from outnumbered beyond belief and doomed to evenly matched and now, almost assured of victory. *Unless . . . unless only* Ala *steps out of that portal*—in which case we were pretty much screwed to *all* hell, no pun intended.

But no—the face and form of Father Defender stepped out of that portal, and my fears were washed away. Stalwart Kamanu, who didn't shrink in the face of his overpowering—and treacherous—wife and remained committed to seeing justice done. Fierce joy soon replaced fear, and I risked a quick glance at Anubis, wanting to see that terror now reflected in *his* expression as it should be, only to find that masked figure's silver-rimmed eyes shining with what looked very much like triumph. That could only mean that Ala had just hopped through—

I whirled but no, neither of the female members of the Triad had put in an appearance. Just Kamanu, who calmly stepped forward and paused beside Adesina, only to just-as-calmly reach forward and snap her neck.

Shock gripped me so hard that, for several interminable seconds, I couldn't process what had actually happened. Adesina was a Nemesis like me, she *couldn't* be killed, not so easily, and surely *not* by the immortal who had championed our cause the most. Any moment now, Kamanu's peaceful mien would fade and be replaced by a spiteful Ala—but no. Kamanu merely let Adesina's surprised body fall to the floor and continued on—straight toward us.

Durra let out an agonized scream the moment *her* frozen brain caught up, showing a grief that seemed way over-the-top considering she knew her mother was immortal and could be only incapacitated, rather than killed. Then all at once sudden realization hit as I realized why Adesina's eyes had seemed off. Kamanu had dispatched the other Nemesis too easily, even for a greater god. He moved on quickly, knowing that her demigoddess body would repair itself, but not soon enough for her to make a difference. I tensed as he made a circle around we three Furies, gave what could be termed a polite nod to Ma'at, and stopped next to Anubis. I let out a small breath. So he *hadn't* realized the truth I just had. It might not matter much, but *any* small advantage might tip the scales in our favor shortly. I *refused* to give up hope, no matter how shitty things looked.

They were about to get shittier.

I touched Durra's shoulder and gave her a sympathetic look, but one that also suggested she needed to buck up. She didn't disappoint; simply gritted her teeth and followed my gaze to the pair of immortals across from us. The unexpected betrayer, Kamanu, and his lesser lover, Anubis. Since I knew neither of them had ever expressed bisexual tendencies, I had to face yet another unpleasant revelation. Anubis had kept his face hidden not out of an overweening pride in wearing his jackal mask, but because he hadn't wanted to give a hint at the true traitor. That necessity no longer applied, so he did what I expected— tore the mask away to reveal something I had heard of but never witnessed firsthand: The proof that true immortals were not bound by mortal constructs of gender.

Anubis's distinctly feminine lips curved into a smile way smugger than any of mine and tossed back her hood to reveal an impressive mane of ebon-dark waves. "Oh, the look upon your face right now is priceless, child. I *did* warn you not to step foot inside my realm again, but you, of course, refused to listen. Now, more than just you will suffer the consequences."

She motioned, and Kamanu chanted in that immortal tongue, causing light to flash and reveal that he'd had a companion magically concealed beside him all the while—not an ally, but rather, a hostage. One of the few who, besides those currently outside his reach, might actually tempt me to throw aside duty in order to keep her safe, my agonizingly mortal partner and cherished friend, Trinity.

CHAPTER SEVENTEEN

TRINITY—WHO MUST REPRESENT THAT EXTRA bit of *insurance* Sean had earlier hinted Anubis would use against me. Charlie let out an angry bellow from behind at the same time I shot a furious glare at Kamanu. Anubis I could have expected to deal such a low blow, but from the supposed *Defender* it seemed unthinkable, especially considering that Trinity likely had ancestors who had once worshipped his traitorous ass. Without them, he would have become nothing, and yet he was perfectly willing to throw all their loyalty and respect aside, not to mention betray his sacred duties to the *Gens Immortalis*—and presumably, his wife—all for what? A piece of Anubian tail? His blackhearted betrayal hurt a thousand times more than Anubis's had because I'd not only trusted him, I had *liked* him.

Him *I liked,* and Ala *I mistrusted. Gods, I need to get my head examined.*

Thoughts of his wife helped me remain calm in the face of his treachery and Trinity's danger. *Nike, we're all doomed if we can't get help from Ala and Epona ASAP.* Her failure to argue showed that she agreed completely, which meant that things *were* every bit as shitty as they appeared. Anubis was going to use Trinity as leverage to get me *out* of the fight, and as much as it pained me to admit—I had no choice but to allow him to do that very thing.

I didn't have to feign frustrated anger. "What the hell are you doing with her?"

Kamanu allowed Anubis to yank Trinity away and simply watched as his lover shoved my bound and gagged friend to her knees before her. "Stacia suggested we would need insurance to gain your cooperation, and I agreed."

I couldn't seem to capitulate too easily. "And you were apparently too weak to take any of my family members hostage, so you resorted to involving a *mortal* in something that should remain among arcanes and immortals."

Her lips tightened, mostly because she knew my insult was all too accurate. Immortals viewed mortals in an even more patronizing manner than most arcanes did. Mortals were to be protected or, at worst, ignored— not drawn directly into our squabbles. Then again, we couldn't exactly expect a god—goddess—who was willing to break just about every immortal law to have the slightest hesitation in violating mere tradition.

"View this in whatever light you choose, but know this: If you strike against me now, your *partner* dies. And even if you are willing to make *that* sacrifice,

Kamanu and I have ensured that her shade will materialize in Duat, where my priests wait to torment her unceasingly unless I send word otherwise."

Well *that* explained how they were getting Fury shades to show up where they shouldn't and arcane shades to retain powers they shouldn't have been able to keep. Add a very powerful Death Lord to a member of the Immortal Triad, and unnatural miracles were possible.

I let out a hiss of my own. "You slimy little bastard— bitch—snake!" Nike didn't protest at that last insult as she otherwise might have. She knew I meant the figurative type of reptile who slithered along on two feet.

Anubis patted Trinity's braid-bedecked head almost affectionately. "I'll forgive you that one moment of disrespect to show my earnest desire to make a bargain with you. I have no desire to murder and torture innocent mortals, not even to punish your most assuredly *not* innocent self. And considering that you stole not just *one* but *two* of my own subjects, that is generous of me." She fisted her hand around several of Trinity's braids and tugged her head painfully upward. "But you will get only one chance at this bargain."

"I will *not* betray my brethren as you have yours."

"Fair enough, and not what is required. Simply stand away from the coming battle, and your partner shall not only live, but be returned whence she came, completely unharmed."

Mom and Durra tensed beside me when I didn't immediately refuse the deal. I couldn't risk warning them ahead of time; their reactions *had* to appear genuine. "You will *swear* to that, and all I need to do is stand down from the battle?"

Several tense whispers broke out from our side, and

Mom sucked in a breath as if I'd kicked her. I might as well have.

Triumph lit inside those silver-edged, neon yellow eyes—too similar to Scott's Hound eyes for my comfort—and she nodded. "I so swear that Trinity Larue will be returned completely unharmed to the mortal realm provided you vacate this field of upcoming battle. Of course, you will understand that I cannot rely upon *your* word alone, not considering the ties you hold to most of the combatants upon your side."

"Marissa, you can't—" Mom's voice choked off when Anubis caressed Trinity's neck in a deliberate reminder of what Kamanu had earlier done to the Megaera. Durra's vengeful gaze met my own when I looked at her and nodded. Realization flickered, but she remained silent in order to prevent anyone else from suspecting. She knew I knew, and hopefully she would trust me the way I was about to trust her.

"What *will* you rely upon, then?"

Anubis gestured to the first portal, the one leading to Duat. "Simply step through to—I am assuming— Ma'at's temple and await the battle's outcome."

I clenched the fingers of one hand while caressing Nike with the other. "That's it? You went to *all* that trouble simply to remove one single person from battle?"

Surprisingly, Stacia was the one to respond. "Don't be so modest, Marissa. People who underestimate you have a habit of winding up dead. *I* should know. And you are not just a single *person*, but a Nemesis."

One of three, and the second lay upon the floor behind us with a broken neck, effectively out of this battle, or so it would appear. Meaning that the number of true immortals on our side would drop to two—and one disembodied Imseti—the moment I quit the field. The thought of leaving my mother and other loved ones—including Scott and my brother—physically hurt, but quit the field I must. I held on to one small ray of hope: Anubis had played right into my hand.

"All right, I'll go."

Not even muffled voices met that pronouncement. Those who knew me were too shocked, while those who didn't merely cursed my weakness beneath their breath. What did *one* person—even mortal—matter against the greater good? A question I couldn't contemplate too closely, or I would take the easy way out and stay there to protect those I loved.

Anubis smirked again but didn't take my words at face value, assigning a contingent of lesser gods to escort me to the portal. I forced myself to meet Scott's gaze as I walked, fearing to see something in his expression that might kill the inner dregs of willpower getting me through. Instead, what I saw humbled— and heartened—me: complete acceptance and faith, followed by him mouthing the words *I love you*. I gave him one short nod, all I could afford, but he nodded back to let me know he understood. Suddenly, it became that much easier to leave those I loved behind to face the swirling storm without me.

FUNNY HOW IT SEEMED EASIER TO TRAVEL by portal the more I did it; either that or it really *did* get easier. I stumbled across the threshold to Ma'at's temple in Duat with only minor disorientation—and the grim determination to do what needed doing. A dozen guardians swarmed me the moment I burst out of the vortex, which evaporated behind me straightaway. The well-armed warriors nearly attacked me before they recognized me as not just Fury, but Nemesis besides. My arms shot up in the universal *I'm unarmed* gesture—something that was never quite true for one of Nyx's children.

Jeserit suddenly ducked out of a nearby doorway and ran over. "What's wrong? Durra said you needed help on the other side of the portal."

"No time for long explanations. Suffice it to say we were wrong about Ala; *Kamanu* is Anubis's lover, and *he* is now a *she*." Jeserit's lips pursed in surprise, but no words emerged. "They took my police partner hostage to force me out of the fight, and I *had* to let them—they're going to slaughter everyone if we can't get the rest of the Triad there immediately."

She nodded in grim practicality, motioning me away from the quiescent mirror. My spirits rose since—while I'd been prepared to *try*—I hadn't been 100 percent sure I could cast a portal to Ala's realm. I didn't know why Jeserit hadn't already fled Duat to protect her unborn child, but I found myself damned grateful she hadn't. As if she'd read my thoughts, Jeserit said, "I don't have the magical strength or finesse of the other priests, but I can manage one measly portal with all the energy running loose from that portal being aborted so abruptly. But I'm afraid the ride's not going to be pleasant."

I smiled fiercely. "Quick and dirty is pretty much my *modus operandi*."

Her hands shot up, and dark energy began writhing in the air, flooding from her straight to the mirror, which began swirling with the telltale mark of a burgeoning portal. She hadn't lied—her spell didn't hold the same beauty and grace I'd seen from Sahana or Mijai—but it most definitely got the job done. Silver light shot through the portal, confirming that she'd managed to break through into Ala's realm.

"Thank you!" I paused long enough to help her sink to the ground when her legs began to collapse. "I'm not sure how this is going to go down so please, some of you escort this woman to safe refuge. She's pregnant, and her husband gave his life for ours."

Jeserit blinked and opened her mouth, perhaps to object, but Ma'at's guardians nodded, with resolve upon their faces. Arcanes valued children even more highly than mortals, especially in the case of posthumous infants. Gods only knew whether I could save anyone else, but these two lives I *would* preserve.

I hurried into the seething portal before anyone could reply, and *damn*, it was *so* not pleasant, worse even than the initial trip to the Underworld from Boston. Magic ripped my body and soul into countless pieces, thrusting them from Duat into the portion of the Underworld ruled by Ala, then reassembling the fragments in a rush more agonizing than dematerialization had been. I didn't *stumble* out of this portal so much as I spilled onto the ground kicking and screaming. Commotion broke out around me. I was too focused on trying to *breathe* to register more than that some of Ala's priests had surrounded me and were demanding answers I couldn't manage to provide—not until I stopped shrieking.

"Leave the Nemesis be!" A cool-but-authoritative voice suddenly ordered. Ala. Never had I thought I would be so grateful to hear *her* voice, and yet I was. She knelt beside me to lay gentle hands upon my brow, murmuring a healing spell that swept across my body and whisked pain and confusion away.

I sat up with a gasp, hands clutching the folds of her robe. "Mother Rebuker, please forgive my urgency, but I need you to come with me to the Hall of Two Truths at once. Anubis is about to slaughter a roomful of Furies and our allies, not to mention Ma'at, for helping me." Okay, so technically he couldn't *slaughter* another immortal, but minor details.

Ala took that pronouncement with her usual cool demeanor, which I was coming to realize was just her natural personality; nothing more sinister. "Oh, clever, clever child. You invoked the Feather against him?"

My cheeks flushed at her praise, so rarely given, now making it that much more prized. "I did, and the Reckoning confirmed everything suspected and more. But we must hurry—Anubis has a—a greater god at h-his side."

Ala's eyes took on a steely glint. "Epona—or Kamanu?"

My mouth dropped open. "You suspected that one of them was working with Anubis?"

She nodded, lips tightening visibly. "Yes, which is why I seemed to object to your appointment as Nemesis so much, to increase their insistence that you be the one to serve. I've seen your dedication to your duties both mortal and arcane, and I believed you would get to the truth no matter what it took. As for why I suspected, Anubis managed to recruit far too many immortals far too quickly to be working alone—not one unremarkable lesser deity, even a Death Lord. When he then managed to close off Duat to not only other parts of the Underworld but also the Divine Realm, I knew that only one of *us* could be helping him amass that much power."

"And you knew *you* weren't the culprit."

The guilt in my voice had her lips quirking. "Oh, peace, Nemesis, I hardly gave you reason to trust me.

I'm impressed you managed to have such success so quickly and to suspect something it took me decades to see. Now, which is it?"

She didn't say it out loud, but her bated breath and clenched fingers told me she was praying I wouldn't say what I had to say. "I'm sorry, but Kamanu is the one helping Anubis."

Immortal she might have been, but not even *she* could hide the sense of betrayal crossing her face. No tears fell, but I could see them lurking beneath the surface, unshed but there all the same. Despite our rocky start, I regretted having to add to her turmoil.

"Everything I've learned suggests the two aren't merely allies—they're lovers."

She recoiled, letting out a hiss that showed she hadn't expected *that* betrayal. Still, Ala caught on faster than me. "Anubis has assumed his —her—feminine aspect once more."

"Yeah, she has." I pushed to my feet, reveling in the fact I could do so without pain, thanks to her. "Can you get Epona here fast so we can get to the Hall before—before it's too late to stop them?"

Another voice sounded from behind us. "That won't be necessary, since I'm already here."

I whirled, assuming a defensive stance that had Nike spitting venom. Epona raised her arms in unconscious—and ironic—imitation of my motion to Ma'at's guardians. Coming from a greater god, it was an even more deceptive gesture.

"Peace, Nemesis, I came in search of you both at the rather insistent demands of the Alecto Prime, who *finally* made contact with me moments ago. I understand we have a mess to clean up." Epona waved behind her, and several dozen lesser gods and Furies, mostly Alectos, stormed into Ala's portal room. I was so happy to see them, I could have cried. Okay, so maybe one or two teensy tears *did* slip down my cheeks, but they were justified. I'd hoped to bring in the figurative cavalry, but never had I expected to drum up *this* much support so quickly.

Ala began issuing orders to the priests around her, and two scurried to the mirror from which I'd appeared to work their mojo. I couldn't help but shudder when their portal swirled into existence, thanks to my recent horrendous trip, but I forced myself to focus on how much more elegant and smooth the vortex raised by Ala's *two*—not one—priests was. Still, only stubborn pride allowed me to grit my teeth, nod to the goddesses beside me, and take the terrifying plunge into the abyss.

My feet hit the floor of the Hall of Two Truths what seemed mere seconds later, fortunately with none of the previous troubles. Chaos surged around me, with combatants battling everywhere I looked and Anubis's forces having the much better time of it. I let out a battle cry and launched myself upon an Anubian darting forward to block the portal, making short work of the man and leaving him dead beneath my feet. The portal spat out Ala, Epona, their divine allies, then Fury after Fury. The two immortals bade me follow, and with an expectant grin, I did so.

I forced myself not to search the crowd for specific faces; either I would see loved ones and be unable to help them, or I *wouldn't* and only worry that they were already beyond help. Rage and Mandate suddenly made themselves felt with a vengeance, making me realize I had somehow been ignoring them both so neither could paralyze me during the unpleasant task of retreating long enough to bring immortal support. That support now bowled through a line of unfamiliar Anubian warriors who must have portaled in after I left. Most of them were shades, a couple of *those* opponents I could swear I had killed during that skirmish where I'd first seen Stacia's spirit.

You probably did *kill them there,* Nike pointed out, then fell silent when we had to defend ourselves from another enemy. I fell into a rhythm of *kick, punch, feint, jab, incapacitate* as we made our way to the front of the Hall. Ala and Epona continued inexorably forward, focused upon Anubis and Kamanu, who were now battling Nyx, Mom, and a dozen other Furies on the dais surrounding the oversized Scales. Nyx and Mom fought with fierce resolve and the knowledge neither of them could be killed; and Mom in Nemesis form managed to make *me* look like an amateur, moving with deadly grace and speed that left no question Anubis would *never* manage to snap her neck the way Kamanu had Adesina's . . .

As if the thought summoned her, Durra appeared at my side, as unharmed and resolute as Mom, and gave me a tight-lipped nod. Her faith in me had been well placed, and—judging by the pile of fallen (though not dead) lesser gods left in her wake—mine had been equally appropriate, which meant she *would* be my ace in the hole.

We reached the dais, and Ala let out one sharply uttered word. "Kamanu!"

All four combatants froze before us, and Kamanu's gaze raced to meet his wife's. Bitter hatred washed over his face, dark emotions that seemed so out of place compared to his usual tranquil façade. Then again, only strong feelings could have inspired such a fearsome betrayal as the one he'd committed. I could only wonder *what* had happened between them over the centuries to bring things to *this*.

Anubis zeroed in on Ala as well, but *her* emotions were much different. She looked at her fellow immortal with what appeared very much like . . . hunger.

Ala and Epona began a back-and-forth exchange with the traitorous duo while I tried to puzzle that out. My eyes moved from Ala to Anubis, then Kamanu, before moving back to Ala. I'd expected my stunning coup of showing up with the remaining two-thirds of the Triad to intimidate the lovers into surrendering or at least temporary withdrawal since two greater gods of their strength easily outclassed one greater god and a lesser. They should have looked worried when Ala and Epona showed up. Instead, they seemed unsurprised and even pleased.

Painful realization flared when I thought about just how eager Anubis had been to get me out of the Hall of Two Truths—ostensibly to even the odds in her favor. But that didn't make a damned bit of sense upon closer inspection. She and Kamanu would have *known* the first action I would take would be to summon the cavalry in the form of Epona and Ala. *They* wanted *me to bring them. Or at least—her!*

Nike hissed. *Ala?*

Yes. This whole thing is a trap!

Ala had suspected treachery for some time—likely one of the primary reasons Anubis had sealed off her realm to the rest of the Underworld. On the flip side, that also meant they couldn't just lure Ala here easily once they were ready to strike—but I'd gone and brought her straight here for them. Of course, Nyx had transported the Hall *out* of Duat, weakening Anubis slightly, but every other immortal except Nyx would suffer a decrease in power as well.

But why? What are they planning—

I spun a moment too late to prevent the trap from springing. Yet *another* group of Furies—this one led by a crazy-eyed Medea inside Nan's body—had leaped out of the portal from the Palladium and spread out to effectively cut the dais off from the rest of the room. I had barely started considering how best to break their blockade when Stacia herded a group of priests through the line of Furies, dragging a struggling Serise while Khenti-Manu manhandled Trinity in his wake. Seeing Khenti-Manu had acid churning inside my belly. He had proven to be particularly skilled at transmutation and been the only priest to succeed at removing an *immortal* from his body.

My gaze zoomed back to Ala, then Anubis, who wore an even greater look of avarice upon her deceptively lovely face. I started to blurt out my sudden flash of suspicion to the immortal next to me, but Trinity's voice let out a scream of agony.

I whirled a second time, only to find Trinity now in Medea's not-so-gentle hands, my partner's gag removed and blood flowing from an awful, gaping wound in her side. Rage surged, and I forgot about everything but Trinity and how I *refused* to watch another friend die before my very eyes. Medea met me with an expression of triumph, but I blocked it from my mind, finding it much easier to assault the Fury wearing my grand-mother's face than I once would have expected. She met my frenzied attacks blow for blow at first, but quickly tired in the face of my enhanced Nemesis abilities. Still, the bitch knew I wouldn't kill her—not when there was a chance to restore Nan to her rightful place. I growled at that thought and mustered my strength and speed to break past her defenses to coldcock her. She slid to the ground with a satisfyingly stunned expression.

I dropped down and ripped off one of Trinity's sleeves to pack against her wound, reminded of another time I'd had to field-dress a serious injury she'd sustained while helping me. She coughed and opened pain-racked eyes, and I cursed. *Gods, you cannot* do *this to me again!*

"Riss, I'll be okay."

The blood soon soaked the sleeve, so I ripped off the other and pressed it tightly to her side, ignoring her ridiculous claim. She winced but didn't complain, instead moving unsteady fingers to push mine away and take up the grisly chore. "I mean it, I'm fine. She missed anything vital, and your mother *needs* your help!"

That was one of the few things that could have gotten me to leave her, especially since cruel reality had set in. Other than applying pressure to her wound—which she could clearly do herself—I was no help. I could *not* heal others. Still, how could I just leave her unprotected? Someone let out a fierce roar nearby and barreled straight through two enemy Furies with little trouble. My eyes widened but then returned to normal when Charlie threw himself down next to us. A Giant whose loved one was in danger made a formidable foe indeed.

He tore off his shirt and took over staunching Trinity's blood loss. "No one shall harm her further, Riss, that I promise. Now go to your mother!"

I turned, expecting to see Mom helping overpower Anubis, only to see the tide of battle had changed once more. Ala and Epona faced off against Kamanu and Anubis while Mom and—Durra—struggled to get through a group of enemy Furies separating them from Khenti-Manu, now chanting over Serise and Stacia, both of whom lay upon the ground; one because she chose to and the other because four Furies were holding her down. Seeing the pregnant Harpy Queen fighting uselessly for not just her freedom but that of her unborn child galvanized me into action.

The line of Furies—outnumbering us four to one—stood no chance against multiple Nemeses, which we proved by mowing them down in double-time fashion. Quick as we were, however, Khenti-Manu had made it most of the way through his spell by the time we loomed over him. When Nike spat venom onto his face, he squealed in terror and slipped away into the fracas. The four traitors holding Serise down vanished just as quickly, leaving her to lurch to her feet and Mom and me to turn our ire upon Stacia—only to find her shade dissipating in front of us.

I let out a harsh breath since nobody had struck her a single blow, then narrowed my eyes. It wasn't a quick dissolution of a slain shade like I'd witnessed firsthand previously, more a slow, lingering process, likely a result of the interrupted transmutation. Still, once her spirit had disappeared completely, and Serise stepped forward to thank me, I remained on edge. She froze when I raised my talons threateningly. "Where did we find my niece when she ran away from the safe house recently?"

Her mouth made a confused O at the seemingly irrelevant question, but then she nodded in realization. "In the alley behind the movie theater near the Boylston T stop."

Not likely that anyone else knew that specific a detail, but I couldn't risk the possibility. "Who was she facing in that alley?"

She gestured. "Why, the Fury standing beside you, the one I saved you from in the subway at your mother's"— another quick gesture—"request."

My body relaxed slightly. Stacia might have ferreted out a detail about one of those occasions, but I doubted she would know that much about the two separate attacks. Durra must have shared my opinion, because she moved to help support the panting Harpy Queen.

I licked my noticeably dry lips. "Please don't tell me the baby's coming *now*!" She remained obligingly silent, but her expression said it all. "Son of a—" I met Durra's sympathetic gaze. "Can you get her over there to Trinity and Charlie? He'll keep her safe so you can rejoin the fight."

Of course, they'd need more than an overprotective Giant to see them through the next few minutes. I glanced at the portal to the Palladium and saw Sahana fighting alongside Scott, Mac, Elle, and a group of loyal Furies. Battle shifted, and I spied another combatant fighting for our side—the Cat shade, Nemesis spitting at enemies from her shoulder. I was pleasantly surprised that the feline hadn't turned tail to fight for Anubis again—especially considering how outnumbered they'd been earlier—but Nemesis riding so close to her exposed neck had no doubt discouraged *that*.

Nike, have Nemesis tell the Cat they need to get Sahana over to Trin and Charlie now. *She's better than nothing and may be able to keep Trin alive and Serise's baby from coming long enough for us to* win *this damned thing.*

Seconds later Scott and Elle began forging a path from the portal to the dais, and I let out a relieved sigh, then turned to Mom at my side. "Mom, we've got to get Nan back to her body *now*, while Medea's out cold, if she's to have any chance of taking it back."

Her expression became uncertain as her sense of duty warred with the personal desire to save her mother. I'd faced that battle myself and knew I *should* have done the right thing and sacrificed Nan for the greater good, but gods damn it, she *deserved* to get her body back, and I still had that ace up my sleeve—or at least close enough to call on for help if need be. I motioned to where Nan could be seen fighting alongside Mijai and their fellow shades. "Go! I'll take care of things here."

She'd always trusted me to do what I said, and that time proved no exception. She patted my shoulder roughly, unfurled her wings, and launched herself into the air, leaving me to lend aid to Ala and Epona. I leaped upon the back of a Fury trying to distract Ala from behind, and the next several moments passed in a frantic blur of kicking, punching, and clawing, the rough-and-tumble Fury way of battle. It seemed like an eternity before I finally dispatched my last opponent, only to turn and find the tides of war had turned once more.

Most of *our* lesser-god allies had either been temporarily knocked out of commission or were desperately battling with certain of *Anubis's* divine minions. Kamanu had lured Epona to the far side of the dais, leaving Ala alone to deal with Anubis. The greater goddess should have had no trouble subduing the lesser, except for one fact: Sean and several other lesser immortals had shown up to bring Ala down to her knees. Anubis knelt next to her, that hungry expression making her face

uncharacteristically ugly. She moved slightly, and I figured out where Khenti-Manu had run off to: straight to
his goddess's side.

He began chanting and weaving Death magic between
the two immortals, confirming my absolute worst fears.
Anubis hadn't ordered an arcane transmuted into a lesser
god's body on a mere whim, she'd done it to be sure she
could safely take the next logical step with greater assurances of success: transmuting a lesser god into the body
of a greater. *That* had been her plan all along, to steal
Ala's body, powers, and godhood, not amassing enough
political and magical power to become a Deity in her
own right. Why do *that* when this method was so much
quicker, easier, and—thanks to her affair with Ala's
husband—more personally satisfying? Besides which,
this way she had a guarantee of taking two-thirds control over the immortal world's chief governing body.

The familiar scent of berries and sandalwood wafted
to my nose just before a hand settled upon my shoulder.
"We have to stop him *now*."

I nodded, feeling renewed determination now that
Scott was by my side. New arrivals pressed close, turning out to be Mac and Elle leading several of Epona's
lesser-god allies, who had gotten separated during the
heat of battle. *Now* we had a better chance of success.
Before I could second-guess the decision, I channeled
Rage to amp up my speed as much as possible, leaped
into the air, flapped my wings, and soared over the group
of lesser gods to land upon Khenti-Manu, slashing my
talons deeply across his throat before anyone could
react. He slid to the ground in a gurgling heap, dead
within seconds. His unfinished spell exploded in a vio-
lent starburst of Death magic, a burst that Anubis took

the brunt of. She collapsed upon the floor without a sound, something that had me frowning until a telltale shimmer of silver and black gave me the vital clue: Her spirit was trapped midway between her body and Ala's, much the way that Imseti was trapped in limbo.

The silver-and-black energy twisted in an angry torrent, zooming toward the figure writhing upon the ground. I grinned when my secret weapon in the form of Durra stepped forward to block its path. Anubis's spirit wasn't particularly intimidated by the lone Fury—until red leather uniform turned to black, and Durra's features were replaced by Adesina's. Anubis finally realized what I had earlier: that Mom and the Megaera had decided I would need another Nemesis by my side in the Underworld and pulled a fast one on us all. The incorporeal immortal sizzled furiously before veering toward Ala, who had taken advantage of the distraction provided by Scott and company to overpower the remaining immortals who had made the mistake of continuing to hold her down. Ala let out a mocking laugh as Anubis's soul buzzed around her impotently. No way would the lesser goddess any longer be able to oust the greater, not without aid from other Deities and her powerful priest to finish the spell that would have made it virtual child's play. She figured out the truth at the same time I did, then flew toward me instead. I scrambled back, unwilling to chance whether Rage-filled Mandate would allow me to ward her off even though I was still in demigoddess form. The cloud of silver-and-black light made what sounded like a very humanlike shriek and arrowed toward the figure who had just stepped in front of me protectively. Scott.

Anubis must have decided he would make a suitable

receptacle because the cloud never slowed, arcing into Scott's body with enough force to knock him off his feet. "No!" I screamed before rushing to his side—too late. Scott stood with a strange expression, blinking several times before his eyes became silver-rimmed neon yellow, even more inhuman than his Hound eyes.

"You have been a plague upon me since ever I first saw your despicable face!" The words spat out in Scott's voice, but I knew they were not his own. A mere arcane had been no match for a true immortal. "I am going to choke the life out of you if it is the last thing that I do!"

I braced myself but had been unable to prepare for just how much she would enhance Scott's strength with her own. Apparently an immortal's magical abilities were split between their physical and spiritual forms, which made sense because Sean clearly possessed many of Imseti's abilities at the same time Imseti's spirit had been able to act, if in a more limited fashion. Scott's body slammed against mine, and Anubis reached *his* hands out to make good her threat. I used the impact to skitter backward, just barely managing to elude his— her—grasping hands. She and I played cat and mouse for several moments—me trying very hard to evade her pointed attempts to kill me. Of course, it wouldn't be a permanent death since ambrosia still flowed through my veins, but *she* was not hampered by the urge to take me unharmed, as I was. I *had* to find a way to incapacitate her that didn't involve killing Scott, and not simply out of my selfish need to see him survive—she would just find a new body to possess and continue wreaking havoc.

My eyes flew wildly around the dais, as if seeking out divine inspiration. All the others were too busy fighting their own battles to offer much hope. Ala was assisting

Mac and Elle in chasing the remaining foresworn immortals away while Adesina maintained grim-faced vigil over Anubis's body. *Her body!* I reacted without conscious intent, reaching forward to snap her unmoving neck as ruthlessly as Kamanu had acted earlier. To my complete and utter shock, Anubis's body fell lifeless before us.

Scott's mouth suddenly let out the most god-awful shriek, one that sounded way too feminine for his vocal cords to manage. Silver-and-black energy roiled around him, letting off freaky little lightning bolts of magic that sizzled in the air. His eyes shifted from silver-rimmed yellow to normal amber and back again as he fought the devastated spirit with a vengeance, neither one quite managing to win the upper hand. Apparently Anubis had been greatly weakened when I killed her corporeal form—a seeming impossibility my brain wanted to shy away from—but evidently not enough for Scott to emerge victor over his own body. This stalemate could go on long enough for Scott to physically tire—and Anubis to take advantage of that fact.

Over my dead body! Which Anubis had already tried and failed to arrange.

I could really only see one chance for Scott, slim though it might have been. I sprinted toward the protective knot surrounding Trinity and Serise, and sure enough, Mijai and his fellow priests had won through to help. Serise lay upon the cold marble floor, deep in the throes of labor, with Mijai and—wonder of wonders—several Furies urging her on. Sahana had her energy and limited healing skills focused upon Trinity—who had freaking *lied* about the severity of her injury, so I would leave her. And, I could tell with certainty, she lay dying.

Sahana met my gaze miserably and shook her head, causing Charlie to let out a low, vicious curse.

"Gods damn it, Trin!" I choked out, tears blinding me. "How could you *do* this to me?"

As if she'd had a choice. She managed the ghost of a smile but couldn't spare the energy to speak. It seemed horribly unfair that she was *there*, bleeding to death, when Scott stood just feet away battling a deity for control of his body, a deity who could have healed Trinity's body in seconds were their roles reversed . . . Although if Scott couldn't stand up to the deity's metaphysical onslaught, what chance would a *mortal* have? My fists clenched as inspiration struck. I zeroed in on Mijai helping Serise and wondered if it would be possible—then decided it didn't matter either way. I damned well had to *try*.

"Mijai! I need your help now, or Anubis wins!" A slight exaggeration, but one I was willing to make. Serise and the Furies shooed him away, and he ran to my side. "How can I help?" I quickly summarized my desperate plan, and to my relief, he agreed to make the attempt. Silver-and-black energy flared, at first terrifying me, until I realized he was being assisted by his patron, Imseti. With him helping Mijai, we might actually have a snowball's chance in hell . . .

I approached Scott moments later with a too-quiet Trinity in my arms and saw with relief that he was still waging that inner war with Anubis. Mijai nodded soberly when I gestured for him to proceed. He stopped midway between Scott and me and, boosted by the assistance of his god, began chanting. That by-then-familiar mix of Death and immortal magic seethed in the air, spreading out from Mijai in two directions: to Scott in one and Trinity in the other.

Scott's body froze, and panicked yellow eyes met my gaze. *She* caught sight of Trinity in my arms, bleeding profusely all over my black leather uniform, and frowned. At first she seemed insulted that we might try and forcibly transmute her spirit into a mere mortal, but then resignation flashed as she realized she'd have more luck overpowering a mortal than she was currently having with Scott—just as I'd hoped. She stopped fighting Scott and surrendered, allowing Mijai's spell to wash over them, not noticing her mistake until it was too late. Mijai didn't transmute *all* of her spirit from Scott to Trinity; he transferred only a *quarter*.

Silver-and-black light sprayed over both Scott and Trinity. Trinity's eyes popped open, no longer unbroken chocolate brown but now rimmed with unnatural silver. She gasped as her fatal injury began knitting itself closed, seemingly of its own volition. I lowered her to the ground carefully, body remaining primed for response should she make any threatening moves, but she didn't. My reckless gamble had paid off. Not only had the quarter of Anubis's soul transmuted into Trinity's body automatically healed its new vessel as I'd hoped; my partner had also proven strong-willed enough to retain control over her body.

I glanced immediately to Scott and let out an explosive huff when silver rimmed amber—rather than neon yellow—eyes met my gaze. He still bore three-quarters of Anubis's essence inside, but that reduction had proven just enough for him to reassert dominance. Thank *all* the gods and goddesses.

Well, *almost* all of them . . .

CHAPTER EIGHTEEN

IRONICALLY, I ENDED UP HAVING TO TAKE A leave of absence from my leave of absence, finding myself helping Scott and Trinity adjust to their new-found statuses as partially immortal. Kale and Mahina took over administrating the MCU while Trinity took up residence inside an unoccupied apartment next door to Scott's so I could help them both learn how to use their new powers. Mom and I put Cori's official swearing-in on hold while I handled that, and Mom worked with Adesina and the Alecto Prime to set things back to rights among the Sisterhood, a much easier task now that Anubis was no longer able to spread dissension among the three classes.

One particular long-standing tradition had apparently gone down in flames without anyone's intending it so. Over the course of the chaos in the Sisterhood the past few days, the identities of the Alecto and Megaera Primes were no longer secret from the other classes. Mom and Ekaterina had found proof that Medea had murdered poor Maylin, then masqueraded as her when necessary over the past few weeks. That explained why the Tisiphone Prime had refused to appear before the Lesser Consensus when summoned: Those fifteen Elders would have sniffed out her deception in short order. Our class would soon have to choose a new Prime so the ceremony to instill the previous Prime's knowledge into the new one could be performed before Maylin's soul moved from the Palladium on to the Underworld. If Mom weren't so set on taking her place on the Conclave, I knew who would have gotten *my* vote.

Speaking of Medea . . . my *darling* great-aunt had managed to slip away in all the confusion—along with Sean, *still* piloting Imseti's body. Stacia, it seemed, we had blown into oblivion by botching the transmutation spell, but I'd feel a heck of a lot better once we confirmed that by tracking down her shade ass wherever it rematerialized.

"You look so pensive, baby; what's up?"

I stretched like a cat when Scott's magic fingers skimmed along my bare shoulders before snuggling me back against his chest. Trinity had gone to bed early, exhausted from learning how to channel magic through her mostly mortal body. Scott and I, on the other hand, had just enjoyed some excellent Chinese takeout and some fine wine in honor of the fact we'd made it out of another mess alive and—mostly—intact. We had spent most of the night re-creating the hot and heavy portion of the night Serise had interrupted us, minus the whole pregnant Harpy busting in unannounced, of course. Much to *her* dismay, Serise remained pregnant. Ala and Epona had worked some of their mojo to make sure Baby Harpy wouldn't put in an untimely appearance because of all the stress Mama Harpy had been put under. They then carted Anubis and Kamanu off to await their trial, letting me know that they would be summoning Scott, Trinity, and me once the trial had been arranged.

"Mmm, that feels *so* good."

"One of the perks to this whole godhead thing, I guess."

Something in his voice had me turning and drawing him into my arms. "You guess? Say the word if you're unhappy, Scott, and we'll find a way to take this away."

He tried for a teasing tone but couldn't quite pull it off. "I thought you said your orgasm tonight was the—and I quote—single-most amazingly spectacular moment of your life."

I tightened my arms around him. "Seriously, Scott, you know we're in this together. If you don't think you can handle this—"

Scott's silver-flecked amber eyes glinted with fierce pride. "Of course *I* can handle it, Riss; I'm just not so sure *you* can."

My mouth dropped open, and I could only sputter wordlessly for several moments.

His lips twisted in amusement, and he continued on as if I hadn't tried and failed to manage a coherent sentence. "*You've* always been the more powerful in our relationship, darling; something I've never minded because I am plenty secure in my own skin. But you're used to that dynamic, and now . . . now it's been flipped around on us both."

I started to vehemently decry his statement as being

absurd, but honesty made me pause. "I—well, I guess the dynamic of our relationship *has* changed, but the way I feel about you hasn't."

Belying his claim to be *plenty secure*, Scott indulged in a moment of sheer vulnerability. "Because I'm mostly immortal now?"

My fingers caressed his cheek tenderly. "No, you big dummy, because you helped me realize that I love you enough to trust you more than anyone or anything, even if that means potentially giving you up or, even better, accepting you just as you are when we've both changed. Now I know we can change together."

All signs of vulnerability leached away, and his lips descended upon mine with crushing—and divine—force, and soon we were weaving our wordless magic once more.

THE NEXT MORNING, ALA AND EPONA SUM-moned us to a Triad session in the Divine Realm to deal with the traitorous god and goddess. *That* particular part of the session was closed to those who were not full-blown immortals, but we three Nemeses, along with Scott and Trinity, were summoned before the Triad, something made possible because each of us was partially divine. Apparently the Triad either fudged the truth about how long the ambrosia would last, or they'd done something to extend its effects, since we Nemeses had slugged it down well over three days earlier.

My first glimpse of the Divine Realm—where all immortals held at least a small portion as their celestial home when not tending to duties in the other realms—was pretty damned impressive. Not surprisingly decorated mostly in the ancient Greek and Roman styles so beloved by immortalkind, touches of colorful accessories and fabrics paid homage to every other culture represented in the *Gens Immortalis*. Everything there was oversized and expensive-looking, even the stark white marble floors and walls that could be seen just about everywhere. Scott and Trinity hovered close to me as full-blown gods and goddesses swarmed the building where official Triad business was conducted. They'd started arriving in numerous waves the moment word went out that the first trial of a Triad member in its very long history was being hastily convened.

Scott leaned in close—those silver-rimmed amber eyes still catching me off guard each time I saw them—to murmur, "Do you think they're going to remove Anubis's soul from us?" He gestured to Trinity, who glanced at me anxiously. Poor Trin. She'd always demanded I involve her more heavily in our arcane investigations and stop sheltering her from the most dangerous aspects, but I could safely say she'd *never* thought she'd find herself the possessor of one-fourth of an immortal's soul, especially considering she'd once refused to believe that either of those two things existed. While she had thanked me for the brilliant if insane gambit that had saved her life, she was completely out of her element, suddenly saddled with abilities she'd never dreamt of having and had no clue how to control.

I opened my mouth to utter some sort of reassuring platitude, but the marble doors separating antechamber from courtroom swung open, and Nyx in black leather and Fury tats—a nice touch to show her solidarity with us—appeared to escort us inside. All five of us not-quite-immortals took deep breaths and stepped forward.

If watching myriad immortals trickle into the court-room in smaller groups had been overwhelming, seeing all several hundred of them packed inside a single cavern-ous chamber took one's breath away. A circular stage sat in the center of the room, upon which a furniture setup much like a modern-day courtroom had been arranged. Epona sat upon the judge's bench, serving the role of Mediator, which was similar to an American court's judge—although she also held the power to break ties once the Tribunal's members finished deliberating and voted upon a transgressor's punishment. Guilt was pretty much a foregone conclusion—providing incontrovertible evidence of guilt being the job of Nemeses—and the death penalty not even an option, but there *were* countless other forms of punishment that could be chosen.

Nemesis and Nike—together once more—slithered along my arms, doing their best to send soothing thoughts as I followed in Nyx's wake. I couldn't resist speaking to them telepathically, since presumably we'd lose that ability once the ambrosia fully wore off. *Is the death penalty still off the table for immortals now? I mean, considering the fact that . . .*

Nemesis didn't hesitate to fill in the blanks. *You mean considering you proved that an immortal's body* can *be killed if the spirit isn't inside it?*

Well, yeah, pretty much.

Nike seemed thoughtful. *If the Triad allowed* that *to become an acceptable form of punishment, They'd be no better than Anubis and Kamanu—and would soon have an even larger-scale mutiny on Their hands.*

True. And besides which, nobody even knows whether Anubis can be safely contained, or if she can eventually resurrect her original body.

We fell silent when Nyx led us straight to the center stage and motioned for us to climb the imposing marble stairs. Ala sat to the right at the Rebuker's table, which I'd expected. More surprisingly, however, Nyx moved to assume the vacant seat reserved for the Defender. While *someone* had to fill the position until a permanent Triad member was chosen—and she'd proven her fitness to serve by defending immortal law even in the face of overwhelming odds—I was surprised at her being chosen since she was still a *lesser* goddess.

I rolled my eyes at my own foolishness. *It's not like you really know the ins and outs of immortal politics— you can barely keep up with* Fury *business.*

We five took up positions in the center of the stage directly facing Epona, Ala to her left and Nyx to her right. Once we settled into place, Epona banged a gavel upon her judge's bench, and silence descended across the room.

Ala rose to her feet behind her table. "The Triad of Immortals has accepted your evidence and the testimony of the Mother Reckoner to confirm judgment against Anubis the Jackal-Headed, whose soul faced Trial by Feather and was found guilty." She gestured to Nyx. "She has suggested what we feel to be a fitting punishment, but first, the penalty must be set before you to see if those directly impacted are willing to serve as required."

Mom, Adesina, and I exchanged glances, certain she must mean us. We were surprised when Ala turned, instead, to Scott and Trinity. "After consulting with Imseti via the priest who has agreed to serve as his avatar until such time as his corporeal form can be recovered, We three agree that Anubis's soul must *not* be transferred until We can be certain she will not break

free to claim an even more powerful victim as her avatar. Further, having her soul split into pieces—while
shocking—can only serve to further keep her in check."
Ala looked gravely from Scott to Trinity. "We understand this is a heavy burden to ask a mortal and arcane to
bear, but We feel you both are capable of carrying the
load. Especially with the help we shall provide."

Scott swallowed before managing to respond. "You're
asking that—that we allow Anubis's soul to remain inside us?"

She nodded, her expression remaining serene.

I couldn't help but protest. "But Mother Rebuker,
with all due respect, wouldn't an immortal be a more
appropriate choice?"

A vigorous headshake met that suggestion. "And risk
Anubis's reunited soul taking control of that being, giving her unfiltered access to the Divine Realm in the
form of her unwilling captive, not to mention access to
that immortal's godhood?"

My eyes widened. "So you *want* her soul kept in
pieces and confined to the earthly realm?" Something
which no immortal could promise to do, even if they
were willing. They all had duties across the realms, even
the dying Otherrealms. Perhaps *especially* there since
some of them still sought to end the mysterious plague
and, if possible, reverse the damage already done. On
earth, where magic itself was at its least potent, Anubis
would be *that* much weaker and thus easier to contain.
Theoretically.

Still, that was a *lot* to ask, especially of a mortal.

"I'll do it!" I blurted out. At Ala's sympathetic look, I
hurried on. "At least let me take up part of the burden;
surely a Fury would be better able to—"

She cut me off, not unkindly. "No, and for the same reasons an immortal is not a suitable vessel, if on a lesser scale." Ala turned to Trinity, who was maintaining a damned fine poker face even though she must have been terrified.

"I will do it, and gladly."

My face took on a comical look of shock at her boldly uttered words. She sounded completely sure of herself, almost eager. She met my gaze and smiled reassuringly, tapping a hand upon the spot where she had been—so it seemed at the time—mortally injured. I blinked and caught her hint. With even a quarter of an immortal's abilities—and the guaranteed self-healing that came along with it—Trinity would no longer be the weakest link of our partnership. Instead, that *honor* would fall to me, at least magically speaking. If that made her practically indestructible, my ego could certainly survive the blow.

Scott, not to be outdone, nodded his own assent. "I, too, will bear this burden so long as there is need."

Ala accepted this pronouncement with a small smile. "Excellent. Now, there is the minor matter of Anubis's godhood. I'm afraid that we've never faced this predicament before, and it was quite a quandary until the Mother Reckoner again provided the perfect solution. Since, as Ma'at, she is quite familiar with the appropriate mythos, she shall act in Anubis's stead as the Jackal-Headed until such time as the two of you have fully learned to control your new abilities, and We are sure Anubis cannot regain control, at which point We shall implement a Persephone solution."

My stomach grew queasy. Just when I'd started to think I wouldn't lose either Scott or Trinity, all of a sudden it looked like I could lose both for significant periods of time. Scott's worried gaze met mine, but Trinity just looked confused. Then again, up until the moment she inherited a portion of divinity, the woman *had* been a die-hard atheist. "Persephone?"

I spoke before Ala could although my voice came out extremely husky. "Persephone, daughter of Demeter, Greek goddess of the harvest. When Hades, lord of the Underworld, stole her away to be his wife, Demeter spread drought across the earthly realm due to her heart-break over losing her daughter."

Trinity let out a sound of recognition. "Okay, I remember that story from lit class. They work out a deal where Persephone stays half the year with Hades—winter—and half with her mother, right?"

"R-right." My anguished eyes moved from hers back to Scott's. *How* could I go half the year without one of them at a time? She was my closest friend and vital partner on the force; Scott was my heart and soul. I couldn't understand how Demeter had been able to bear making such a horrible deal with that asshole Hades.

Is it not better than losing one or both to death?

There Nike went, being all logical again and, damn her, *right*.

Scott, formerly perfectly willing to make up for his treacherous deity, started showing that mercenary streak that typically drove me crazy. "No *way* can I afford to spend half a year at a time in the Underworld, begging your divine pardon. And I thought the goal was to keep Anubis's soul *out* of the nonearthly realms."

Nyx rose smoothly. "The goal is to keep *all* of Anubis's soul out of the nonearthly realms at any one time, which a Persephone solution accomplishes quite

neatly, while still allowing Anubis's followers to be tended to. The only other alternative would be to completely eradicate her worship, which poses problems of its own."

Unhappy murmurs broke out among the assembled immortals. Religions *did* die out completely whenever arcanes lost faith as much as mortals did—but it was rare. Even then, most gods and goddesses made sure to cultivate multiple aspects—such as Nyx-as-Ma'at—to ensure *someone* would always be worshipping them. Arcanes were also a stubborn lot when it came to carrying on the old ways—as with Scott's Warhound family tradition of serving Anubis even today.

"Okay fine," Scott said. "But that doesn't change the fact that Trinity and I have lives and duties of our own on earth. We can't just be leaving them for *six months* at a time."

Epona's turn to rise gracefully. "A Persephone solution does not have to follow the story literally; We are free to set our own terms."

Hope stuttered to life inside my chest. Were it up to me, the immortals would have gotten the better end of the deal from sheer gratitude. Luckily, Scott was a *way* better negotiator. He and Trinity exchanged silent looks—or *were* they silent? The way they kept looking at each other suggested they *could* be communicating on some Wonder Twins type of level. I had to admit that any sort of telepathy would certainly make it easier for them to share the duties of Anubis's godhood . . .

Although thinking of those two—even partially—as immortal was *really* starting to trip me out.

The newly minted Wonder Twins nodded, and Scott spoke up again. "We'll agree to one day on, one day off."

Another buzz swept the room, ended only when Epona banged her gavel again. "Impossible. Switching back and forth so often will be entirely too disruptive."

He shrugged. "Perhaps. But you are asking for a *very* large sacrifice with no guarantees that Anubis will not someday steal control—and possession—over our bodies *and* souls."

The three Triad members consulted silently, cementing my belief that Scott and Trinity *did* have some weird Wonder Twin telepathy going on. Epona turned her implacable stare back on Scott. "Three months at a time."

"Three *days*, and we *might* have a deal."

Gods, only *my* mate would have the audacity to price-gouge immortal beings who had existed since before his earliest ancestor.

Epona shook her head. "One month on and off."

Hope grew even stronger. *Surely* I could endure a month at a time without them if I had—

"One week on and one off—our final offer."

As audacious as it seemed, I knew that he and Trinity had them between a rock and a hard place. Nothing guaranteed Anubis *could* be safely transmuted in pieces to other arcanes or mortals—or that new recipients would have the necessary strength of mind to hold firm. And these two had proven their dedication to justice and the Triad in ways no one else had.

"Deal," Epona agreed without further dickering, suggesting that had been what they had hoped for all along.

My heart soared as realization set in. Sure, going seven days at a time without seeing one or the other of them would be hard, but *not* impossible. Plenty of people had to travel constantly for their jobs. We could make this work!

Apparently considering that matter settled for the moment, Ala turned her attention to the Nemeses in our group. "Both the Triad and *Gens Immortalis* as a whole owe the three of you a debt of gratitude." She glanced at Adesina with an actual look of sorrow marring her typical serenity. "Please accept our condolences on the loss of your daughter, who was a true Fury to her last breath. As your reward for bringing the traitors to justice, know this: Durra has agreed to serve as the new Jackal-Headed Duality's chief guardian in Duat. You will also be allowed to speak with her once every seven days via mirror so long as you live."

Tears of both pride and gratitude shone in Adesina's eyes. I couldn't help a smile of my own. As huge a pain in my ass as Durra had been, Ala was right; she *had* been a true—and loyal—Fury to her dying moment.

Ala turned to Mom. "As *your* reward, Allegra Holloway, we offer this boon: the same right to speak with your mother Maeve once a week since she has requested to serve the Jackal-Headed Duality in Duat until such time as she can be restored to her body—or dies a true death."

Mom's eyes glittered with emotion, but she held back the tears. I couldn't say the same for myself, and I wasn't ashamed a damn bit. Mom *deserved* the chance to speak with Nan after all they'd been through, and Nan deserved the chance to get her own body back. Selfishly, I couldn't help but be pleased that Scott and Trinity would have her to depend upon in the time to come as they settled into their duties.

Ala's gaze fell upon me, and I held my breath. I couldn't imagine what reward they could give that would top having Trinity and Scott still, on whatever abbreviated schedule, or the knowledge that Nan would be provided for while stuck in the limbo caused by her evil sister.

"You, Marissa Holloway, we owe perhaps the greatest debt to. Your ingenuity in invoking the Feather against Anubis the Once-Jackal-Headed and perseverance in seeing both the traitor immortals defeated ensured that divine law was upheld. *Your* reward comes, as seems appropriate, in three parts. First: that you immediately ascend to Elder Fury status, several decades sooner than usual."

Okay, on the one hand that meant getting sucked further into Fury politics sooner than I wanted, but on the other it meant Nifty! New! Powers! like keeping my enhanced telepathy with my Amphisbaena, who seemed just as enthused about that prospect as I.

"Second: We will champion your brother's cause once your mother assumes her place upon the Conclave and puts him forward for entrance to the—ah—*Sister*-hood of Furies."

I didn't need to ask *how* they knew any of that, just found myself grateful for the assist. We were going to *need* the divine intervention since there'd never been a male Fury in all the millennia since Nyx birthed the first three.

"Third: something We have not considered implementing in the past but now feel is absolutely crucial going forward. A second Persephone solution needs must be put into place, especially considering that your mate is now three-quarters divine."

I froze as her words sank in. I hadn't truly considered the ramifications of Scott's being mostly immortal as far as our relationship went, not beyond the fact that we'd be neatly, while still allowing Anubis's followers to be tended to. The only other alternative would be to completely eradicate her worship, which poses problems of its own."

Unhappy murmurs broke out among the assembled immortals. Religions *did* die out completely whenever arcanes lost faith as much as mortals did—but it was rare. Even then, most gods and goddesses made sure to cultivate multiple aspects—such as Nyx-as-Ma'at—to ensure *someone* would always be worshipping them. Arcanes were also a stubborn lot when it came to carrying on the old ways—as with Scott's Warhound family tradition of serving Anubis even today.

"Okay fine," Scott said. "But that doesn't change the fact that Trinity and I have lives and duties of our own on earth. We can't just be leaving them for *six months* at a time."

Epona's turn to rise gracefully. "A Persephone solution does not have to follow the story literally; We are free to set our own terms."

Hope stuttered to life inside my chest. Were it up to me, the immortals would have gotten the better end of the deal from sheer gratitude. Luckily, Scott was a *way* better negotiator. He and Trinity exchanged silent looks—or *were* they silent? The way they kept looking at each other suggested they *could* be communicating on some Wonder Twins type of level. I had to admit that any sort of telepathy would certainly make it easier for them to share the duties of Anubis's godhood . . .

Although thinking of those two—even partially—as immortal was *really* starting to trip me out.

The newly minted Wonder Twins nodded, and Scott spoke up again. "We'll agree to one day on, one day off."

Another buzz swept the room, ended only when Epona banged her gavel again. "Impossible. Switching back and forth so often will be entirely too disruptive."

He shrugged. "Perhaps. But you are asking for a *very* large sacrifice with no guarantees that Anubis will not someday steal control—and possession—over our bodies *and* souls."

The three Triad members consulted silently, cementing my belief that Scott and Trinity *did* have some weird Wonder Twin telepathy going on. Epona turned her implacable stare back on Scott. "Three months at a time."

"Three *days*, and we *might* have a deal."

Gods, only *my* mate would have the audacity to price-gouge immortal beings who had existed since before his earliest ancestor.

Epona shook her head. "One month on and off."

Hope grew even stronger. *Surely* I could endure a month at a time without them if I had—

"One week on and one off—our final offer."

As audacious as it seemed, I knew that he and Trinity had them between a rock and a hard place. Nothing guaranteed Anubis *could* be safely transmuted in pieces to other arcanes or mortals—or that new recipients would have the necessary strength of mind to hold firm. And these two had proven their dedication to justice and the Triad in ways no one else had.

"Deal," Epona agreed without further dickering, suggesting that had been what they had hoped for all along.

My heart soared as realization set in. Sure, going seven days at a time without seeing one or the other of them would be hard, but *not* impossible. Plenty of people had to travel constantly for their jobs. We could make this work!

Apparently considering that matter settled for moment, Ala turned her attention to the Nemeses in group. "Both the Triad and *Gens Immortalis* as a who owe the three of you a debt of gratitude." She glanced a Adesina with an actual look of sorrow marring her typical serenity. "Please accept our condolences on the loss of your daughter, who was a true Fury to her last breath. As your reward for bringing the traitors to justice, know this: Durra has agreed to serve as the new Jackal-Headed Duality's chief guardian in Duat. You will also be allowed to speak with her once every seven days via mirror so long as you live."

Tears of both pride and gratitude shone in Adesina's eyes. I couldn't help a smile of my own. As huge a pain in my ass as Durra had been, Ala was right; she *had* been a true—and loyal—Fury to her dying moment.

Ala turned to Mom. "As *your* reward, Allegra Holloway, we offer this boon: the same right to speak with your mother Maeve once a week since she has requested to serve the Jackal-Headed Duality in Duat until such time as she can be restored to her body—or dies a true death."

Mom's eyes glittered with emotion, but she held back the tears. I couldn't say the same for myself, and I wasn't ashamed a damn bit. Mom *deserved* the chance to speak with Nan after all they'd been through, and Nan deserved the chance to get her own body back. Selfishly, I couldn't help but be pleased that Scott and Trinity would have her to depend upon in the time to come as they settled into their duties.

Ala's gaze fell upon me, and I held my breath. I couldn't imagine what reward they could give that would top having Trinity and Scott still, on whatever

viated schedule, or the knowledge that Nan would
provided for while stuck in the limbo caused by her
sister.

"You, Marissa Holloway, we owe perhaps the great-
st debt to. Your ingenuity in invoking the Feather
against Anubis the Once-Jackal-Headed and perseverance in seeing both the traitor immortals defeated ensured that divine law was upheld. *Your* reward comes, as
seems appropriate, in three parts. First: that you immediately ascend to Elder Fury status, several decades
sooner than usual."

Okay, on the one hand that meant getting sucked further into Fury politics sooner than I wanted, but on the
other it meant Nifty! New! Powers! like keeping my
enhanced telepathy with my Amphisbaena, who seemed
just as enthused about that prospect as I.

"Second: We will champion your brother's cause
once your mother assumes her place upon the Conclave
and puts him forward for entrance to the—ah—*Sister-*
hood of Furies."

I didn't need to ask *how* they knew any of that, just
found myself grateful for the assist. We were going to
need the divine intervention since there'd never been a
male Fury in all the millennia since Nyx birthed the first
three.

"Third: something We have not considered implementing in the past but now feel is absolutely crucial
going forward. A second Persephone solution needs
must be put into place, especially considering that your
mate is now three-quarters divine."

I froze as her words sank in. I hadn't truly considered
the ramifications of Scott's being mostly immortal as far
as our relationship went, not beyond the fact that we'd be

forced to spend so much time apart. Stupid, considering the lengths Anubis and Kamanu had taken to put themselves on an even level, metaphysically speaking. It only made sense that they would be concerned about the new disparity between Scott and me—which would hit the moment my ambrosia wore off. The whole *second Persephone solution* thing did *not* sound good, however.

"Marissa Holloway, the Triad of Immortals bestows upon you the first permanent position as Our Nemesis and calls upon you to serve as such for no less than one-twelfth of each year as needed, during which time you shall be charged with such duties as restoring Imseti's body to him and recovering the traitorous Fury, Medea Holloway, so she may face justice and your grandmother be restored to *her* body."

Shock at the potential ramifications of accepting this charge— which hadn't *really* sounded like a choice— battled admiration for how neatly they'd boxed me in. Not surprising that they wanted to engage me in returning Imseti to his corporeal form in light of my previous success (and luck!)—even less surprising that they dangled the carrot of saving my grandmother from permanent death to ensure I'd cooperate. Honestly, it was the kind of crazy, brilliant scheme *I* might have come up with.

Scott and I exchanged looks again. *That* was another potential benefit: As a full demigoddess, I could visit him in Duat during his times there if needs—or overwhelming Fury hormones—be. My gaze went back to Ala, and I slowly nodded. The situation was not ideal— immortal rewards often hid double-edged blades, and who knew exactly how long *no less than one-twelfth of each year* would play out logistically. Still, the potential price was one I was willing to pay. To secure their help in acceptance for my brother, to bring both Sean and Medea—blackhearted betrayers—to justice, and to ensure Scott and I maintained the delicate divine balance allowing us to be together, I would dare far worse.

I crossed my arms and strove to sound nonchalant. "So, where do I sign up?"